What Happens to Me
When the Moon Changes . . .

I turned around and threw myself on my bed; only by the time I hit it, I knew something was seriously wrong.

For one thing, my nose and my head were crammed with these crazy, rich sensations that it took me a second to even figure out were smells, they were so much stronger than any smells I'd ever smelled. And they were—I don't know—*interesting* instead of just stinky, even the rotten ones.

I opened my mouth to get the smells a little better and heard myself panting in a funny way, as if I'd been running, which I hadn't, and then there was this long part of my face sticking out and something moving there—my tongue. I was licking my chops . . .

—from "Boobs," the Hugo Award–winning story by Suzy McKee Charnas

"Profoundly intimate fears . . . new, forbidden territories of the psyche . . . This collection must be taken seriously."

—*The Listener*

SKIN OF THE SOUL

This is for my sister, who likes scary stories, and for Ismay, when she's old enough to like them, too.

CONTENTS

INTRODUCTION

Lisa Tuttle

Fear is a basic and universal emotion, usually something we try to avoid, but not always. Although we might prefer daily life to be safe and predictable, most of us discover as children that fear can be fun. As Sigmund Freud wrote in his essay "The Uncanny": "Much as we ask for it, the *frisson* of horror, among the many oddities of our emotional life, is one of the oddest." The Romantics had their "aesthetic of terror," the belief that terror and beauty were linked, and that frightening, "awe-ful" experiences could lead to enlightenment.

Part of the appeal of horror fiction is that it allows the thrill of terror without physical danger. But good horror fiction provides more than a shock to the system, more than a rush of adrenaline. Unlike a ride on the fairground ghost-train (or its cinematic equivalent), really effective horror fiction is a way of exploring areas of experience we normally access only in our dreams, if at all. In *Danse Macabre*, his personal examination of contemporary horror films and books, Stephen King says that the work of horror is not interested in "the civilized furniture of our lives" but seeks out another, hidden, and deeply primitive place: "The good horror tale will dance its way to the center of your life and find the secret door to the room you believed no one but you knew of. . . ." From a very different background and philosophical stance, Julia Kristeva defines horror in a similar way, suggesting in *Powers of Horror* that it deals with material on the borderlines of the unconscious, material that is almost but not quite repressed.

Horror fiction has been in existence for as long as people have told stories. It has been given such labels as dark fantasy, ghost stories, strange stories, tales of the macabre, supernatural stories, weird tales, thrillers, shockers, gothics, or nasties, but "horror" is probably the most wide-ranging and useful term. It's not as classy as "dark fantasy," or as socially respectable as "ghost story," but I agree with editor David Hartwell, who favors the term "horror" because "it points toward a transaction between the reader and the text that is the essence of the experience of reading horror fiction, and not anything contained within that text (such as a ghost, literal or implied)." It is the reader's experience, not generic trappings, atmosphere rather than subject matter, that defines horror.

To ask whether women write horror seems absurd; yet this question is asked, and apparently in all seriousness. Having outlasted the time when women were outsiders in the science fiction field, I now discover I'm an oddity for writing horror stories. Jessica Amanda Salmonson, author and editor (of *What Did Miss Darrington See? An Anthology of Feminist Supernatural Fiction*), has told of the "unpleasantly comic experience" of observing an all-male panel of experts at a World Fantasy Convention "addressing the problem of 'Why Women Don't Write Horror.' " But of course we do! We always have, from the beginning. What about the mother of Frankenstein, the mother of us all, Mary Shelley?

Ah, but that was then, and this is now. And now . . . now

horror is a lucrative and popular genre less often identi-
fied by the textual transaction mentioned above than by
glossy black covers and symbolic imagery like blood,
teeth, and claws. Since the 1970s and the rise of such
best-selling authors as Stephen King, Ira Levin, William
Peter Blatty, and Peter Straub, horror has become not
one strand within the weave of literature, but a market-
able category like the mystery, the western, or the histor-
ical romance. And all the best-selling authors have been
men. Well, almost all: there were, of course, "exceptions" like Anne Rice, V. C. Andrews, Daphne du Maur-
ier, Anne Rivers Siddons, Chelsea Quinn Yarbro . . .
But, increasingly, not only the mass market but the
small presses have been dominated by men; not only
the best-sellers and the cult classics, but the imitative
hackwork and the critical assessments were written
almost entirely by men. They have defined the genre (if
it *is* a genre) for themselves. Women writers tend either
to be seen as rare exceptions, or to be redefined as something else—not horror but gothic; not horror but sus-
pense; not horror but romance, or fantasy, or something
unclassifiable but different. It has almost become a circu-
lar, self-fulfilling argument: Horror is written by men,
so if it's written by women, it isn't horror.

Critic and author Douglas E. Winter (called by his
publishers "the conscience of horror and dark fantasy")
edited the collection *Prime Evil* (1988), which invited
contributions from "the masters of modern horror" writing at the top of their form. Not only are the contribu-
tors all men, but Winter's introduction, despite
promoting the "heresy" that horror is not a genre but
an emotion ("It can be found in all literature") and giving long and very diverse lists of sources for it, contains
the name of only one woman ("Child abuse is the relentless theme of the best-selling novels of V. C. Andrews . . .") and seems curiously, innocently unaware
that males might not comprise the whole of "mankind."

Sometimes women's contributions to the field of horror have been noted and acclaimed—who could forget

Shirley Jackson, Edith Wharton, Charlotte Perkins Gilman, May Sinclair, or Patricia Highsmith?—but only to construct a pattern of difference separating them from the male-dominated mainstream. In the introduction to *Haunting Women* (1988), Alan Ryan concludes that horror stories by women are different from those by men: less gruesome and lacking monsters, with the fear of a domineering man (husband, father, or lover) recurring (wonder why?). The stories proving his point were chosen by him from the many thousands available, and although he claims, "I did not set out to prove anything or to illustrate patterns," he also admits that anthologies "reflect the editor's thoughts as much as a novel reflects the novelist's thoughts," without, apparently, recognizing any contradiction. Of course he found what he was looking for.

I don't know how many times I have heard it suggested that although there are a few women writing horror, they write gentler or less visceral or more subtle or softer horror than their male colleagues. The same "soft/hard" dichotomy that haunts women writing science fiction and fantasy plagues us as horror writers. What it comes down to is just another way of saying women don't write horror.

And of course we do. Why shouldn't we? Horror is a human emotion, like desire, felt by both women and men, and it can be expressed in writing through subtle hints or graphic details. The choice of how it is expressed has more to do with individual inclination and skill than with gender. How we define horror, the specific details of what frightens us—these are also individual, personal things . . . but there, women may tend to have more in common with each other than with men. Some fears are universal (death), some are individual (spiders), and some fears appear to be part and parcel of our sexual identities. It is in that area that a woman's conception of horror will differ from a man's.

The connection has been made before between horror and pornography, that other male-dominated field. It's an obvious comparison, and not simply because of the increasing nastiness of much pornography, or the way that violence toward women is so often sexualized or even defined *as* sex in our culture. Another connection is that both horror and pornography have extraliterary aims; both are produced with the intent to arouse feelings in the reader, whether of fear or desire. Assumptions have sometimes been made about the difference between male and female sexuality based on the different ways men and women respond to pornography: that men are more voyeuristic, or that female response is not triggered by visual cues, or that women are repulsed by hard-core pornography because they prefer a gentler, more subtle, less visceral, *softer* approach to sex. What this overlooks is the fact that most pornography is created not only for and by men, but according to male-oriented, and largely unconscious, notions about what is sexy and what sex is. The idea that women's experience of sex might be profoundly different than its accepted representation in our culture has been expressed, mostly by feminists, but this is an area that has barely begun to be explored. And so it is with women's sense of horror.

We all, men and women, begin at the same place, in the same world in our common humanity, but that world begins to split along the line of gender as soon as we are born and labeled male or female. Our deeply buried, almost subconscious memories must be very much alike: the experience of being expelled from the safety of the womb, of being warm and fed and satisfied, of being cold and wet and abandoned, of utter powerlessness, of facing the terrors of life for the first time alone. But even before we're fully conscious, male and female babies have different places in the world, different relationships to others, and that difference is constantly reinforced as we grow up. For example, although both boys and girls may be sexually abused by male relatives, and for both the experience is deeply and probably permanently damaging, they will not respond to or deal with that experience in precisely the same way, nor will it be incorporated into their later lives in the same way. Boys are expected to grow out of their powerlessness as girls are not; and girls, unlike boys, are expected to find sexual fulfillment with men. Territory that to a man is emotionally neutral may for a woman be mined with fear, and vice versa. For example, the short walk home from the bus stop of an evening. And how to understand the awesome depths of loathing some men feel for the ordinary human (female) body? We all understand the language of fear, but men and women are raised speaking different dialects of that language.

The impulse behind this anthology was not to prove that women can and do write horror (because I don't think that needs to be proven), nor to try to establish a new category of "women's horror." Men don't write only for men, nor women only for women, nor should they. The best writers can be androgynous—or do I mean bisexual?—imagining other lives for themselves, speaking in other tongues. Personal experience counts for something, but so does a sympathetic imagination, and I am not sure there is anything that *only* a man, or *only* a woman could write. To cite a few of the most popular horror writers: Stephen King and Ramsey Campbell show insight into female characters, while the male narrators of works by Tanith Lee and Anne Rice are always convincing.

According to literary critics Cynthia Griffin Wolff and Anne K. Mellor, the gothic novel (a forerunner of contemporary horror) was always particularly attractive to women writers because its conventions permitted them to explore the forbidden experiences of female sexual desire. It seems to me that men today find the horror genre appealing for a similar reason. Expressions of heterosexual desire and practice are certainly not prohibited in our culture—quite the opposite!—but there are, often unacknowledged, restrictions as to what is acceptable. In most areas of life, men's doubts about their own masculinity, their fears of female sexuality or of their own, have to be denied. In horror fiction these things come bursting out.

There's no reason why men should not explore their own fears and fantasies, but when they lose sight of the existence of an encultured male bias and mistake it for universal "human nature"; when they forget there are other ways of being and feeling; when they confuse patriarchal social structures with natural law; when they perpetuate stereotypes and mistake their own fantasies for objective reality—then we're all imprisoned by their limitations, and horror becomes another kind of pornography.

Horror fiction offers the same dangerous freedoms to women writers, but not if the male definition of horror dominates the field and closes off dissent, not if male editors, critics, and readers refuse to listen to female voices that do not echo their own limited experience. If horror is to be more than disposable, boys-own junk—as I think it can be—then it must listen to voices from both sides of the night.

The idea behind this book was to begin to open up the field; to try to provide some alternatives, some sort of counterbalance, to what is currently a man-dominated, largely man-defined genre, and to let some more women be heard. And in addition to their stories, I wanted to know *why* they wrote horror (if they thought they did!), which is the reason for the personal afterwords by the authors. I approached established writers whose horror stories had frightened me in the past and some good writers who had never before thought of writing horror, and was also pleased to discover some very promising new writers. My criterion for selecting a story was that it should produce that particular, unmistakable *frisson* by which I define a horror story. Intellectual arguments aside, in the end it comes down to a personal response. I like these stories because each one chilled or disturbed me in its individual way.

LIGHTNING ROD

Melanie Tem

Her body spasmed. The newspaper flew in pieces from her hands, and the lamp swayed. She was flung hard against the wall; amid all the other surging pain, the impact barely registered.

Heat sizzled from her fingertips, then shot back through the pathways of her nervous system. Her eyes teared and her nose stung from the familiar, bitter odor of her own singeing flesh and hair.

"Mom?"

Kevin was standing by the bed. Instinctively, Emma reached for him. Then, appalled by her own carelessness and selfish need to heal, she snatched her hands back. Just in time: She saw electricity spark between them, but it didn't quite reach Kevin. "I'm all right," Emma managed to say.

"But what's wrong?"

As the shock subsided, Emma found herself tingling with resentment. Self-absorbed teenager or not, how could Kevin ask such a question? Reminding herself that maternal sacrifices often go unnoticed—that, in fact, in

1

order to work they must go unnoticed—she said only, "I was missing your father," which, she'd come to understand, was not precisely true.

"Oh. Still?"

Emma pulled herself up to a shaky sitting position against the hot pillows and pressed her knuckles against the buzzing in her temples. Sometimes it seemed to her that, if she could create a complete circuit, the current traveled more smoothly through her, with less painful arcing. She knew it was dangerous to try to make things easier for herself, but for the moment Kevin seemed safe enough.

"You have another headache, huh?"

Emma nodded. "Not a really bad one, though." It had, in fact, been much worse, and would be again before Kevin was grown.

Kevin hesitated, then reached toward her. "Want me to rub your neck?"

"No!" Emma cried in alarm, then added more gently, "It's already getting better." To keep her son from guessing that the headache still raged, she forced her hands open and to her lap.

Kevin settled himself companionably among the rumpled bedclothes but didn't try to touch her again. From this distance, Emma studied him: downy thighs, cheeks and chest with no hint of hair, Adam's apple as yet apparent only to the touch, iridescent gray eyes so much like Mitchell's before the cancer had flooded them. So far, Emma concluded again, it seemed she was doing her job with this one; at thirteen, Kevin had suffered no real pain in his life.

The thought of Mitchell missing his little boy growing up brought Emma a burning sadness, and she thought about it with deliberate regularity, the only thing left that she could do for her husband. The sorrow of Kevin's fatherlessness was actually heart-stopping. Holly had already been grown and living across town with her grandfather when Mitchell died, but Emma still had a duty to protect her son from ever understanding how much he'd lost.

"I was thinking about him, too," Kevin said now, dry-eyed, even smiling a little. "But just when I was starting to get really sad, I heard you yelling and I had to come in here and make sure you were okay."

Emma closed her eyes in relief. Disaster averted one more time. This, at least, she could do.

"I don't think about him like you do, though. I never did," he said.

Kevin was regarding her warily. Ears still ringing, vision still blurred, breath still coming short, Emma managed to nod approval.

"Most of the time I'm pretty happy, you know? Even right after he died, a few days or so, I was okay."

Those first few thunderous days, before Emma had regained her bearings, she hadn't been able to stop Kevin from crying and vomiting and calling for his father. "That's good, honey," she told him now. "That's what I want for you."

"Or I'm worried about other stuff. Normal stuff, like grades or something."

"But not *too* worried," Emma protested. "You don't worry *too* much, do you?"

"Or girls." He blushed. Emma caught her breath at how beautiful he was, how perfect and innocent and utterly vulnerable without a mother's protection.

"You're too young to worry about girls."

"Is it okay to still be happy even if your father died?"

"That's exactly the way it's supposed to be."

"But my life didn't really change. Don't you think that's weird? It's like he never died. Or never lived."

A slight contraction marred his face; Kevin was sad. Emma's throat prickled, but she was able to say, "You're going on with your life. That's what you're supposed to do."

"But what about you? What about your life?"

"This *is* my life." Emma judged it an acceptable risk now to hug her son. He buried his face childishly against

3

her, rubbing the new wounds on her chest, but she didn't wince.

"I don't miss him! I don't know how, and I want to!" Kevin burst into tears. Confused, Emma held him until the sobbing had stopped, which didn't take long. Almost immediately, he grew restless, sat up, wiped his nose with the back of his hand, and asked, "Are Holly and Grandpa coming over for dinner tonight?"

"Of course."

"Gee, they're here every day. Good thing they live close."

"Holly's only twenty-one. She can't be expected to do everything for him. It's enough that she lives there."

"When I grow up, I'm not gonna take care of anybody."

Emma smiled fondly at her son and said nothing.

"What time are they supposed to get here?"

"About six o'clock." Emma felt the brief surge of panic that always accompanied the realization that she was not ready for her father. "What time is it?"

Kevin shrugged.

"Oh, Kevin, what happened to the brand-new watch I just bought you?"

"Lost it, I guess. How come you don't wear a watch?"

"I can't. They stop."

"You used to wear watches. You had that real pretty one with the diamonds that Dad gave you for your anniversary that year." Without warning, the smooth little face registered a slight tremor, and the gray eyes glistened with tears. "Oh, I wish Daddy—"

Emma clenched her teeth. The hair on her arms stood up, and she was hot, then cold. It didn't last long and, when she relaxed from it, all traces of Kevin's own sadness had been overridden by concern for her. "We better get dinner started," she told him.

"Spaghetti, right? I'll get the pans out."

He clattered off down the stairs. Emma called after him, "Don't turn the stove on till I get there!" though she knew he wouldn't; he was afraid of the burners, as she intended him to be.

Gingerly, Emma swung her legs over the edge of the bed. For as long as she could remember her body had ached, and the aching had worsened since Mitchell died, joints stiffening and muscles tearing little by little. She made her way across the room, carefully rolling up her shirt so that, by the time she was standing in front of the full-length mirror on the door, the entire front of her torso was exposed to her own view.

Three new scars twisted among the hardened and raised edges of older ones, bright pink amid darker red and brown and white. One descended along her breast-bone for an inch or two; one disappeared into her thin-ning pubic hair; the largest branched out into the vulnerable pale underside of her left arm. The absorbent flesh around her heart was so thickly patterned that she could neither see nor find by tracing with her fingertips where the new marks began.

Below all the other scars, most of which nested together on her chest like those terrible photos of the backs of slaves after the Civil War, was the birthmark that coiled like a red-brown tail out of her navel. Emma touched it. It didn't hurt. She seemed to remember that it had once, but that couldn't be right; she knew birth-marks didn't hurt. It had always embarrassed her until she'd met Mitchell, who used to kiss it with tender awe.

For just an instant, Emma missed Mitchell. But she pushed it away; there was no room for her own sadness amid the sadness of everyone else.

She hadn't saved Mitchell from the cancer. She thought now that she should have seen it coming, should have known he was in danger before he did, before the doctors had given the danger a name. If she'd been braver or more skillful, she could have taken the disease into her own body.

It gave her some comfort to know that she had been able to absorb much of his pain and his fear of dying.

Because of her, he'd been peaceful at the end, while Emma's terror of his leaving her had spread and hardened like scar tissue.

She had stayed in bed with him those last long days and nights. Kevin had brought them his homework and the morning paper. Holly had brought them soup: "Why don't you take a break, Mama? I'll stay with him." But Emma knew better than to leave. If she left him, Mitchell would hurt, and he would be afraid. She could feel the wounding and scarring across her internal organs and in the cavities of her mind and body. Finally the circuit had made itself continuous, a self-perpetuating loop, and she'd felt closer to Mitchell than ever before.

Just before he died, Mitchell had whispered, "Something's wrong. I feel like it's somebody else who's dying." Emma had accepted that as a measure of how well she'd done her job.

Emma's father had come to the funeral. He'd never paid much attention to Mitchell, and he didn't seem to be paying much attention now. He was safe this time. He hadn't lost anyone he loved.

Emma's father had no name.

She knew he had a given name, of course, and a surname that related him to generations of people besides her, but she never thought of herself as that named man's child. She did her best not to call him anything, to keep him where she could watch him, in direct relationship to her—"my father," and nothing else. On the few occasions that had required some form of address, "Dad" and "Daddy" and "Pa" had frightened her, and always a bad shock and deep scarring had followed. For a long time, Emma hadn't known what the pain was that threatened her father at those times, but she could always feel it gathering.

"We can't let your father be hurt anymore."

Mama had told her that from as early as she could remember, in lullabies and fairy tales and happy birthday songs. Emma didn't remember what Mama looked like or anything they'd done together, just the two of them, but she remembered the sound of her voice saying that, and the scarring on the older woman's chest and stomach like a blooming thorn tree. Mama had never been shy about letting Emma see her body, and every time it seemed there was a new branch on the scar tree, a new pink flower.

"That's what you do when you love somebody like him. You protect him. He can't take any more pain."

Her father's father had died when Emma was six. She'd never met him, and Mama said she never had, either; he lived hundreds of miles away and had been estranged from his son for years. In the car all the way to the funeral, Emma and her mother had cried, and Emma, in the backseat, had watched the occasional twitching of Mama's head, the tensing of her shoulders. Her father hadn't said anything, except that they'd have to stop for gas, and wasn't that the juncture of Route 36 where they were supposed to turn? He'd looked at his father's body in the coffin without expression, while Mama wailed. Without comment and without taking a thing, he'd cleaned out the house he'd grown up in; by this time Mama had been so upset that she couldn't help, and Emma's chest had hurt for days.

"He's been hurt enough."

Emma knew the story, although not from her father. She would have been afraid to hear it from him. Before she'd even existed, before there'd been any need for her, he'd had another family, a wife named Maryellen and two little boys named Joseph and John. They'd all died when their house burned down while he was away at work. Just thinking their names made Emma catch her breath painfully; she tried to remember to think their names every day, and she'd made sure to teach them to Holly.

"Our job is to bring him joy and to keep pain away from him." Mama had still been saying that the day she left; Emma was thirteen, no longer a child.

She'd been awakened in the night by her father's cry,

7

followed almost at once by a flash of lightning that lit her room purple, a fierce thunderclap, the acrid smell of ozone, and a jolt of electricity that pinned her for long moments to her bed. She'd felt the progress of the burn, traveling from the base of her throat to her lower abdomen in split seconds; she'd cried out, but weakly, and her father hadn't heard. The burn had scarred badly, her first scar, and had formed the trunk and roots for all the other scars to come.

Grief threatened her father constantly that first year, and Emma was terrified that she wasn't good enough, that some of it would get through to him and he'd explode. But she learned. "I'm learning, Mama." Before long, she could sense when he was in danger of being sad even if she was away from him. The school nurse thought she was having seizures; the doctor concurred and gave her medicine, which she pretended to take, afraid that even the pretense of self-protection would make them stop.

Once, not looking, she'd crossed the street too close in front of a speeding car. She'd heard its frantic honking and her father shouting her name at the same moment, and by the time he reached her on the other side of the street Emma had been trembling violently, holding on to a signpost, and panting, "I'm sorry! Oh, I'm so sorry!" But her father had been utterly calm; later, she wondered if he'd even realized that she'd been in danger.

The fall of her senior year in high school, her father was transferred to California. Emma had barely started to think about all she was leaving behind when she'd come upon her father standing desolately in the backyard. "I built this house," he told her. She hadn't known that. "I've lived here twenty-three years. Your mother—" Emma had collapsed on the grass. Her father helped her to her feet. When her head had cleared, they'd finished packing their belongings, and both of them had left the emptied house without a backward glance. Now Emma could not remember how one room had opened into another in that house, or how sunlight had come into the backyard.

Her father reminded her of a sock puppet with no face, a thumb-smoothed lump of modeling clay. Approaching eighty now, he was very nearly featureless. He had no hair left, no residue of mustache or beard. His sparse eyebrows were almost the same color as his flesh. He had no wrinkles. It had been years since Emma had seen him laugh or frown or even yawn and, since the night Mama'd left and she had understood her job, she had never seen him cry.

"We take his pain away. That's why he married me. That's why you were born."

Abruptly, Emma stepped closer to the mirror and peered at the birthmark that spun like thin red wire from her navel. She touched it. It didn't hurt, but it once had. This, she suddenly realized, was what connected her to her father. This was her first scar.

Emma lowered her shirt and tried to bring her reflection into focus. Since Mitchell's death she could hardly see herself, but she didn't think any of the scars showed.

The shirt, however, was badly wrinkled, and a faint brownish burn pattern spread like charred twigs across the front. Her father and Kevin wouldn't notice, but Holly would. Emma changed quickly into a clean shirt and ran a comb through her hair without really looking, trying to smooth the static with her palms. Her father would be here soon and, although Holly took care of him now, Emma would have to go downstairs.

Emma kept looking around the dinner table. Again and again she studied each of these people she loved, trying to gauge their shifting mental states. Her taut nerves keened like wires in a hot, mounting wind. She hardly ate; she wasn't hungry, and she dared not divert any attention away from her father, son, daughter, father, son. Again and again she focused on each of them; loving them, she was charged with keeping them safe from pain.

Mitchell should have been sitting at the end of the table. His place had been gutted, as if by fire. Emma should have been able to stop that from happening.

Across the table, Holly was watching, too, and Emma saw how little she ate. Now and then, the glances of mother and daughter crossed like antennae; once, for an instant, they locked, and Emma felt a tiny reverberation of loss, something drained away from her, before she looked away.

"Neat, huh, Grandpa?"

Emma snapped her attention back to her son, afraid she was too late and he'd already been hurt by her father's blankness. Kevin was leaning sideways in his chair and ducking his head childishly to see up into his grandfather's averted face.

"Mmm," said Emma's father, which was virtually all he seemed to say these days. When he took another forkful of salad, he bent his head even farther, and Kevin nearly fell off his chair.

Pain was gathering around her son. Emma readied herself. At a very early age she'd stopped trying to interest her father, seeing how uncomfortable it made him; stopped saying she loved him because it put him in danger. Holly had done the same. But Kevin, oblivious or stubborn, wouldn't give up. "I love you, Grandpa," he still insisted, and his grandfather, if he said anything, said, "Mmm."

He hadn't yet stopped demanding of her, "Does Grandpa love us?"

"Of course he does."

"Why doesn't he say it? Or act like it?"

"He can't, sweetheart. At first he was too afraid, and now he's forgotten how."

Kevin had just told a joke. Emma had missed most of it, but she smiled encouragingly at the punch line. Holly chuckled. Kevin was looking expectant and pleased with himself. Emma's father sipped impassively at his coffee.

"You know any good jokes, Grandpa?"

The old man regarded him flatly and then, minimally, shook his head. His face caught the light like the surface of an egg.

"Wanna see my turtle?"

Kevin was taking too many chances. Emma intervened. "Kevin. Let Grandpa finish his meal."

"He's finished! He's just sitting there!"

"Kevin. Stop."

Her son left the table scowling then, close to tears. But before he was out of the room, the soft spot just below Emma's breastbone tingled, and she saw Holly flinch. A moment later, Kevin went out the back door whistling.

"He's okay," Emma found herself saying to Holly, and then for the first time saw the faint red line emerging from her daughter's open collar. A scratch, she told herself, or the edge of a sunburn. But she knew what it was.

Emma stood up and carried her dishes into the kitchen. Kevin was safely outside; she heard him playing with the dog, whooping like a much younger child. The others were out of her line of sight, but she could hear her daughter talking gently to her father, could hear his silences.

Emma leaned heavily against the counter and sobbed. She pressed her fingers over her mouth to still the noise, but it burst through like a frantic Morse code. *I miss Mitchell. I want my mother.* Quite unexpectedly, this was no one else's grief but her own.

The pain was enormous and exquisite. Emma embraced it, claimed it, fell with it to her knees.

Then it was gone. As if a switch had been thrown, a current diverted.

"No!" she whispered. "It's mine!"

She raised her head and saw Holly in the doorway, collapsed against the jamb. Her sturdy young body jerked, and her hair stood out wild around her head. Emma thought she smelled burning, and her ears rang as if from a loud close noise. Long red burns were steadily

11

making their way along the undersides of her daughter's outflung arms.

"Holly, don't!"

"Oh, Mama, let me. You always take care of everybody else. Let me take care of you. I know how."

"Give it back to me."

Holly shook her head fiercely, and her hair flew. "I love you. I don't want you to be sad."

"It's *mine!*" Emma cried. "It belongs to *me!*"

She lunged at her daughter and tried to take her in her arms. But Holly was stronger. She forced Emma into her lap and cradled her like a baby. She stroked her, and Emma felt her facial muscles going limp as Holly's fingers twisted and splayed.

"I miss them," she whimpered, but she no longer knew whom she meant. Holly had taken it all.

Afterword

I write horror fiction because it seems to me that coming at human nature from that angle illuminates it in ways that more direct approaches miss or obscure. My other profession is social work, and I was trained to take a theoretical, not to say analytical, attitude toward human nature. I'm not discounting that, because I think there's something to be learned about myself and about life in that way, but fiction—and, at this point in my life, dark fantasy especially—adds another resonant dimension. I like to start with a literal psychological "truth" that I don't understand—say, the very strong urge (felt particularly but by no means only by women; particularly but by no means only by wives and mothers) to protect people they love from grief, to the point of denying both themselves and the people they love the vital human experience of grieving. By extending this idea a little, pushing it a little. I hope to look at it in a new and expanded way.

Melanie Tem

BOOBS

Suzy McKee Charnas

The thing is, it's like your brain wants to go on thinking about the miserable history midterm you have to take tomorrow, but your body takes over. And what a body! You can see in the dark and run like the wind and leap parked cars in a single bound.

Of course, you pay for it next morning (but it's worth it). I always wake up stiff and sore, with dirty hands and feet and face, and I have to jump in the shower fast so Hilda won't see me like that.

Not that she would know what it was about, but why take chances? So I pretend it's the other thing that's bothering me. So she goes, "Come on, sweetie, everybody gets cramps, that's no reason to go around moaning and groaning. What are you doing, trying to get out of school just because you've got your period?"

If I didn't like Hilda, which I do even though she is only a stepmother instead of my real mother, I would show her something that would keep me out of school forever, and it's not fake, either.

But there are plenty of people I'd rather show that to.

14

I already showed that dork Billy Linden.

"Hey, Boobs!" he goes, in the hall right outside Homeroom. A lot of kids laughed, naturally, though Rita Frye called him an asshole.

Billy is the one that started it, sort of, because he always started everything, him with his big mouth. At the beginning of term, he came barreling down on me hollering, "Hey, look at Bornstein, something musta happened to her over the summer! What happened, Bornstein? Hey, everybody, look at Boobs Bornstein!"

He made a grab at my chest, and I socked him in the shoulder, and he punched me in the face, which made me dizzy and shocked and made me cry, too, in front of everybody.

I mean, I always used to wrestle and fight with the boys, being that I was strong for a girl. All of a sudden it was different. He hit me hard, to really hurt, and the shock sort of got me in the pit of my stomach and made me feel nauseous too, as well as mad and embarrassed to death.

I had to go home with a bloody nose and lie with my head back and ice wrapped in a towel on my face and dripping down into my hair.

Hilda sat on the couch next to me and patted me. She goes, "I'm sorry about this, honey, but really, you have to learn it sometime. You're all growing up and the boys are getting stronger than you'll ever be. If you fight with boys, you're bound to get hurt. You have to find other ways to handle them."

To make things worse, the next morning I started to bleed down there, which Hilda had explained carefully to me a couple of times, so at least I knew what was going on. Hilda really tried extra hard without being icky about it, but I hated when she talked about how it was all part of these exciting changes in my body that are so important and how terrific it is to "become a young woman."

Sure. The whole thing was so messy and disgusting, worse than she had said, worse than I could imagine, with these black clots of gunk coming out in a smear of pink blood—I thought I would throw up. "That's just the lining of your uterus," Hilda said. Big deal. It was still gross.

And plus, the *smell*.

Hilda tried to make me feel better, she really did. She said we should "mark the occasion" like primitive people do, so it's something special, not just a nasty thing that just sort of fell on you.

So we decided to put poor old Pinkie away, my stuffed dog that I've slept with since I was three. Pinkie is bald and sort of hard and lumpy, since he got put in the washing machine by mistake, and you would never know he was all soft plush when he was new, or even that he was pink.

Last time my friend Gerry-Anne came over, before the summer, she saw Pinkie lying on my pillow and though she didn't say anything, I could tell she was thinking that was kind of babyish. So I'd been thinking about not keeping Pinkie around anymore.

Hilda and I made him this nice box lined with pretty scraps from her quilting class, and I thanked him out loud for being my friend for so many years, and we put him up in the closet, on the top shelf.

I felt terrible, but if Gerry-Anne decided I was too babyish to be friends with anymore, I could end up with no friends at all. When you have never been popular since the time you were skinny and fast and everybody wanted you on their team, you have that kind of thing on your mind.

Hilda and Dad made me go to school the next morning so nobody would think I was scared of Billy Linden (which I was) or that I would let him keep me away just by being such a dork.

Everybody kept sneaking funny looks at me and whispering, and I was sure it was because I couldn't help walking funny with the pad between my legs and because they could smell what was happening, which as far as I knew hadn't happened to anybody else in Eight-A yet. Just like nobody in the whole grade had anything real in their stupid training bras except me, thanks a lot.

Anyway I stayed away from everybody as much as I could and wouldn't talk to Gerry-Anne, even, because I was scared she would ask me why I walked funny and smelled bad.

Billy Linden avoided me just like everybody else, except one of his stupid buddies purposely bumped into me so I stumbled into Billy on the lunch line. Billy turns around and he goes, real loud, "Hey, Boobs, when did you start wearing black and blue makeup?"

I didn't give him the satisfaction of knowing that he had actually broken my nose, which the doctor said. Good thing they don't have to bandage you up for that. Billy would be hollering up a storm about how I had my nose in a sling as well as my boobs.

That night I got up after I was supposed to be asleep and took off my underpants and T-shirt that I sleep in and stood looking at myself in the mirror. I didn't need to turn a light on. The moon was full and it was shining right into my bedroom through the big dormer window.

I crossed my arms and pinched myself hard to sort of punish my body for what it was doing to me.

As if that could make it stop.

No wonder Edie Siler had starved herself to death in the tenth grade! I understood her perfectly. She was trying to keep her body down, keep it normal-looking, thin and strong, like I was too, back when I looked like a person and not a cartoon that somebody would call "Boobs."

And then something warm trickled in a little line down the inside of my leg, and I knew it was blood and I couldn't stand it anymore. I pressed my thighs together and shut my eyes hard, and I did something.

I mean I felt it happening. I felt myself shrink down to a hard core of sort of cold fire inside my bones, and all the flesh part, the muscles and the squishy insides and the skin, went sort of glowing and free-floating, all shining with moonlight, and I felt a sort of shifting and balance-changing going on.

I thought I was fainting on account of my stupid period. So I turned around and threw myself on my bed, only by the time I hit it, I knew something was seriously wrong.

For one thing, my nose and my head were crammed with these crazy, rich sensations that it took me a second to even figure out were smells, they were so much stronger than any smells I'd ever smelled. And they were—I don't know—*interesting* instead of just stinky, even the rotten ones.

I opened my mouth to get the smells a little better, and heard myself panting in a funny way as if I'd been running, which I hadn't, and then there was this long part of my face sticking out and something moving there—my tongue.

I was licking my chops.

Well, there was this moment of complete and utter panic. I tore around the room whining and panting and hearing my toenails clicking on the floorboards, and then I huddled down and crouched in the corner because I was scared Dad and Hilda would hear me and come to find out what was making all this racket.

Because I could hear them. I could hear their bed creak when one of them turned over, and Dad's breath whistling a little in an almost-snore, and I could smell them too, each one with a perfectly clear bunch of smells, kind of like those desserts of mixed ice cream they call a medley.

My body was twitching and jumping with fear and energy, and my room—it's a converted attic space, wide but with a ceiling that's low in places—my room felt like a jail. And plus, I was terrified of catching a glimpse of myself in the mirror. I had a pretty good idea of what I would see, and I didn't want to see it.

Besides, I had to pee, and I couldn't face trying to deal with the toilet in the state I was in.

So I eased the bedroom door open with my shoulder

and nearly fell down the stairs trying to work them on four legs and thinking about it, instead of letting my body just do it. I put my hands on the front door to open it, but my hands weren't hands, they were paws with long knobby toes covered with fur, and the toes had thick black claws sticking out of the ends of them.

The pit of my stomach sort of exploded with horror, and I yelled. It came out this wavery "wooo" noise that echoed eerily in my skullbones. Upstairs, Hilda goes, "Jack, what was that?" I bolted for the basement as I heard Dad hit the floor of their bedroom.

The basement door slips its latch all the time, so I just shoved it open and down I went, doing better on the stairs this time because I was too scared to think. I spent the rest of the night down there, moaning to myself (which meant whining through my nose, really) and trotting around rubbing against the walls trying to rub off this crazy shape I had, or just moving around because I couldn't sit still. The place was thick with stinks and these slow-swirling currents of hot and cold air. I couldn't handle all the input.

As for having to pee, in the end I managed to sort of hike my butt up over the edge of the slop-sink by Dad's workbench and let go in there. The only problem was that I couldn't turn the taps on to rinse out the smell because of my paws.

Then about 5 A.M. I woke up from a doze curled up in a bare place on the floor where the spiders weren't so likely to walk, and I couldn't see a thing or smell anything either, so I knew I was okay again even before I checked and found fingers on my hands instead of claws.

I zipped upstairs and stood under the shower so long that Hilda yelled at me for using up the hot water when she had a load of wash to do that morning. I was only trying to steam some of the stiffness out of my muscles, but I couldn't tell her that.

It was real weird to just dress and go to school after a night like that. One good thing, I had stopped bleeding after only one day, which Hilda said wasn't so strange for the first time. So it had to be the huge greenish bruise on my face from Billy's punch that everybody was staring at.

That and the usual thing, of course. Well, why not? *They* didn't know I'd spent the night as a wolf.

So Fat Joey grabbed my book bag in the hallway outside science class and tossed it to some kid from Eight-B. I had to run after them to get it back, which of course was set up so the boys could cheer the jouncing of my boobs under my shirt.

I was so mad I almost caught Fat Joey, except I was afraid if I grabbed him, maybe he would sock me like Billy had.

Dad had told me, "Don't let it get you, kid, all boys are jerks at that age."

Hilda had been saying all summer, "Look, it doesn't do any good to walk around all hunched up with your arms crossed, you should just throw your shoulders back and walk like a proud person who's pleased that she's growing up. You're just a little early, that's all, and I bet the other girls are secretly envious of you, with their cute little training bras, for Chrissake, as if there was something that needed to be *trained*."

It's okay for her, she's not in school, she doesn't remember what it's like.

So I quit running and walked after Joey until the bell rang, and then I got my book bag back from the bushes outside where he threw it. I was crying a little, and I ducked into the girls' room.

Stacey Buhl was in there doing her lipstick like usual and wouldn't talk to me like usual, but Rita came bustling in and said somebody should off that dumb dork Joey, except of course it was really Billy that put him up to it. Like usual.

Rita is okay except she's an outsider herself, being that her kid brother has AIDS, and lots of kids' parents don't think she should even be in the school. So I don't hang around with her a lot. I've got enough trouble, and anyway I was late for math.

I had to talk to somebody, though. After school I told Gerry-Anne, who's been my best friend on and off since Fourth Grade. She was off at the moment, but I found her in the library and I told her I'd had a weird dream about being a wolf. She wants to be a psychiatrist like her mother, so of course she listened.

She told me I was nuts. That was a big help.

That night I made sure the back door wasn't exactly closed, and then I got in bed with no clothes on—imagine turning into a wolf in your underpants and T-shirt—and just shivered, waiting for something to happen.

The moon came up and shone in my window, and I changed again, just like before, which is not one bit like how it is in the movies—all struggling and screaming and bones snapping out with horrible cracking and tearing noises, just the way I guess you would imagine it to be, if you knew it had to be done by building special machines to do that for the camera and make it look real; if you were a special effects man, instead of a werewolf.

For me, it didn't have to look real, it *was* real. It was this melting and drifting thing, which I got sort of excited by it this time. I mean, it felt—interesting. Like something I was doing, instead of just another dumb body-mess happening to me because some brainless hormones said so.

I must have made a noise. Hilda came upstairs to the door of my bedroom, but luckily she didn't come in. She's tall, and my ceiling is low for her, so she often talks to me from the landing.

Anyway I'd heard her coming, so I was in my bed with my whole head shoved under my pillow, praying frantically that nothing showed.

I could smell her, it was the wildest thing—her own smell, sort of sweaty but sweet, and then on top of it her perfume, like an ice pick stuck in my nose. I didn't actually hear a word she said, I was too scared, and also I had this ripply shaking feeling inside me, a high that was only partly terror.

See, I realized all of a sudden, with this big blossom of surprise, that I didn't have to be scared of Hilda, or anybody. I was strong, my wolf body was strong, and anyhow one clear look at me and she would drop dead.

What a relief, though, when she went away. I was dying to get out from under the weight of the covers, and besides I had to sneeze. Also I recognized that part of the energy roaring around inside me was hunger.

They went to bed—I heard their voices even in their bedroom, though not exactly what they said, which was fine. The words weren't important anymore, I could tell more from the tone of what they were saying.

Like I knew they were going to do it, and I was right. I could hear them messing around right through the walls, which was also something new, and I have never been so embarrassed in my life. I couldn't even put my hands over my ears, because my hands were paws.

So while I was waiting for them to go to sleep, I looked myself over in the big mirror on my closet door.

There was this big wolf head with a long slim muzzle and a thick ruff around my neck. The ruff stood up as I growled and backed up a little.

Which was silly, of course, there was no wolf in the bedroom but me. But I was all strung out, I guess, and one wolf, me in my wolf body, was as much as I could handle the idea of, let alone two wolves, me and my reflection.

After that first shock, it was great. I kept turning one way and another for different views.

I was thin, with these long, slender legs but strong, you could see the muscles, and feet a little bigger than I would have picked. But I'll take four big feet over two big boobs any day.

My face was terrific, with jaggedy white ripsaw teeth and eyes that were small and clear and gleaming in the moonlight. The tail was a little bizarre, but I got used to it, and actually it had a nice plumy shape. My shoulders were big and covered with long, glossy-looking fur, and I had this neat coloring, dark on the back and a sort of melting silver on my front and underparts.

The thing was, though, my tongue, hanging out. I had a lot of trouble with that—it looked gross and silly at the same time. I mean, that was *my tongue,* about a foot long and neatly draped over the points of my bottom canines. That was when I realized that I didn't have a whole lot of expressions to use, not with that face, which was more like a mask.

But it was alive, it was my face, those were my own long black lips that my tongue licked.

No doubt about it, this was *me.* I was a werewolf, like in the movies they showed over Halloween weekend. But it wasn't anything like your ugly movie werewolf that's just some guy loaded up with pounds and pounds of makeup. I was *gorgeous.*

I didn't want to just hang around admiring myself in the mirror, though. I couldn't stand being cooped up in that stuffy, smell-crowded room.

When everything settled down and I could hear Dad and Hilda breathing the way they do when they're sleeping, I snuck out.

The dark wasn't very dark to me, and the cold felt sharp like vinegar, but not in a hurting way. Everyplace I went, there were these currents like waves in the air, and I could draw them in through my long wolf nose and roll the smell of them over the back of my tongue. It was like a whole different world, with bright sounds everywhere and rich, strong smells.

And I could run.

I started running because a car came by while I was sniffing at the garbage bags on the curb, and I was really scared of being seen in the headlights. So I took off down the dirt alley between our house and the Morrisons' next door, and holy cow, I could tear along with hardly a sound, I could jump their picket fence without even thinking about it. My back legs were like steel springs and I came down solid and square on four legs with almost no shock at all, let alone worrying about losing my balance or twisting an ankle.

Man, I could run through that chilly air all thick and moist with smells, I could almost fly. It was like last year, when I didn't have boobs bouncing and yanking in front even when I'm only walking fast.

Just two rows of neat little bumps down the curve of my belly. I sat down and looked.

I tore open garbage bags to find out about the smells in them, but I didn't eat anything from them. I wasn't about to chow down on other people's stale hot-dog ends and pizza crusts and fat and bones scraped off their plates and all mixed in with mashed potatoes and stuff.

When I found places where dogs had stopped and made their marks, I squatted down and pissed there too, right on top. I just wiped them *out*.

I bounded across that enormous lawn around the Wanscombe place, where nobody but the oriental gardener ever sets foot, and walked up the back and over the top of their BMW, leaving big fat pawprints all over it. Nobody saw me, nobody heard me, I was a shadow.

Well, except for the dogs, of course.

There was a lot of barking when I went by, real hysterics, and at first I was really scared. But then I popped out of an alley up on Ridge Road where the big houses are, right in front of about six dogs that run together. Their owners let them out all night and don't care if they get hit by a car.

They'd been trotting along with the wind behind them, checking out all the garbage bags set out for pickup the next morning. When they saw me, one of them let out a yelp of surprise, and they all skidded to a stop.

Six of them. I was scared. I growled.

The dogs turned fast, banging into each other in their hurry, and trotted away.

I don't know what they would have done if they'd met a real wolf, but I was something special, I guess.

I followed them.

They scattered and ran.

Well, I ran too, and this was a different kind of running. I mean, I stretched, and I raced, and there was this joy. I chased one of them.

Zig, zag, this little terrier kind of dog tried to cut left and dive under the gate of somebody's front walk, all without a sound—he was running too hard to yell, and I was happy running quiet.

Just before he could ooze under the gate, I caught up with him and without thinking I grabbed the back of his neck and pulled him off his feet and gave him a shake as hard as I could, from side to side.

I felt his neck crack, the sound vibrated through all the bones of my face.

I picked him up in my mouth, and it was like he hardly weighed a thing. I trotted away holding him up off the ground, and under a bush in Baker's Park I held him down with my paws and I bit into his belly, which was still warm and quivering.

Like I said, I was hungry.

The blood gave me this rush like you wouldn't believe. I stood there for a minute looking around and licking my lips, just sort of panting and tasting the taste because I was stunned by it, it was like eating honey or the best chocolate malted you ever had.

So I put my head down and chomped that little dog, like shoving your face into a pizza and inhaling it. God, I was *starved*, so I didn't mind that the meat was tough and rank-tasting after that first wonderful bite. I even licked blood off the ground after, never mind the grit mixed in.

I ate two more dogs that night, one that was tied up on a clothesline in a cruddy yard full of rusted-out car parts down on the South Side, and one fat old yellow dog out snuffling around on his own and way too slow. He tasted pretty bad, and by then I was feeling full, so I left a lot.

I strolled around the park, shoving the swings with my big black wolf nose, and I found the bench where Mr. Granby sits and feeds the pigeons every day, never mind that nobody else wants the dirty birds around crapping on their cars. I took a dump there, right where he sits.

Then I gave the setting moon a good-night, which came out quavery and wild, "Loo-loo-loo!" And I loped toward home, springing off the thick pads of my paws and letting my tongue loll out and feeling generally super.

I slipped inside and trotted upstairs, and in my room I stopped to look at myself in the mirror.

As gorgeous as before, and only a few dabs of blood on me, which I took time to lick off. I did get a little worried—I mean, suppose that was it, suppose having killed and eaten what I'd killed in my wolf shape, I was stuck in this shape forever? Like, if you wander into a fairy castle and eat or drink anything, that's it, you can't ever leave. Suppose when the morning came I didn't change back?

Well, there wasn't much I could do about that one way or the other, and to tell the truth, I felt like I wouldn't mind; it had been worth it.

When I was nice and clean, including licking off my own bottom which seemed like a perfectly normal and nice thing to do at the time. I jumped up on the bed, curled up, and corked right off. When I woke up with the sun in my eyes, there I was, my own self again.

It was very strange, grabbing breakfast and wearing my old sweatshirt that wallowed all over me so I didn't stick out so much, while Hilda yawned and shuffled around in her robe and slippers and acted like her and Dad hadn't been doing it last night, which I knew different.

And plus, it was perfectly clear that she didn't have a clue about what *I* had been doing, which gave me a strange feeling.

One of the things about growing up that they're careful not to tell you is, you start having more things you don't talk to your parents about. And I had a doozy.

Hilda goes, "What's the matter, are you off Sugar

Pops now? Honestly, Kelsey, I can't keep up with you! And why can't you wear something nicer than that old shirt to school? Oh, I get it: disguise, right?"

She sighed and looked at me kind of sad but smiling, her hands on her hips. "Kelsey, Kelsey," she goes, "if only I'd had half of what you've got when *I* was a girl—I was flat as an ironing board, and it made me so miserable, I can't tell you."

She's still real thin and neat-looking, so what does she know about it? But she meant well, and anyhow I was feeling so good I didn't argue.

I didn't change my shirt, though.

That night I didn't turn into a wolf. I lay there waiting, but though the moon came up, nothing happened no matter how hard I tried, and after a while I went and looked out the window and realized that the moon wasn't really full anymore, it was getting smaller.

I wasn't so much relieved as sorry. I bought a calendar at the school book sale two weeks later, and I checked the full moon nights coming up and waited anxiously to see what would happen.

Meantime, things rolled along as usual. I got a rash of zits on my chin. I would look in the mirror and think about my wolf face, that had beautiful sleek fur instead of zits.

Zits and all I went to Angela Durkin's party, and next day Billy Linden told everybody that I went in one of the bedrooms at Angela's and made out with him, which I did not. But since no grown-ups were home and Fat Joey brought grass to the party, most of the kids were stoned and didn't know who did what or where anyhow.

As a matter of fact, Billy actually did get a girl in Seven-B high one time out in his parents' garage, and him and two of his friends did it to her while she was zonked out of her mind, or anyway they said they did, and she was too embarrassed to say anything one way or the other, and a little while later she changed schools.

How I know about it is the same way everybody else does, which is because Billy was the biggest boaster in the whole school, and you could never tell if he was lying or not.

So I guess it wasn't so surprising that some people believed what Billy said about me. Gerry-Anne quit talking to me after that. Meantime, Hilda got pregnant.

This turned into a huge discussion about how Hilda had been worried about her biological clock so she and Dad had decided to have a kid, and I shouldn't mind, it would be fun for me and good preparation for being a mother myself later on, when I found some nice guy and got married.

Sure. Great preparation. Like Mary O'Hare in my class, who gets to change her youngest baby sister's diapers all the time, yick. She jokes about it, but you can tell she really hates it. Now it looked like it was my turn coming up, as usual.

The only thing that made life bearable was my secret.

"You're laid back today," Devon Brown said to me in the lunchroom one day after Billy had been especially obnoxious, trying to flick rolled-up pieces of bread from his table so they would land on my chest. Devon was sitting with me because he was bad at French, my only good subject, and I was helping him out with some verbs. I guess he wanted to know why I wasn't upset because of Billy picking on me. He goes, "How come?"

"That's a secret," I said, thinking about what Devon would say if he knew a werewolf was helping him with his French: *Loup. Manger.*

He goes, "What secret?" Devon has freckles and is actually kind of cute-looking.

"A *secret*," I go, "so I can't tell you, dummy."

He looked real superior and he goes, "Well, it can't be much of a secret, because girls can't keep secrets, everybody knows that."

Sure, like that kid Sara in Eight-B who it turned out her own father had been molesting her for years, but she never told anybody until some psychologist caught on from some tests we all had to take in seventh grade. Up till then, Sara kept her secret fine.

And I kept mine, marking off the days on the calendar. The only part I didn't look forward to was having a period again, which last time came right before the change.

When the time came, I got crampy and more zits popped out on my face, but I didn't have a period.

I changed, though.

The next morning they were talking in school about a couple of prize miniature schnauzers at the Wanscombes' that had been hauled out of their yard by somebody and killed, and almost nothing left of them.

Well, my stomach turned a little when I heard some kids describing what Mr. Wanscombe had found over in Baker's Park, "the remains," as people said. I felt a little guilty, too, because Mrs. Wanscombe had really loved those little dogs, which somehow I didn't think about at all when I was a wolf the night before, trotting around hungry in the moonlight.

I knew those schnauzers personally, so I was sorry, even if they were irritating little mutts that made a lot of noise.

But heck, the Wanscombes shouldn't have left them out all night in the cold. Anyhow, they were rich, they could buy new ones if they wanted.

Still and all, though. I mean, dogs are just dumb animals. If they're mean, it's because they're wired that way or somebody made them mean, they can't help it. They can't just decide to be nice, like a person can. And plus, they don't taste so great, I think because there's so much junk in commerical dog-foods—antiworm medicine and ashes and ground-up fish, stuff like that. Ick.

In fact, after the second schnauzer I had felt sort of sick and I didn't sleep real well that night. So I was not in a great mood to start with; and that was the day my new brassiere disappeared while I was in gym. Later on I got passed a note telling me where to find it: stapled to the bulletin board outside the principal's office, where everybody could see that I was trying a bra with an underwire.

Naturally, it had to be Stacey Buhl who grabbed my bra while I was changing for gym and my back was turned, since she was now hanging out with Billy and his friends.

Billy went around all day making bets at the top of his lungs on how soon I would be wearing a D cup.

Stacey didn't matter, she was just a jerk. Billy mattered. He had wrecked me in that school forever, with his nasty mind and his big, fat mouth. I was past crying or fighting and getting punched out. I was boiling, I had had enough crap from him, and I had an idea.

I followed Billy home and waited on his porch until his mom came home and she made him come down and talk to me. He stood in the doorway and talked through the screen door, eating a banana and lounging around like he didn't have a care in the world.

So he goes, "Whatcha want, Boobs?"

I stammered a lot, being I was so nervous about telling such big lies, but that probably made me sound more believable.

I told him that I would make a deal with him: I would meet him that night in Baker's Park, late, and take off my shirt and bra and let him do whatever he wanted with my boobs if that would satisfy his curiosity and he would find somebody else to pick on and leave me alone.

"What?" he said, staring at my chest with his mouth open. His voice squeaked and he was practically drooling on the floor. He couldn't believe his good luck.

I said the same thing over again.

He almost came out onto the porch to try it right then and there. "Well, shit," he goes, lowering his voice a lot, "why didn't you say something before? You really mean it?"

I go, "Sure," though I couldn't look at him.

After a minute he goes, "Okay, it's a deal. Listen, Kelsey, if you like it, can we, uh, do it again, you know?"

I go, "Sure. But, Billy, one thing: This is a secret,

between just you and me. If you tell anybody, if there's one other person hanging around out there tonight——"

"Oh, no," he goes, real fast, "I won't say a thing to anybody, honest. Not a word, I promise!"

Not until afterward, of course, was what he meant, which if there was one thing Billy Linden couldn't do, it was to keep quiet if he knew something bad about another person.

"You're gonna like it, I know you are," he goes, speaking strictly for himself, like usual. "Jeez. I can't believe this!"

But he did, the dork.

I couldn't eat much for dinner that night, I was too excited, and I went upstairs early—to do homework, I told Dad and Hilda.

Then I waited for the moon, and when it came, I changed.

Billy was in the park. I caught a whiff of him, very sweaty and excited, but I stayed cool. I snuck around for a while, as quiet as I could—which was real quiet—making sure none of his stupid friends were lurking around. I mean, I wouldn't have trusted just his promise for a million dollars.

I passed up half a hamburger lying in the gutter where somebody had parked for lunch next to Baker's Park. My mouth watered, but I didn't want to spoil my appetite. I was hungry and happy, sort of singing inside my head, "Shoofly pie, and an apple pandowdy . . ."

Without any sound, of course.

Billy had been sitting on a bench, his hands in his pockets, twisting around to look this way and that way, watching for me—for my human self—to come join him. He had a jacket on, being it was very chilly out.

Which he didn't stop to think that maybe a sane person wouldn't be crazy enough to sit out there and take off her top, leaving her naked skin bare to the breeze. But that was Billy, all right, totally fixed on his own greedy self and without a single thought for anybody else. I bet all he could think about was what a great scam this was, to feel up old Boobs in the park and then crow about it all over school.

Now he was walking around the park, kicking at the sprinkler heads and glancing up every once in a while, frowning and looking sulky.

I could see he was starting to think that I might stand him up. Maybe he even suspected that old Boobs was lurking around watching him and laughing to herself because he had fallen for a trick. Maybe old Boobs had even brought some kids from school with her to see what a jerk he was.

Actually that would have been pretty good, except Billy probably would have broken my nose for me again, or worse, if I'd tried it.

"Kelsey?" he goes, sounding mad.

I didn't want him stomping off home in a huff. I moved up closer, and I let the bushes swish a little around my shoulders.

He goes, "Hey, Kelse, it's late, where've you been?"

I listened to the words, but mostly I listened to the little thread of worry flickering in his voice, low and high, high and low, as he tried to figure out what was going on.

I let out the whisper of a growl.

He stood real still, staring at the bushes, and he goes, "That you, Kelse? Answer me."

I was wild inside, I couldn't wait another second. I tore through the bushes and leaped for him, flying.

He stumbled backward with a squawk—"What!"—jerking his hands up in front of his face, and he was just sucking in a big breath to yell with when I hit him like a demo-derby truck.

I jammed my nose past his feeble claws and chomped down hard on his face.

No sound came out of him except this wet, thick gurgle, which I could more taste than hear because the sound came right into my mouth with the gush of his blood and the hot mess of meat and skin that I tore away and swallowed.

He thrashed around, hitting at me, but I hardly felt anything through my fur. I mean, he wasn't so big and strong lying there on the ground with me straddling him all lean and wiry with wolf muscle. And plus, he was in shock. I got a strong whiff from below as he let go of everything right into his pants.

Dogs were barking, but so many people around Baker's Park have dogs to keep out burglars, and the dogs make such a racket all the time, that nobody pays any attention. I wasn't worried. Anyway, I was too busy to care.

I nosed in under what was left of Billy's jaw and I bit his throat out.

Now let him go around telling lies about people.

His clothes were a lot of trouble and I really missed having hands. I managed to drag his shirt out of his belt with my teeth, though, and it was easy to tear his belly open. Pretty messy, but once I got in there, it was better than Thanksgiving dinner. Who would think that somebody as horrible as Billy Linden could taste so *good*?

He was barely moving by then, and I quit thinking about him as Billy Linden anymore. I quit thinking at all, I just pushed my head in and pulled out delicious steaming chunks and ate until I was picking at tidbits and everything was getting cold.

On the way home I saw a police car cruising the neighborhood the way they do sometimes. I hid in the shadows and of course they never saw me.

There was a lot of washing up to do in the morning, and when Hilda saw my sheets she shook her head and she goes, "You should be more careful about keeping track of your period so as not to get caught by surprise."

Everybody in school knew something had happened to Billy Linden, but it wasn't until the day after that that they got the word. Kids stood around in little huddles trading rumors about how some wild animal had chewed Billy up. I would walk up and listen in and add a really gross remark or two, like part of the game of thrilling each other green and nauseous with made-up details to see who would upchuck first.

Not me, that's for sure. I mean, when somebody went on about how Billy's whole head was gnawed down to the skull and they didn't even know who he was except from the bus pass in his wallet, I got a little urpy. It's amazing the things people will dream up. But when I thought about what I had actually done to Billy, I had to smile.

It felt totally wonderful to walk through the halls without having anybody yelling, "Hey, Boobs!"

There are people who just plain do not deserve to live. And the same goes for Fat Joey, if he doesn't quit crowding me in science lab, trying to get a feel.

One funny thing, though, I don't get periods at all anymore. I get a little crampy, and my breasts get sore, and I break out more than usual—and then instead of bleeding, I change.

Which is fine with me, though I take a lot more care now about how I hunt on my wolf nights. I stay away from Baker's Park. The suburbs go on for miles and miles, and there are lots of places I can hunt and still get home by morning. A running wolf can cover a lot of ground.

And I make sure I make my kills where I can eat in private, so no cop car can catch me unawares, which could easily have happened that night when I killed Billy, I was so deep into the eating thing that first time. I look around a lot more now when I'm eating a kill, I keep watch.

Good thing it's only once a month that this happens, and only a couple of nights. "The Full-Moon Killer" has the whole state up in arms and terrified as it is.

Eventually I guess I'll have to go somewhere else, which I'm not looking forward to at all. If I can just last until I can have a car of my own, life will get a a lot easier.

Meantime, some wolf nights I don't even feel like hunting. Mostly I'm not as hungry as I was those first times.

I think I must have been storing up my appetite for a long time. Sometimes I just prowl around and I run, boy, do I run.

If I am hungry, sometimes I eat from the garbage instead of killing somebody. It's no fun, but you do get a taste for it. I don't mind garbage as long as once in a while I can have the real thing fresh-killed, nice and wet. People can be awfully nasty, but they sure taste sweet.

I do pick and choose, though. I look for people sneaking around in the middle of the night, like Billy waiting in the park that time. I figure they've got to be out looking for trouble at that hour, so whose fault is it if they find it? I have done a lot more for the burglary problem around Baker's Park than a hundred dumb watchdogs, believe me.

Gerry-Anne is not only talking to me again, she has invited me to go on a double date with her. Some guy she met at a party invited her, and he has a friend. They're both from Fawcett Junior High across town, which will be a change. I was nervous, but finally I said yes. We're going to the movies next weekend. My first real date! I am still pretty nervous, to tell the truth.

For New Year's, I have made two solemn vows.

One is that on this date I will not worry about my chest, I will not be self-conscious, even if the guy stares.

The other is, I'll never eat another dog.

Afterword

Years ago someone invited me to contribute to a pro-
posed collection of werewolf stories for and about teenagers. I said (as I generally do), "Well, I don't usually
write short work, but if something pops into my head,
I'll let you know," and I forgot the whole thing. As far
as I am aware, that collection never did see publication;
but three or four years later, along came "Boobs," spin-
ning itself rapidly out of my machine; a story designed
for a buyer long since gone on to other projects and a
difficult story to sell anywhere else. I thought it really
ought to get out there and find a general audience, since
it addresses a matter of concern to one-half the human
race (menstruation, not werewolfery), so I went looking
for a general outlet. But "Boobs" is not exactly suitable
for *Redbook* or *Mademoiselle*, *Seventeen* wouldn't
touch it, and *Ms.* told me they weren't taking fiction.
So it was back to the usual places or into the drawer. I
kept getting answers from female editors that went like
this: "God, I really *loved* this story—how well I remember!—but it just isn't right for our readership."

BOOBS

In the end, Gardner Dozois bought "Boobs" for *Asimov's*. He asked for a minor rewrite of the ending, something to take a little of the chill off, so to speak. He said that both he and his editorial assistant found our heroine a bit too "unsympathetic," and he suggested a change that seemed appropriate to counter that feeling without doing serious violence to the story.

My stepdaughter had reacted in a similar fashion, objecting that Kelsey is too cold-blooded about wolfish violence. I reminded her of, a) the tendency in the young toward a very, very narrow morality ("What hurts me is unforgivably awful and what I do is okay"); b) the surprising failures of empathy in children that can lead to the most shockingly loathsome behavior committed in a very casual manner; for example, c) the true beastliness of teenage boys in packs. Personally, I am pleased to see the original ending restored in this collection, for readers who may be disinclined to have their angry young heroines sweetened.

It may be of interest that the people at the word processing center at my husband's office, where I did my final edit of this story (as of all my work), had a very different reaction. These are (for the most part) working women in their twenties and thirties. I left a copy of the story for them to read, as usual—these are, after all, the people who kindly fly to my aid when I sit foaming at the screen, screaming, "HELP WHAT DO I DO NOW I HAVE LOST MY CURSOR?" or whatever.

They said they liked the story very much, but several of them objected to the killings of the dogs.

Suzy McKee Charnas

WALLS

R. M. Lamming

Walls that collapse, and something rushes in.

Walls that collapse to reveal, standing just behind them, something bone-white that has waited very patiently.

Walls that collapse inward, blocking off the light; and all the lights go out. Darkness. Then, picking through the rubble comes the sound of something with a long fingernail.

Walls that collapse neither inward nor outward but to thinness, so that one walks through them accidentally and doesn't know it until, on turning round—there the walls are, a barrier at one's back.

Walls that creep, closing in around one with eyes and feet, although they look—they insist—they are perfectly normal.

Walls that shout, or boom with groans, or weep in the night, inconsolably.

WALLS

Walls that sing, especially before dawn, giving out a faint, high-pitched singing from somewhere round the skirting board.

Walls that sweat.

Walls that shake with laughter.

Walls that crack open like an eggshell to let some blind, hatchling thing come wriggling through.

Walls that crack open like an eggshell, and a sharp parent beak reaches in.

Walls that turn to dust.

Walls that melt, oozing gently down round whoever the wick is.

Walls that breathe: in-out, in-out.

Walls like lungs, soaking up the air.

Walls that run like rats suddenly through the shadows when no one's looking.

Scavenger walls.

Hunter walls.

Walls like gods, demanding sacrifices.

Walls that are as jealous as lovers, hugging one like lovers.

Walls like owls, evacuating tiny pellets of skin and gristle.

Walls that are like death, lasting forever.

Afterword

Our sense of horror is skin-of-the-soul stuff. Horror is always in us; it defines our soul-shape as much as, say, our sense of beauty does—another part of the soul-skin. But whereas so-called everyday life sometimes offers us encouragement to be articulate about our sense of beauty, we are taught to ignore what seems individual about our sense of horror, and for good reason: this planet is crammed with terrible events, persecutions, and sufferings, and to articulate a horrified response to those is of far greater immediate moral value than is the exposing of our personal "skin." Yet the "skin" exists, and by acknowledging these individual senses of horror and exploring them, we can strengthen our understanding of each other and also our respect for life—vital gains if we want to stop terrible events and persecutions at the source. Surely the function of this individual sense of horror is essentially moral; it celebrates life, by which I mean a natural balance whether in environment or living entities or in the relationship between the two; it celebrates by activating an alarm when one or the other of these territories is violated. But, like much of the soul-skin, the most personal layer of our sense of horror can be numbed or perverted by social codes, all the anesthetics of expediency and overfamiliarity; and this increases the importance of exposing it from time to time and taking a look at it and prodding it to be sure that it is still functioning healthily.

R. M. Lamming

ANZAC DAY

Cherry Wilder

We could see Aunt Madge's house through the macrocarpa trees: a red corrugated iron roof, white verandah posts. My brother Billy, six years old, said it was like Nan's house and I contradicted him sharply. I could not bear it when he was homesick for our former life, for our own farm and the homestead where our grandmother had lived. My mother said:

"Rachel, we must make ourselves presentable again!"

An old man in a Ford had given us a lift to this gate in the middle of nowhere. It was a perfect April day; a lone oak tree on the drive showed that the season was autumn, the fields were a thick, juicy green on either side of the dusty road. Behind the farmhouse rose a green hillside flecked with the gray skeletons of dead trees, then other hills clothed in bush, a rich blue-green. Barbed-wire fences and a ditch ran parallel on both sides of the road; the green grass grew thickly outside each fence, with reeds and wildflowers springing up in the ditch. The barbed wire sagged across the road; a young jersey cow put her head through the fence and munched buttercups. They would taint her milk.

Uncle Len's name, FELL, was on the mailbox. We perched on a roofed platform for cream cans. I combed my hair, wiped my face—I had been eating biscuits—and shined my shoes with a handful of grass. My mother dealt with Billy first of all. Then she took out her compact, powdered her nose, and put rouge on her lips with the tip of her finger. She wore a navy costume and a pert felt hat trimmed with grosgrain ribbon. I wore a pleated skirt of Royal Stewart tartan with a cotton bodice and over it a blouse of cream tussore silk with a Peter Pan collar and a navy cardigan. Billy wore gray serge short pants, almost to his knees, a long-sleeved blue shirt, and a Fair Isle pullover with a pattern of fawn and green horseshoes and four-leafed clovers. We had been down on our luck, however, and it was beginning to show.

We had left Te Waiau without paying the lady at the boardinghouse. It was not so much a midnight flit as a teatime one, but it had meant an uncomfortable night in the station waiting room. The early train from Te Waiau to Claraville had contained a number of returned soldiers in uniform, others in their best suits with rows of medal ribbons. Today was Anzac Day. After the solemn mystery of the dawn service by the cenotaph, the town was gathering itself together for a midmorning parade. In spite of the Depression, the people in the streets looked cheerful and well fed. The memorial pyramid with its list of the fallen was draped in purple; at its base were piled wreaths of flowers.

We set off through the streets of Claraville; my mother knew the way. The shops were shut today; all shops had been more or less shut to us for a long time now. Even the sight of a Woolworth's or a Milk Bar meant little to Billy. We wandered on past hedges and gardens and came to a much larger house, a Victorian mansion set among smooth lawns. A sign read: BETHANY, HOME FOR THE AGED.

There was the usual problem of where we should wait. I wanted very much to stay with Billy in the garden. We stared at some old people and an attendant, a woman in a starched mauve uniform.

"Better not," said my mother.

We took the gate that said TRADEMEN'S ENTRANCE and went down a drive separated from the garden by a tall hedge. Bethany was dark inside, brown-varnished with brown linoleum on the floors. We were engulfed by a warm smell of food as we passed the kitchen. There was an uncushioned wooden bench for us to wait on outside the door of the matron, Mrs. McCormack. Billy was tired and hungry; he whined and could not keep still.

Life had become an endless train journey full of discomforts that Billy and I had no right to complain about, as children. We waited, we could not be left alone too much, our care and feeding were a constant worry. The adults we met demanded certain behaviour: "Speak up! You like that, don't you, girlie? Have you wiped your feet? Make a fist, young fella!" They were giving a performance for children, like the ladies who leaned over a baby's pram making goo-goo noises, and we must react accordingly. In fact, I did not like waiting alone; it was safer with Billy. Special behaviour was demanded of a girl child by men—strangers and drunks but also friendly acquaintances like the gardener at the boardinghouse. Not much more, in most cases, than familiarity, an insidious change of attitude, but I suffered great embarrassment and dread. How thin the line was between something that could be shrugged off and the need to scream or tell my mother.

As we sat in the corridor, a Maori maid came past mopping the floor with a strong solution of Jeyes fluid.

"You kids wipe your feet?" she asked.

A hideous old woman in a pink kimono chattered to Billy, patted his head, and gave him a caramel. An old man with a walking stick and a white moustache demanded our names, then mimicked our replies. When we stopped answering him he became excited, whacking at our suitcase with his stick. A nurse appeared and said, leading him off:

"This is not a place for children!"

At last my mother came out smiling with Mrs. McCormack, an enormously dignified woman in gray silk; I knew at once that she had got the job.

"So these are your two," said Mrs. McCormack, coming straight to the point. "What are you going to do with them, Mrs. Tanner?"

"We are going to my cousin's farm," said my mother proudly. "Mrs. Fell. Just out along this road."

"I'm hungry," said Billy.

"Oh!" Mrs. McCormack laughed. "Oh, indeed. Well, we don't want to spoil your dinner."

She caught my eye.

"But this *is* a special day," she conceded.

As we passed the kitchen, she put her head in the swing doors and said:

"Alma—some of those lovely Anzac biscuits."

As we went down the drive munching, my mother said to Billy:

"Don't you ever say that again!"

"Why?" he asked with his mouth full.

My mother ate one of the biscuits herself. We were faced with a walk of unknown length along a country road. The footpath soon gave way to a track, then the track disappeared. We stopped at this point, and the Ford came roaring along in the right direction. The old man, whose name was Wilson, took us to the Fell farm. He deposited us in the middle of nowhere and we watched him drive on, out of sight. There was another house on the other side of the road, just visible from where we stood, but it wasn't his place.

When we were presentable again, we opened the gate, closed it after us, and negotiated the cattlestop. The cows in the field raised their heads as we went past. As we reached the oak tree, Mother said:

"Wait on!"

She enacted a little parody of exhaustion.

"I can't carry this thing another inch."

Then she headed for the tree with our suitcase. It struck terror into my heart. We would have nowhere—no bed, no food, not even a lavatory—unless Aunt Madge and Uncle Len took us in. Mother was so uncertain of our reception that she wasn't game to march up to the house suitcase and all.

My mother pressed on into the long grass at the foot of the tree and suddenly drew back with a horrified squeak.

"What is it?" I asked.

"Nothing," she said. "Nothing, just cow manure."

She walked in a wider arc round the tree and set down the case. We plodded up the drive; no dogs barked. The house was larger and more handsome than it looked from the road, a spreading bungalow, its weatherboard newly white, its roof a deep crimson. I yearned for the house, for its wide verandahs and the cool, beautiful rooms inside. The front garden was surrounded by a white picket fence and a privet hedge to protect the lawn and flower beds from the livestock. A window blind in one of the front rooms was caught up crookedly at a sharp angle across the pane. The perfection of the swept brick garden path was marred by a large cane doll's pram lying on its side. I thought with dull envy of my cousin Beryl, nine years old to my eleven; she had a house, expensive toys, a father who had *not* cleared out.

We came toward the macrocarpa trees, which had thick low-hanging branches above worn patches of earth, as if children had played there, riding and swinging on the trees. In black shade the leaves stirred as if a little girl might step out. I was suddenly filled with an entirely inappropriate emotion, a wave of fear and sadness that seemed to come welling up from the ground on which I stood. It was not part of me at all.

We did not think of going to the front door but followed the wider track to the backyard. Billy went lolloping on ahead, then came to a dead stop.

"Hey, look! Hey, look!" he cried.

The body of a kelpie cattle-dog lay in the grass; I heard my mother's horrified squeak for the second time.

"Come away," she said. "Poor thing."

"We must tell Aunt Madge," I said.

"No!" said my mother. "We don't want to come rushing in with bad news. Not a word, Billy."

Billy stared at the dead dog with great concentration. There was no telling how it had died; the small amount of blood at its brown muzzle was almost hidden by a shiny mass of bluebottle flies.

"Come on!"

I dragged him by the wrist. We went along the side of the house into a picture-book backyard with Canterbury bells, delphiniums, and gladioli, fruit trees, a big puriri tree with a swing, two dog kennels; the whitewashed privy was half covered with sweet-smelling honeysuckle. My mother patted her hair and tugged at her costume coat. She went up two steps and knocked at the back door, calling cheerily:

"Oo-hoo! Madge, dear! Look who's here!"

She had to repeat the ritual before heavy steps sounded inside the house and the door was flung open. A soldier stood in the doorway. He wore khaki breeches, puttees, neatly wrapped, and army boots, but his tunic was slung over his shoulders. He had been shaving in his braces and a flannel vest; there were still specks of lather on his face and a cutthroat razor glistening in his hand.

"Oh, Len!" said my mother. "Oh, I'm sorry to catch you . . ."

"Caught me on the hop . . ." he echoed.

He wiped his lantern jaw with the towel he carried around his neck. Uncle Len was older and wore a mustache, but he was not unlike our own father: a tall, rangy, muscular man, pale-skinned with black hair. I saw that his eyes were a much lighter blue with a curious darker ring around the iris.

"I'm Madge's cousin Grace Tanner," said my

47

mother. "You remember, we all met at Violet's wedding. And these are my two . . . Rachel and Billy."

His eyes did not move; he stared over the top of my mother's head.

"Madge's cousin Grace," he said. *"Gracie*. Gracie Tanner."

He looked into her face for the first time and backed away awkwardly.

"Come in," he said, "I'll put on the kettle."

My mother was already in, making gestures behind her back for us to follow. The kitchen was unbearably hot; the stove was burning fiercely with the grate open and the windows were shut. A black iron kettle was boiling away. There were dishes piled in the sink and a smell of burnt food. Uncle Len stood with his back to the sink, a dark figure against the windows, buttoning up his tunic. My mother gave a laugh.

"Well, I can see you're doing for yourself, Len," she said. "Suppose *I* make the tea."

She went at it with great efficiency, finding the teapot, the caddy, clean cups and saucers, milk, and sugar in Aunt Madge's kitchen without a second's help from him. She wiped down the kitchen table, spread a checked cloth, found bread, butter, and jam, took off Billy's pullover and rolled up his sleeves, shut the stove, altered the damper, put two burnt pots to soak, and opened the windows. As she reached round him to do this, Uncle Len shuddered like a nervous horse; I saw the whites of his eyes.

"Madge . . ." he said, clicking his razor shut.

"Madge and Beryl must be on a visit," said my mother. "What a pity. Are they down in Auckland with Violet?"

"With Violet," he said. "I'm on my own."

She motioned us to our chairs and poured the tea.

"Take off your cardigan," she said to me. "It's hot in here."

Len lowered himself into a captain's chair at the head of the table.

"Well, Anzac Day," said my mother, "in this sad year."

I could not take my eyes off Uncle Len. I thought he would echo her again in his hollow twang: "Sad year." Instead, he cocked his head on one side, looking more or less at the clock on the wall, and said brightly:

"Yes, Anzac Day!"

"Were you one of the Anzac soldiers, Uncle Len?" burst out Billy.

Uncle Len became suddenly alert; his expression was wolfish and cunning. He grinned at Billy and stretched his legs.

"Gracie's boy," he said. "Wants to know if I was one of the Anzacs. No harm in saying that I was."

"Did you kill any Turks?" cried Billy.

My mother, still smiling, shook her head at him.

"Kill Turks?" echoed Uncle Len. "That's what they told us to do. Orders came from above. Johnny Turk was a good soldier, he knew how it was done. Learned a lot from him, Johnny Turk. Killed him and saw him die. Shot him down like a dog. Better still, used the bayonet. . . ."

My mother made a low sound of protest and rattled her white breakfast cup into its saucer. Len shut up. My mother cut us all some bread, then spread it thickly with butter and tinned raspberry jam.

"You need to see red!" exclaimed Uncle Len. "Then you can really give it to them. What's your name, sonny?"

"Billy!"

"Don't talk with your mouth full!" said my mother. She wiped her fingers daintily on a tea towel, passed it to me, then excused herself.

"I'll just be a minute."

She went out the back door. I heard her steps on the brick path to the privy. We were alone with Uncle Len.

"Like a knife through butter!" he said. "A bayonet is sharp enough to cut off your hand. I seen that, too.

Pile of little hands. The hands of the Belgian babies. You hear what old Jerry did with the Belgian babies?''

"It wasn't true!" I gasped.

Uncle Len glared at me.

"Shut your trap, girlie!" he said. "Who asked you? Now, Billy, show us the size of *your* hand. . . ."

"*Billy!*" I shrieked.

"Shut your trap, I said!" roared Uncle Len. "By Christ, Beryl, I've had enough of your shenanigans. We'll see who's boss around here!"

"I'm not Beryl!" I said.

My mother came back into the kitchen. Uncle Len controlled himself, his nostrils dilated with the effort.

"Is that your girl, Gracie?" he asked. "She better mind her p's and q's."

"Why, Rachel," said my mother, "have you been giving cheek to Uncle Len?"

I saw what was going to happen and I was terrified.

"No," I said.

"No what?"

"No, I didn't give him cheek."

"No, *mother!*" said my mother severely.

She flung herself down onto her chair and said in a trembling voice:

"Oh, Len, it's so difficult to manage all alone. Poor old Will is down in Auckland looking for work. The farm has gone. Did you know that? I've just got this job at the old people's home here in Claraville, and I hope and trust you won't mind putting us up for a few days. Madge was always offering us the spare room."

Uncle Len reached casually into the sink and produced a small meat cleaver. He wiped it clean with the corner of the tablecloth and said:

"Hold out your hand, Beryl. . . ."

He winked at my mother.

"Well, go on," said my mother, "he's only teasing."

"Hold out *your* hand, Mum," I said. "Make Billy hold out his hand."

"Oh, Rachel," said my mother, "can't you take a joke?"

Uncle Len lunged at me with the cleaver held flat, like a fish-slice, and I backed away so hard that I over-turned my chair. He roared with laughter, Billy joined in, my mother took the descant. Uncle Len raised the cleaver high in the air and cut the loaf of bread neatly in two on the breadboard with a hollow thunk.

"Oh, Len!" scolded my mother. "Now it will go stale. Put that thing away."

"Blunt anyway," said Uncle Len.

The cleaver rattled into the sink.

"About the spare room . . ." said my mother. "I have to be back in Claraville at four for the night shift."

"Just through there," said Uncle Len. "It's open."

My mother relaxed and smiled. Uncle Len sprang up from his chair.

"Have to get to work."

"Are you going to the parade, Len?" asked my mother.

"Parade?" he said.

"For Anzac Day," said Billy.

"Come along, Sonny," said Uncle Len. "You can give me a hand. No time for a parade. We'll make our own little celebration."

Billy got down from his chair.

"What do you say?" murmured my mother.

"Excuse me!"

Billy called it over his shoulder as he followed Uncle Len into the yard. I stood up and sat down again, feeling the blood drain from my face. The kitchen darkened before my eyes.

"Mum," I whispered, "please . . ."

I clutched at her.

"Please, Mum, we can't stay here with him. You can't leave us with him!"

She put an arm around me, squeezing too tightly.

"It's all been too much for you," she said.

"Mum," I said, "he keeps saying dreadful things. He keeps calling me Beryl."

"Poor man," she whispered. "I think I know what has happened."

I lacked words to express my fear of Uncle Len.

"He's gone funny," I said. "He's mental. He's shell-shocked."

"You're a big girl, Rachel," said my mother. "You know the facts of life. You should be able to understand."

"Understand what?"

"I think Madge has cleared out and left him," she said. "Taken Beryl with her. Things haven't been going too well in this part of the world either."

She left me slumped over the table and began washing up. She found Aunt Madge's dishmop and soap strainer. I staggered to my feet and began to dry the dishes. My mother rattled about in the pantry, then checked the oven and built up the fire. She went to work at the table and I saw that she was making a bacon and egg pie. Before it was in the oven, she said, wheedling:

"Why not go and look at the room?"

I finished wiping the bench and went into the passage. The house was dark and cool after the kitchen. . . . I could see the door of the spare room standing ajar, but first I went exploring. There was a sitting room next to the kitchen with a wireless set and comfortable chairs. The house was divided by a wooden archway filled with a bead curtain; beyond this point it grew very much colder.

There was a large linen cupboard and opposite it a bathroom that was locked. In a little strip of corridor was a room with a pink ceiling to be seen through its fanlight—Beryl's bedroom, I guessed, but it was locked, too. At the front of the house I found the "best room," with a gleaming black piano, a china cabinet, a small bookcase. On the mantelpiece was a photograph of Uncle Len in full uniform with his peaked cap and Sam Brown belt. In the empty grate lay a mess of broken glass and cardboard; I made out two framed photographs of Aunt Madge and Beryl, smashed and twisted and smeared with something like brown varnish. The room with the crooked blind was the front bedroom, and it was locked, too.

There were panels of coloured glass in the front door; I looked at a green world, then a red one. I could see the doll's pram on the path, the trees, the picket fence, the sky, all red as blood. I took fright then and ran for the spare room. When I looked back, I thought again of a child, a little girl, standing just beyond the flickering strings of beads in the half-darkness.

The spare room was perfect for the three of us; it had a double bed and a smaller bed on the glassed-in sunporch. The double bed was made up with a thick white cotton counterpane. There was an old washstand with a basin and ewer patterned with water lilies. I moved like a sleepwalker through the quiet room to the dressing table and opened the left-hand top drawer. It was lined with newspaper and empty except for a gold bangle. I didn't have to read the engraving; it was Beryl's bangle. My eye was drawn to any kind of print; I turned my head and read the headline of a copy of *Truth,* lining the drawer: HACKED TO PIECES. I unfolded the paper to find out the first words, but part of the page was torn away, only three letters remained: . . .HER. Her hacked to pieces? Saw her hacked to pieces? The few lines of bold print under the headline told of a Mrs. Emma Palmer, dying in a grisly sawmill accident. I heard steps in the passage, shut the drawer, and moved away from it as my mother came in.

"Ohhh . . ." she sighed. "Oh, isn't it lovely. We've really fallen on our feet this time!"

She sat in the wicker chair at the bedside and took off her shoes, resting her stockinged feet on the polished floor. She took my hand and drew me down until I sat on the edge of the bed.

"Let me look at you," she said reproachfully. "You haven't got a scrap of colour in your face."

She took off my patent leather shoes and began to unbutton my blouse.

"Lift up!"

She rolled back the counterpane and one soft green blanket and bundled me into bed. I laid my head on the cool pillow. She brushed the hair out of my face and laid her hand on my forehead.

"Billy . . ." I said.

"Ssh," said my mother. "He needs to go out with his uncle. Remember how his dad used to take him everywhere? I'm making them a nice lunch. Len hasn't been looking after himself."

Her eyes were dark and glistening; she began to sing me an Anzac song:

> "There's a long, long trail a-winding
> Into the land of my dreams,
> Where the nightingales are singing
> And the white moon beams . . ."

I felt my fear slip away gradually like a black tide going out.

"Wake me up before you go!" I said.

"I'll save you a piece of bacon and egg pie," said my mother.

As I drifted off to sleep, I thought of the missing word: MOTHER HACKED TO PIECES. I slept deeply and was brought half awake by voices in the kitchen. I could not make out exactly who was there. At first I thought it was my mother and father and Billy, but I knew that couldn't be true. Then it sounded like three completely different people. I turned and saw that our suitcase was in the room and then I fell asleep again.

I dreamed of doors banging and a slow, heavy tread that echoed through the whole house. A voice said quietly, *"Dead to the world . . ."* I was filled with terror in the dream and my heart pounded in my throat. The slow, purposeful footsteps went on, another door was shut, there was a sound of hoarse breathing. The voice said:

"Keep still!"

Then there was a dull chopping sound and another voice screamed loudly, then dwindled to an inhuman moaning, which abruptly stopped. I was standing in the passage, in the icy coldness of the house, beyond the bead curtain. The little girl, Beryl, stood at the front door; I could see her white nightdress and her curly mop of golden hair. I was more frightened than ever. She opened the door and ran out to her doll's pram in bright sunshine. She bent over the pram, and then a shadow blotted her out. The terrible voice said:

What are you up to now?

I tried to scream but I could not. The dream doubled back on itself. Beryl stood in the hall again, at the front door; she looked back at me over her shoulder.

"Run!" she said. "Run to the road! I can't open the door!"

Then she turned toward me and I saw that her pretty white nightdress was smeared with blood from head to foot. She held her arms up awkwardly, pressed against her chest, and her hands had been cut off.

I came up out of the dream, and it was dark. I knew where I was and knew what had awakened me. Someone had shut a door heavily. I was wide awake, unnaturally alert, tingling to my fingertips.

"Billy . . . ?" I whispered.

The room was not so dark; light came in from the passage, through the fanlight over the door. I could see our suitcase flung open. My mother had gone off to work and let me sleep. I reached for my cardigan, which was on the chair back, but did not put on my shoes.

There was a heavy galumphing tread that I recognised: Someone was wearing gumboots. I opened the spare room door just a crack and saw Uncle Len in the kitchen. He was alert, as I was, full of purpose. He wore gumboots now and an old blue jersey in place of his khaki tunic. He carried, at the trail, a rifle with a fixed bayonet. He crossed to the back door and went out.

I slipped into the corridor and said as loudly as I dared:

"Billy?"

I followed a thread of sound to the living room. There was a pool of light from the standard lamp and another from the dial of the radio. Billy lay curled up on the couch under a blanket. When I ran to him, he sat up and said:

"What's the password?"

"Gallipoli!" I said.

"Wrong!" he crowed. "It's 'Slit their bellies'!"

On the radio a lady was singing "Roses of Picardy." I saw that Billy was as dirty and untidy as it was possible for a boy to be. The smears of mud on his cheeks made him look like a little kid in the pictures—like the Kid himself or a member of Our Gang.

"What did you do out there?" I asked.

His eyes were open very wide, his teeth clenched, his hair bristling. He flattened his stained hands and beat upon the gray army blanket. I knew that he was hurt, maimed; a day with Uncle Len had left him shell-shocked at six years old. I was filled with a tearing anxiety for my little brother. I gripped his hands and knelt by the couch.

"Tell me . . ." I said. "Billy! Billy-boy!"

"The cows came in," he said. "Uncle Len did the milking."

"Before that?"

"Dug holes . . ." he said.

"He made you dig holes?"

"Put the dead dogs in . . ."

He was still tense.

"Had to . . . had to . . . cut them up first . . ."

"Don't!" I said. "Don't think about it. He shouldn't make you do things like that!"

"Being soldiers!" he whispered.

"Where has Uncle Len gone now?"

"On patrol," he said.

Uncle Len came in far away, at the front door. He began to look into every room. The good front room, then the front bedroom with the crooked blind. I heard him unlock the door. He didn't raise his voice, but it carried through the whole house:

"You asked for it," he said.

His heavy tread went on into the room, a piece of furniture fell over. Then Uncle Len made a sound of disgust, a kind of whinny, and came out cursing under his breath. He unlocked the bathroom and I heard water gushing, a clatter of metal. He came back into the passage, close now, just beyond the bead curtain.

"Now then, my little miss," he said. "Did I deal with you? Girlie?"

I tried to pull Billy off the couch.

"Come away!" I whispered.

The big sash window on to the verandah was wide open; I could see the wind stir the curtains.

"We have to get away," I said. "He's after us!"

"Not me," said Billy reasonably. "Only you. You're a girlie."

He raised his voice and called.

"In here, Uncle Len! Here's one!"

He tried to hold my hands. As I scrambled to my feet, the tall standard lamp swayed and fell down. Perhaps I had tugged on the carpet. I half-crawled across the dark room and went through the open window onto the verandah. I heard Uncle Len stride into the room. Billy challenged him:

"What's the password?"

"Is that my little cobber?" Uncle Len laughed.

I ran softly along the verandah to the front of the house. The front door was open—I quickly slipped inside and went into the front bedroom with the crooked blind. I went into that room because it was a good place to hide: He had been in that room, he hadn't liked it. I was also looking for evidence.

It was hard to be in that room. The overhead light

was on; it had a pink fringed shade. A chair had fallen over and there was a large star-shaped crack in the long mirror on the wardrobe door. The drawers of the dressing table hung open; handfuls of clothing had been used to wipe up the blood. It was dark and sticky like paint on the mats; it had risen up in a fountain from the bed. In places it was still scarlet in the light, but mostly darker. There were congealing pools of blood in the middle of the bed where the mattress dipped. Aunt Madge had been lying in bed; her head was still on the pillow, a wide band of bloodstained pillow slip visible between her head and her trunk. One arm was severed at the shoulder and at the elbow, the other had fallen in three pieces to the floor. She lay disjointed like a big doll and there were stab wounds like dark holes in her chest. The door of the little pedestal cupboard beside the bed had been torn off, it lay on the other pillow; Uncle Len had used it as a chopping board.

I flattened myself against the wall beside the sticky doorway and wiped my hand on my skirt. The room was filled with the smell of blood; a red mist rose before my eyes. For a moment I was floating free, I was high in the corner of the dreadful room gazing down at the dismembered woman on the bloodstained bed and the girl in the tartan skirt, pressed against the wall beside the door. "Run!" I ordered the girl. "Through the front door again! Now! Stop a car—make them get the police!"

Then I was back in my body again; the experience had lasted only a few seconds. I was out the front door, on the path, among the trees, on the grassy drive, running as hard as I could go for the road in the clear night air. There were the cars, two, three, four cars, a stream of traffic driving home from Anzac Day in Claraville. I climbed over the gate and crouched in the grass beside the mailbox, waiting to stop a car. Too many were driven by lone men; running from one sort of madman, I did not want to risk an encounter with another.

In my dream I try to stop one car, then another, but

they pass me by and the one that stops is wrong. The horror will never end, has never ended to this day. In fact, it was the best car that stopped—the Reti family from the farm down the road who knew old Len Fell was a bit gone in the head. He had shot one of *their* dogs once. They believed my story at once, but I am not sure if the police would have been convinced. George Reti clinched the matter by going up the drive and hailing Uncle Len from the shelter of the macrocarpa trees. Uncle Len put on the outside lights and fired shots into the darkness; it was a matter for the police.

In another dream, sometimes a daydream, I save Billy, he runs with me, I never enter the first of the "death rooms," as *Truth* called them. I certainly never entered the second death room, Beryl's pink bedroom, yet I have heard and read that she lay very peacefully in her bed, golden head on the pillow. Nothing much to be seen until the bedclothes were stripped back; then strong men quailed. This was long after the sergeant had come out carrying Billy and put him into our mother's waiting arms. Not a mark on him. He grew up in the Gillworth Home for Boys, Auckland, trained as a carpenter, and cut his throat at the age of twenty "while the balance of his mind was disturbed."

When I first saw my mother that night, brought from Bethany to the Claraville police station, she flew at me and clawed my face, screaming:

"You left Billy! You didn't take care of him! He's still in there with that man!"

She was right, of course, but I didn't see what else I could have done. The policemen were shocked by her behaviour. My mother went on to contradict much of what I had told the police. She denied that I had ever mentioned Uncle Len's strange behaviour. She had no memory at all of the incident with the cleaver and the loaf of bread. She had never suggested that Aunt Madge and Beryl had "cleared out." She also lied with genteel persistence about money. In fact, she lied so desperately and pointlessly about everything to do with our lives and the circumstances at the Fell farm that she aroused suspicion. Had she been invited or not? How close was she to Len Fell? ". . . *a woman with two children staying in the murder house* . . ." hinted the newspapers. She lost her job, of course, and had the first of her nervous breakdowns. None of our remaining cousins and aunts stood by her. My father got a divorce. Billy and I were both put into homes.

When the brave sergeant went up to the house at first light, ahead of the spreading cordon of armed constables, he found that Len Fell had run off into the bush. Billy, sound asleep, was the only person alive in the house. There was a long hunt for the fugitive, all through the backblocks. Distant shots were heard now and then; after three months, the search was called off. The police believed their man was dead; the kids in Claraville are still told to watch out or Old Len Fell will get them.

In my dreams, I go hunting for Uncle Len with my trusty 303.22, a newer weapon. Beryl is there, too, and even Aunt Madge. We are like furies, wild and bloodstained, stalking our helpless prey through the green twilight. I know this is an evil dream. In the gentle forests of New Zealand there are no harmful creatures, no snakes, no predators.

Afterword

Looking back, I realize that there has always been a touch of the weird and strange in my stories, even in the mainstream stories that I wrote before I saw the light and turned to science fiction and fantasy in about 1973. Now I am writing quite a lot of ghost/horror, including a recent novel, *Cruel Designs* (Piatkus, 1988). I still don't know how full-time horror writers such as Ramsey Campbell and Stephen King keep up the grue for years on end. I often reach the point where I say, "No, you can't put *that* in!" and then remind myself firmly, "Cherry, this is a *horror* story. . . ." Lisa Tuttle had to urge me to submit something "confrontational" for this anthology; the result was "Anzac Day."

Cherry Wilder

THE NIGHT WOLF

Karen Joy Fowler

Sometimes the cracks on Anna's bedroom ceiling turned into a wolf's head. It wasn't always easy to see. You couldn't see it when you first went to bed, when your mother had just turned the lights out and you couldn't see anything clearly. You couldn't see it in the morning when you saw everything *too* well and the wolf's head was just cracks in the ceiling, like all the other cracks in the ceiling. When you saw it, it was the middle of the night and you'd woken up suddenly, and you especially saw it when the moon was bright and came in at your window. Then it was right above your head as you lay and looked up. The head never looked back at you. It was turned to the side, looking away, so you didn't even see the eyes, but you saw the dark spot where the nose was and all the little triangles of its teeth.

Anna made her mother move her bed all the way across the room, away from the door to the other wall, even though her mother thought she was being silly. What was there to be afraid of? Anna's mother had said. Cracks on the ceiling that didn't look like a wolf to

Anna's mother no matter what Anna said. Anyway, by then it was too late. By then the wolf had found his way into Anna's room in the middle of the night, in the middle of her dreams, and especially on those nights when the moonlight was bright. By then the wolf had found his way to Anna, and he came anytime he wanted to.

An empty rectangle of light shone suddenly where the closed door should have been. It wasn't the wolf; the wolf never came in with a light behind him. It was Anna's mother. "Are you still awake?" she asked Anna in a whisper.

"Yes," said Anna.

"Why?" Her mother came to Anna's bed.

"I can't sleep."

"School tomorrow."

"I just can't sleep. Stay with me?"

"Be a big girl," Anna's mother said, kissing her. "Tell that imagination of yours to work on some sweet dreams." She didn't quite close the door when she left; Anna saw the bright strip of the opening before her mother turned off the light in the hall. Anna was no safer with the door closed. A real wolf couldn't turn the slippery doorknob with his paws, and maybe, but maybe not, with his teeth. But a wolf who had the magic of the moon behind him, and darkness, too, could always get in. Huffing and puffing. Who's afraid? Who wouldn't be?

"Name a vegetable," Emily said.

"What?" said Anna.

"No, quick. Any vegetable."

"Squash."

"You're weird," Siri told her. "But I said celery, so I'm weird, too."

The three girls were walking home from school together and there was nothing at all weird about Siri, whose mother took her to the Esprit outlet for clothes and braided her hair every morning in one long french braid down her back and whose father called her "princess," but let her go all by herself on a plane to her grandmother's house. Anna thought if she got to Siri's early enough the next morning, Siri's mother might braid Anna's hair, too. Sometimes she did. Anna's hair was all different lengths and Anna's mother couldn't braid it. "What's weird about squash?"

"It's not orange," said Emily. Emily was getting breasts and you could see them under her T-shirt, little lumps right where the nipples were. Anna felt sorry for her and always tried not to look. It was funny how hard it was not to look at something if you were thinking about not looking. You'd think it would be easy. There were always lots of other things you could look at. "A normal person, if they have to name a vegetable fast, they name an orange vegetable."

"Isn't squash orange?" Anna asked. "Sort of orange."

"What color is squash?" said Siri.

"It's not orange," said Emily.

Michael Paxton came up behind them on his skateboard. He cut down over the rounded curb and then back up to the sidewalk in front of them. The front wheels caught on a crack and he fell forward, landing on his hands and knees. He got up, looking at them defiantly. Siri laughed. "Squash," she said.

"You couldn't ride a skateboard." Michael wouldn't look at Siri. He examined his palm. Anna thought it was bleeding, but it was a dirty hand and she couldn't tell for sure. Anna didn't want to know if it was blood. "I'd like to see you try." Michael looked at Anna, pressing his palm against his shirt so that it left a smudge. "Your mother makes you wear a helmet and ride your bike on the sidewalk." This was true. There was nothing Anna could say. Michael was such a *little* boy. Who cared what Michael Paxton thought? "She'd never even let you on a skateboard." Michael's tone made it sound like something pretty bad. He turned to Emily. "*You'd* have to wear a chest protector."

"You're scum, Michael," Siri said. "You're the scum scum scrape off their shoes." He skated away, took the jump off the curb without falling. "Talk about your orange vegetables," said Siri. The girls laughed behind him just loudly enough to be sure he heard.

They had reached Emily's house. "Call me tonight," she told Siri. "I'll call you," she said to Anna. She ran inside. Anna could hear her shouting to her mother that she was home, that she was hungry.

"Do you know what she said about me?" Siri told Anna. They crossed the street. The sunshine through the leaves made a wallpaper pattern on the sidewalk. It moved around Anna's feet like she was walking in water. "She says I talk about people behind their backs. That's what she told Debbie. *She's* the one."

"You don't talk about people behind their backs," Anna agreed. Anna didn't talk about people.

"Call me tonight." Siri pretended she was Emily, her voice high and dishonestly sweet. "So two-faced," she said in her own voice again. "You wait and see. When she calls you she'll say something mean about me."

"I'll tell you if she does," said Anna.

"She always does," said Siri. "She pretends to be your friend and then she tries to get everyone else to turn against you. Will your dad let you talk on the phone tonight?"

"Fifteen minutes if I've finished my homework."

"We can hardly say *anything* in fifteen minutes. I'll call you," said Siri. She opened the gate to her yard. A muddy cocker spaniel was waiting, leaping about in excitement. "Don't jump, Pumpkin," Siri told him. She turned back to Anna. "After I talk to Emily, I'll call and tell you what she said. But don't tell her I told you."

"I won't tell," said Anna. Anna could keep a secret. Although, in fact, it was unlikely her dad would let her talk to both Emily *and* Siri. "You see them all day at school," he would say to her. "Anything you need to talk to them about, you have the whole day to do it."

* * *

65

Anna's father put his fork and then his knife into his steak. "This is good," he told Anna's mother, chewing. "I'm surprised we can afford it, but this is good."

"This once," said Anna's mother. She passed a bowl of peas to Anna. Anna passed them on. "Take some peas, Anna," her mother said. "How was school?"

"Fine," said Anna.

"What did you do?"

"Nothing."

"You were at school for six hours and you did nothing?" Anna's mother said.

Anna looked at her plate, letting the peas fall one at a time from the serving spoon, wondering just how many she had to take. One pea, two peas, three peas. She looked at her mother, looked back at her plate. Four peas, five peas. "Nothing special," she said. She put the spoon back in the bowl and passed the peas to her father. In the window behind her mother, the sky was just beginning to darken. You could already see the moon. From now on it would only get brighter.

"So tell me some of the things you did that weren't special," Anna's mother said.

"Leave her alone," said Anna's father. "She doesn't want to talk, don't make her talk. Nothing wrong with not talking." He cut another bite of steak. "God knows, the world can always use a few more women who don't talk."

Anna heard the door pushed open. The door didn't creak or anything. It was such a small sound. Just a movement of air. You could dream it. Maybe Anna was dreaming it. The setting moon made a blue pool on the ceiling, a large dreamy pool of light, its shape cut by the window. It stretched all the way across the room to where the wolf's head still looked down whether anyone saw it or not. Anna didn't see it, but she closed her eyes anyway, or dreamed that she did, because if she was dreaming then she had never really opened her eyes. The wolf entered the dream. He knew exactly

66

where she was. There was no way to make herself so small in the bed that he would miss her. The darkness hid him, but it didn't hide her. It didn't change her into someone else. He could smell her, her Anna smell. She could smell him. She could feel his breath and his hair. The bed creaked with his weight.

Anna made herself dream about traps. It was hard work to dream this. It took her entire attention. She dreamed she was trapping the wolf. She saw the triangular teeth of the trap, like a wolf's mouth, closing over the wolf's paw. Just when he thought he was safe. Just when he was saying to himself, Anna would never hurt me. Not Anna. The trap would hold him until night and the darkness were over. Until hard, bright sunlight found him in his vulnerable sunshine shape.

Anna had heard a story somewhere about a wolf who stepped into a trap and chewed off his own foot so that he could escape. Could he do that? How could anyone do that?

The house was quiet and filled with sunlight. Anna dressed and passed her father, shaving before the bathroom mirror. He put a white beard of shaving cream onto his chin and then scraped it off again. He dipped the razor into the sink of water. "Good morning, Sunshine," he said. "How's my little girl?"

Anna's mother was making oatmeal. "Sleepyhead," she said to Anna. "Raisins or bananas?"

"Raisins," said Anna. The whole day stretched ahead of her. A whole day before night came. Anna's father stood in the kitchen doorway and wiped the rest of the shaving cream from his face with his T-shirt sleeve. He smelled of bay leaves. Anna's mother scraped the oatmeal pan into the sink.

Anna ate quickly. "Can I go to Siri's?" Anna asked. "I've finished breakfast."

"You stay here," her father said. "You're always running off to Siri's. Give us the pleasure of your company for a change." After breakfast he would put on a shirt with buttons and a tie over his T-shirt. Anna's mother would put on stockings and low heels and makeup on her face. They would change into their working selves. Anna would be the person she was at school. It was the same Anna. Everywhere she went.

Siri's mother braided Anna's hair for her at the breakfast table while Siri finished her eggs and toast. "It's easier when your hair isn't so clean," Siri's mother said. She was still in her bathrobe, an old pink terry-cloth robe with shiny patches and patches of nap. "Let me go put some water on the brush." She went to the sink. "Not that I'm advocating dirty hair," she said.

Anna yawned. She sometimes did this deliberately, because Siri absolutely couldn't help yawning back, but this was a real yawn. Siri put her fork down and covered her mouth. "I won't," she said, but she did and the two girls laughed.

"Early in the morning to be yawning," Siri's mother said.

"Anna made me do it."

"Hold still now, Anna," Siri's mother said, brushing the water through Anna's hair. "We have two minutes to turn this wet mess into a thing of beauty before you'll be late for school. Siri, your job is to finish your egg. And keep track of the rubber band." Anna winced as the brush caught on a snarl. "Am I hurting you, angel?" Siri's mother said. "I'm sorry. The price of beauty is very high. Are you done eating, Siri? Have you lost the rubber band yet?" Siri held it out to her. Her mother took it, twisting it around the finished braid. "There," she said. She kissed them both. "You are very good girls," she told them. "Now *run* to school."

Anna put her desk chair in front of her bedroom door. The wolf pushed it aside in the middle of the night. It fell to the floor with a loud noise. "Anna?" Anna's mother called down the hall from her bed.

"Anna?" Anna's father was at the door. "Are you all right, Anna? What's going on?"

"What's going on?" Anna's mother's voice moved closer. The light went on in the hall. "I heard a noise in Anna's room."

"Anna, are you all right?" Anna's father said. He pushed the door open as far as it would go. The chair wedged between the door and the wall. Her father and her mother squeezed through the half-open door. Her mother came to sit on the bed. Her father picked up the chair and put it back by the desk.

"You scared me," her mother said to Anna. "I heard this crash. What were you doing out of bed?"

"I wasn't out of bed," Anna said.

"*Someone* knocked the chair over," Anna's mother said.

"I was sleeping," said Anna.

"Sleepwalking," Anna's father suggested.

Anna's mother stroked her hair back from her forehead. Anna caught her hand. "And dreaming," Anna's mother agreed. "We all should be." She stood up. "Let's go back to bed," she said to Anna's father. "You sure you're all right?" she said to Anna.

"The wolf knocked the chair over," Anna said. She whispered it.

"There's no wolf here, sweetheart," said Anna's mother.

"Nobody here but us chickens," said Anna's father. He stood in the shadow of the door.

Anna's mother leaned down and kissed her. "You had another one of your bad dreams," she said. "It's over now. You can go back to sleep." She stood by the bed and waited another moment until Anna let go of her hand.

"I think he's cute," said Siri. She and Anna sat together in the back-porch swing at Anna's with their history books open on their laps. They swung slowly with the movement of a clock pendulum. It was Saturday, early afternoon. Nightfall was many swings away. "Don't tell *anyone* I said so, though."

Anna was always being told not to tell. Not to tell anyone. "All right," she said. "Anyway, I think he likes you."

"Why do you think so?"

Anna's father stepped out on the porch and walked past them. He was wearing his Red Sox hat. Siri picked up her book hastily. "So, who was in command at the Alamo?" she asked Anna.

"Bowie," said Anna.

"Travis," said Anna's father. "Am I right, Siri? I'm right, aren't I?"

"Travis," Siri confirmed, nodding.

"Give the man in the baseball cap a gold cigar." Anna's father smiled at Anna. He continued down the walk and into the toolshed. Anna could hear him inside, whistling the theme from Davy Crockett: "Raised in the woods so he knew every tree. Killed him a bar when he was only three."

"Why do you think he likes me?" Siri asked.

"I just think so. He's awfully nice to you."

"He never talks to me at all."

"He never talks to me, either, but he's not nice about it."

"So he likes *you*," said Siri. "My mother says that's how boys this age are."

Anna's father pushed the lawn mower out of the toolshed, knelt, and poured it full of gasoline.

"Travis," said Siri loudly, turning her book so that Anna could see it, pointing out the relevant line. "Travis was the commander. Bowie got sick or something before the battle. He ended up having to fight from his bed." The power mower started. Anna's father stood up.

"Don't be silly." Anna leaned toward Siri so that she could be heard over the mower. Anna was angry and she wasn't sure why. "People who like you are nice to you. If they're not nice, they don't like you. No matter what they say. He doesn't like me at all," Anna said.

Anna left the TV and went into the kitchen. She was trying to braid her own hair like Siri's mother did. Her father stood at the sink. Her mother was slightly behind him, watching. "What did you want, Anna?" her father asked.

"Just some water." She came and stood beside him, holding out her brush.

"Give me a minute. The disposal isn't working," Anna's father told her. He reached down, his hand almost too large for the drain. He had to wiggle and rotate it in. "Your mother put something down it."

"I don't think so," said Anna's mother apologetically.

"I can feel it. Something stringy. Celery hair or something." Anna's father tried to pull his hand back out. "You're not going to believe this," he said.

"Your hand is stuck," said Anna's mother.

"I can't pull it out." Anna's father and mother looked at each other.

"Soap," said Anna's mother brightly. "We can try to soap it." She knelt and opened the cupboard under the sink.

Anna looked at her father's hand. "Pretty embarrassing," he told her. "Caught in my own kitchen sink. I hope we don't have to have the fire department out to see." He put his other hand on his wrist and tried to pull. The sink had swallowed him all the way to his watch. Anna reached to the disposal switch. "Anna," he said in surprise. She flipped the switch.

"Anna!" Anna's mother stood staring at her. She had dropped the dish soap and the plastic bottle spun slowly at her feet until it pointed at Anna. Her eyes were big. Her face was pale.

"It's all right," said Anna's father. "She knew it was broken. Flip the switch back, sweetheart, so I can work on it."

"You could have hurt your father," Anna's mother

said. "If the disposal had gone on, you could have hurt him badly."

"She knew it was broken," Anna's father said. "She didn't mean anything by it. Anna wouldn't hurt me, would you, Anna?" He looked at her. "Flip the switch back." Anna couldn't face him. She looked up from the soap bottle to where her father's hand disappeared into the dark and silent sink. Her own hand was shaking on the disposal switch. She flipped it down.

"I'm sorry," Anna said. Of course she was. Of course she wouldn't want to hurt her father.

"You're a very lucky girl." Anna's mother's voice was clipped and angry. "If that disposal had gone on, your father might have lost the use of his hand. You would have carried that guilt for the rest of your life."

"Let's forget it. Nothing happened. No one is hurt," said Anna's father. "Pour the soap. Get me out of here."

A little thing like a chair doesn't stop the wolf anymore. He opens the door slowly, and if it catches on something, he reaches one paw inside and removes the obstacle so softly no one wakes up. "You wouldn't hurt me, Anna," he says. He whispers, almost voiceless. "You don't want to hurt me. You know I love you. You can keep a secret. You won't tell."

He comes while she dreams, and creeps from the room in the darkness to hide in his daytime shape. No one can see the wolf but Anna, and she tries not to look. It is exhausting her. It is so hard. Like not looking at Emily's breasts, but much harder because the wolf comes so close.

Once Anna found one of his hairs on her pillow. She threw it away at once, down the sink with lots of water, but it was too late. She had seen it, and then there were other hairs, often. Sometimes she throws them away, but sometimes she saves them. She puts them in an envelope in her desk drawer and sometimes she even looks at them again. She has five of them now. She is building a trap. Maybe she will show them to someone. Guess what these are, she will say, but they will never guess. And she is not supposed to tell.

Get me out of here, the wolf says, get me out of here, but he is not really trapped. He can change his shape and go anywhere he wants to. The trap is Anna's. Anna is caught here and she cannot dream an escape until she figures out what piece of herself to chew off and leave behind.

Afterword

Three pieces of reading shaped this story. The first was an article I read a few years ago that contended that Freud deliberately refused to believe his female patients who came to him with stories of incest, choosing instead to dismiss their experiences as wishful fantasies. The second was a statistical study suggesting that one in every five women has been molested. The figure may be too low, the study said, because so many women can't remember the experience. The third was a poem by Lucille Clifton. The story owes its shape to this poem, which I only heard once but was unable to forget. It was called "Shape Shifters"; Clifton read it in 1989 at a workshop in Brockport, New York.

The piece that resulted is, I think, a sort of mirror image of a horror story. I don't write horror, as a rule, because I am easily frightened and I have always felt that if I were doing it properly, I would be too frightened to finish, and if I were able to finish, then I must not be doing it properly.

Karen Joy Fowler

THE ANCESTRESS

Josephine Saxton

(For Clarice, my mother,
an unforgettable person—with love.)

Clare had finally found the temple in Stanley, on the
south shore of Hong Kong Island. She had walked miles
in the steaming heat, seeking images of Kum Yin, the
goddess to whom Chinese women pray, in much the
same spirit that Roman Catholic women pray to the Virgin. Kum Yin is much older and more powerful than the
Virgin, but Clare, neither Taoist nor Catholic, was not
in any case seeking help. She was illustrating a book on
porcelain figurines of this sweetly smiling deity.

The keeper of the temple was a very old woman with
the remains of her hair scraped up into a hard little knot.
She slouched farther down in her deck chair, lit a cigarette, turned up her transistor, coughed and hawked
violently, and spat expertly into a cardboard box several
feet away. By the sound of it, she would soon be one
of the ancestors who were propitiated in this brilliantly
painted shrine, so gaudy it might with little effort turn
into a roundabout from a carnival. The main interior

was filled with little grottoes lighted with coloured bulbs and candles, decorated with wonderfully ugly masks, flowers, lanterns, streamers. Incense from the huge brazier made Clare cough as she wandered around looking at the gifts to the gods and the dead. Mouldering oranges, sweeties, drinks. Some of the statuary was papier-mâché, but there were some nice gilded carvings, and also porcelains, one of which was Kum Yin. Not a large effigy, but very beautiful. Clare would have loved to pick her up and feel the delicate surface, which absorbed the coloured lights like pearly rainbows on her enigmatic expression. Temples in Hong Kong were unashamedly materialistic, visited to propitiate the demons who prevented wealth and to keep well in with those powers that conferred prosperity. Dear Santa Claus.

Clare did not feel well, recovering from a violent chest infection that had got her as soon as she landed in this June steam. At home in England she had monthly sessions with an acupuncturist, to keep her health reasonably stable, but some viruses just took no notice of all that. Besides, she did not trust a practitioner who could speak no English, so had submitted to a course of antibiotics prescribed by a clinic that had actually taken proper samples and made tests before doling out the pills. It had been expensive, of course.

She had not gone to bed with the virus, but dragged herself around in a feverish haze that somehow seemed appropriate. It enhanced her paranoia in hostile back streets where white woman never trod. She had been shrieked and flapped at while watching a Chinese funeral on one of the islands. Many Chinese still thought of white people as devils—*gwai los*—and very bad luck, especially at funerals.

There were fortune-telling sticks on the altar, so Clare, who sometimes used the I Ching her ex-husband had given her long ago, threw them and asked, "Please, will I be free of depression?" The sticks came down: no.

76

Behind her she felt a flurry of disapproval and turned to see three women around the brazier, burning paper effigies of furniture and clothes for the dead. Clare thought: Oh, belt up, you think I am just an ignorant tourist but I know what goes on here, and where I come from the I Ching is far from esoteric! But she was impassive, expressionless. She knew that the Chinese thought even a slight European smile to be a frightful grimace more suited to a baboon. The women went on unfolding the paper packets, which could be bought in temple shops: bright coats and trousers, hats, bags, dresses, printed upon tissue and decorated with gold paper lace more usually seen improving the status of cakes. Clare would have liked to talk with the women, ask about the religion firsthand, but the language problem was insuperable, and as a white woman wandering about alone she was to be ignored at best.

She took some photographs, and wished that Kum Yin could really be helpful. Her spirits were low after her illness, but she was depressed a great deal and had always been so. She had tried everything and decided that it was hereditary temperament about which nothing could be done. She was fortunate, with her crazy father, her awful mother, two crackpot cousins, a barmy aunt, not to be downright doolally! Sometimes, too often, a deep abyss sucked in all her joy and happiness. Her marriage, over. Depressives are difficult to love. Love.

Approaching middle years, young-looking for all her miseries. No porcelain goddess was going to help—she was in the grip of the inevitable. She went outside, past the spitting guardian, who did not acknowledge the coins Clare paid for a stick of incense to light and leave. Chinese incense was not very fragrant, but it made plenty of smoke. Eyes streaming, she went to lean on the harbour wall to recover.

She felt a deep fatigue and leaned heavily, taking slow breaths to induce a return of strength. She watched two fishermen in a rotten little boat. They looked remarkably like a Chinese watercolour, in which the filthy water could not be smelled. Everyone ate fish from this water, it was delicious. They ate anything that moved, here. They skinned frogs and snakes alive at the market so they would stay fresh. Clare thought, This culture is so different that at last I am in a truly alien place. No European city had felt so alien. But we are all human, can we really be so different? It would seem, yes. Here, ancient practises fitted in perfectly with modern; businessmen called in the *feng shui* man to arrange things with the architect of a new skyscraper, so that demons would not interfere with the successful work. The furniture was arranged not according to usefulness or aesthetics, but to *feng shui,* to get things on dragon lines, to deflect the ever-present evil influences; it was a part of life. She thought of her own flat back in England; how would it be arranged according to good *feng shui*? It might be amusing to get a book and try—perhaps she was depressed because the furniture was not right. Lots of depressed housewives perhaps felt this unconsciously as they kept on trying the sofa and telly first here, then there.

On the face of it, especially in the modern city and Kowloon, there was nothing important but large banks, department stores, commerce, food, artifacts. The Europeans were all wealthy, some of the Chinese were extremely wealthy. And in the shantytowns and doorways lived Chinese people who appeared to be extremely poverty-stricken, but a rich, loudmouthed expat had told Clare, at a party resembling a sixties display of success, that they lived like that by choice, and that they invariably had a fortune in the bank. Clare watched the street traders, and did not know; perhaps it was true, but who could possibly choose to live like that? It was an alien place, one might be on a distant moon; not only a different place, but a different time. To be poor and white here was to die, ignored by both races.

She gathered together some strength and wandered along to the market. In a temple shop, which was a sort of shack under an awning, she bought dozens of packets of dead-clothes, some demon-deflecting mirrors with the I Ching trigrams around the borders, lots of incense in pretty packets, and a few lanterns. The dead-clothes would look very chic pinned to the bathroom walls of her friends at home, in amongst political posters and naked women. The shopkeeper was clearly hostile to her presence; even from behind his impassive mask she saw dislike and fear. Clare stood her ground, mentally saying, Screw you, too. And then she took an expensive cab back to the skyscraper block where her host lived, her friend of many years now working in Hong Kong. Expat life was cushy, they paid you a lot to be very hot and damp, alienated and far from home.

Anne, younger than Clare, fair and attractive and ambitious, opened a bottle of chilled Australian white wine and filled two very large glasses, which immediately misted.

"Cheers. How was it?" Anne was a journalist and fashion writer now, but they had studied at the same college at different times. Ex-art students often have much in common.

"Great. Really grotty, of course, but some nice pieces. A vicious temple-keeper—she spat at me, I think!"

"White devil! I got a letter today from my mum." Anne's mother had recently visited. "She thoroughly enjoyed everything, she says, but feels the cold back home. In June!"

"Those Pennine summers can be hellish." Clare shivered. She had no nostalgia for her birthplace or any of the people there, or her family, now mostly dead or emigrated. She had escaped. Anne had moved, but liked her roots.

"How did she get on with the food here?" Clare thought of her own mother, who had never touched anything even remotely un-English, food or otherwise. "Oily muck," "chinks," "wops," "dagos"—these words had decorated her mother's vocabulary of hatred.

"She tried everything—she even brought some fresh snake back here and cooked it. I didn't eat it myself. She even ate durum fruit." This same fruit had been offered to Clare, and now it stood on the balcony because of its odour, closely resembling sewage. Her mother would have gone on about the smell for years. Clare's mother was dead, and Clare was glad.

"There's a party tonight, remember. We have about two hours to get ready, no rush." The wine had hit Clare, so she thought, Good, get in some dancing. Anne said there would be lots of guys. Clare didn't care about that. She felt that she had finished with "guys." But they pursued her even more than when she had been young. She did not want another close relationship, and she did not want to screw around, so that took care of that. She withdrew. But loved dancing at parties. Dancing filled the inner emptiness, as did this excellent Aussie plonk. The two women chatted for a while, then Anne went off to get ready. There were two bathrooms, but Clare was in no hurry.

"I'll be showered, changed, painted, and half-cut by the time you are, and also twenty years younger!" she called out, and they laughed together. Anne returned to replenish her glass to take to the bathroom.

"You're not depressed, are you?" she asked with a wistful little grimace. Clare reassured her, no. But she was, as always at the mention of mothers. Her own returned to haunt her. She had been a man-hater who aped the persona of Mae West, when in a good mood. At other times she had hated most people and most things, and poured scorn like strong acid on men and anything unusual, or "fancy," or "jumped up"—on everything she had ever wanted and failed to have. She had been witty with her loathing but had ended up utterly alone, avoided and feared. Consumed with bitterness and anger.

One night there had been a phone call, long distance, from a social worker, asking Clare's permission to forcibly take her mother to a hospital. A psychiatrist and a doctor were present, but it had needed Clare's permission, which she had given. The alternative would have been the police, because her mother had attempted to set fire to the block of flats where she lived alone, ignoring the neighbours as always.

The fire had consisted of mostly new things, a fact that seemed to cause more of a crack of upset in the voice of the social worker, who clearly had never enjoyed visiting Clarinda, than the fact of an old woman losing her mind and perpetrating some utterly illogical and dangerous act. Clare knew that her mother was likely to burst out into some desperate act from time to time; she had witnessed shouting and hurling of objects ever since she could recall. Threatening to burn down the house was an oldie—actually lighting matches up against new clothes and knickknacks was just the one step too far.

The next day, after a night of almost excited speculation interrupting her sleep, Clare had driven north to visit her mother in Sheepscar Dene, the local loony bin of which anyone even remotely eccentric had been told, "You'll end up in Sheepscar." Her mother had prophesied that she herself would end up there, "driven mad by you all!" but she had really meant that everyone else should go there, to be straightened out into her own, Clarinda's, point of view.

Clare would never forget the way her mother had looked that day. Her once beautiful face was bloated with water, caused by the chemical sedation, and, flickering in and out of a puzzled or blank expression, there had shot vicious glances of malice and hatred, triumphant evil.

"Now look what you have done. But I haven't finished with you yet!" Had she said that, or had Clare imagined it? She had slid into total silence, and Clare had eventually managed to get her transferred to a comfortable home where she stalwartly ignored everyone. She had later suffered a broken hip and pneumonia, and died in hospital the day after one of Clare's visits, during which Clare had drawn a portrait in between administering little drinks of water and measuring the urine. Her sole attempt at physically caring apart from gifts of clothes and goodies to eat. The drawing was the most potent she had ever done, and now it was hidden away. On the wall it had scared people and upset herself. Guilt, of course. Clare knew she should have looked after her mother herself. But nobody could have survived that, everyone who had known her had said that Clare "had done the right thing."

Anne danced in, almost ready. Clare pulled herself together and, staggering slightly, rushed off to effect a transformation in herself. An artist at dressing up, she soon produced an image suitable for impressing people at lavish expat parties, and then off they went together, giggling like schoolgirls and as high as Chinese kites.

On the plane going home, work completed and holiday at an end, in the high that can come only from free airplane wine, Clare got chatted up by her neighbour. As luck or synchronicity would have it, he was a Jungian psychiatrist and a collector of porcelain. At first it was interesting to discuss his ideas on the Virgin Mother aspects of Kum Yin, but they eventually began to talk about real mothers, laughing at his self-deprecatory jokes on being a thoroughgoing, unashamed mother's boy, and then her mother, her guilt, her depressions. She knew better than to do this, but he seemed to be drawing her out and she succumbed once more to the telling, which never changed anything. It came out: her mother's scorn and malice, how her ex-husband had once told her—and dug his own grave in that instant— "The trouble with you is that you are just a carbon copy of your mother." It was quite the most cruel thing he could have said. It filled her with fear that it might be true. She had tried so hard to be otherwise.

Clare and her new companion drank, ate, laughed, and he drew from her gradually, almost without her realising, a description of a certain dream that had haunted her for many years. It was like a doctor being interested in her cough, a lawyer in her divorce—most unlikely, and yet he seemed fascinated. Perhaps he fancied her? Too bad, buster, I'm off it. Let's have some more plonk.

Clare had not dreamed so much nor so vividly for some time. There had once been frequent days when she had woken from realities more lucid than the feel of sheets, the taste of coffee, running water. These had been shadows thinly veiling the reality in which she had walked in low-angled sunbeams, conversing with the spirits in her coloured nights. Then, the colour and life had returned to her mornings painfully, like the veins of a butterfly filling and forcing in life. The night had been her time, peopled with figures of a clarity not seen even in pre-Raphaelite paintings. Sometimes she dreamed strangers, and sometimes those she knew, so that if she met them the next day, she felt she had seen beneath their masks and knew them for who they really were. Such a one had been her mother in the dream she related, as they flew over India.

She had been standing on a green by a school back in her hometown, a school out of a novel by Angela Brazil, with a clock tower, where they played lacrosse. Her mother had brought her up to believe that she would attend that school, but when the time came and Clare had passed the scholarship, it had been scorned as "too fancy," and expensive, and what was the point of educating women—look at Cousin Lorna; to be a private secretary, now, that was a good ambition. Cousin Lorna had got herself some higher education, costing her mother a great deal of money, and then got married! What was the use of it?

Clare had made her own way through education much later, without lacrosse, but there she was, in the dream. A funeral was in progress; mourners stood in black with veils and flowers on the green, which was more vivid than verdigris, than moss, than algae, than any green on earth. Each blade of grass sharply defined. By the grave, inconsequentially far from a church, lay an empty coffin, its opened lid revealing a phosphorescent silk lining with tiny pleats fit for the wedding dress of a princess. And by the coffin Clare's mother had appeared, her hard jaw thrusting, her thick and hard-worked hand outstretched, the shiny pinkness of her scoured skin reflecting a passing cloud, a tiny white cloud, the only one in a watercoloured sky painted by some perfectionist with a large sable brush, using Prussian, cerulean, cobalt, oxgall, and the speed of light. The finger outstretched and pointing down, at the coffin. Her mother's eyes, bitter and dark like those of the incontinent Pekingese she had once had put down, held Clare in a gaze of such force that she felt paralysed, like a windup doll without a key. Her mother had opened her mouth in a smile of dreadful dentist perfection, and then the teeth had parted to articulate a monstrous birth of sound that seemed to fill the sky and echo, as if it were the inside of an opaque glass bowl and not the clear infinity.

"Get in," commanded her mother, and Clare had looked at the wonderful coffin. She had not been married very long, she had escaped her mother forever, she was happy, her mother could no longer touch her heart and soul with her Gorgon stare. Or so Clare had believed.

"Get in, Clare. You belong to me!"

Clare had known that she was in a dream, and that if she could wake up she would be saved, so she struggled to evade the pull toward the coffin, struggled to emerge from that world, writhing inside her carcass, to resist the silky womb in which she would be buried forever. A gravedigger stood waiting with a long spade. Veils moved slowly as if underwater, mourners concealed their impatience.

Clare made an inner twist, warped herself into a sidewise loop, and was suddenly awake, looking into the concerned eyes of her husband. He had told her, "Your eyes have been open for several minutes, but I couldn't get you to respond, it was frightening." Frightening for him! Clare shook, and wasted half that night in calming down, explaining. And she had seen: So, I am still in thrall to my mother, I have not escaped enslavement after all, for I have married a man who actually seems to like my mother, they are in league with one another. There is nowhere I can go to be myself. But when she is dead I shall be free. And eventually she had thought: When I am divorced, I shall be free.

Her listener, good-looking and fashionably dressed, poured plonk and said that many young women had dreams of that ilk, they had not yet found themselves, individuated, had made the mistake of equating marriage with freedom. How did she feel now that her mother was dead and she was single again?

"No different, really, in my deepest self."

He had no reply of any consequence, but they laughed uproariously, attracting attention from across the aisle and from the air hostess, whose little frown he turned to a bland smile by asking for ice cubes, in a very cool and sober manner. They laughed at that, too, Clare elated at finding one other who found the same dark jokes and a certain triviality hilarious. They exchanged addresses.

A couple of weeks later he invited her to a party and she accepted, thinking she would not go. She was tired, had not slept well since Hong Kong. Perhaps it was a long jet-lag. She had the sense of having dreamed a great deal but could never recall anything, and this was somehow worse than having clear dreams, however disturbing. The sense of having forgotten something important bothered her often, distracted her when she was working. She often woke feeling worse than when she had gone to bed, her energy drained.

And then, three days before the party, she dreamed very clearly. Her mother was back.

"You should have looked after me in my old age," said the hard, voluminous voice. Clare was standing on a beach looking out to sea, and the voice had blown down from a mountain behind her. She looked around to see her mother standing naked, as Clare had never

85

seen her in life. The large bones showed clearly through old skin, her breasts withered, a large vertical scar that Clare knew nothing about. The dark eyes regarded her accusingly as a cold wind stirred her sparse hair, and the voice reflected from a glassy sky: "It was your duty."

Guilt can be a very destructive force. Clare fought it down, shivering and very angry in the cold night, brewing oolong and munching a handful of muesli, muttering aloud her memory of a certain bleak day. "I told the doctor, I *can't*. I just can't have her with us, she fights and moans the whole time, she causes quarrels, my children hate and fear her, she spreads a horrible atmosphere. Even if she is my own mother, I can't handle it, she will break up my home and wear me out." He had replied, to Clare's amazement, "But your mother is still a very attractive woman, you know," and Clare, amazed, had thought, Well, if she's so damned attractive, you look after her.

Clarinda, her mother, had certainly been attractive once. In the twenties she had resembled Clara Bow, she had been a femme fatale. Although she was small and dark, the Mae West persona had suited her; she had the tough way of speaking out of the side of her mouth when putting men down, which they seemed to love. Clare recalled this vicious humour with a wry smile. He mother had lacked tact and grace, but she had made men laugh even as they shrank in pain. Clare had been told that she, too, could be like that, but Clare did not believe it at all. Although she did not bullshit, for sure; men did not pander, why should she? Sure, peel me a grape. Then bugger off. She could almost hear the clench-jawed delivery of "hips like a snake"—as a child Clare had not understood this, for snakes have no hips, they wriggle slowly. Exactly. Undulate, and disappear into the undergrowth.

Clare had let the oolong go cold, so she poured herself a glass of Chablis at four in the morning, standing shivering by the open fridge, smelling grave dust in the delightful mustiness of the wine. She carefully peeled the label off the bottle and put it into the kitchen drawer alongside many other labels and clippings. This one had a realistic coloured picture upon it of a bunch of grapes.

She went to the party and had a nice time. The psychiatrist, named Phil, was attentive and amusing, but she got chatted up by three other men as well, and lied to them that she had a committed relationship with someone else, who was not present. She thought, I must be barmy, what is the matter with me, when I was married I thought it would be nice to move around a bit after my divorce. Men, presentable, well-heeled—most women of my age would be delighted. Committed relationships, nothing; she hardly had any friends at all these days, she discouraged them all—like Garbo, another of her mother's role models, she wanted to be alone most of the time.

She went home alone and changed into a kimono, filled a large glass with wine, and went into her sitting room to play a video, for sleep was gone until dawn approached; this was always the same if she had been drinking and eating late. The same old thoughts came back into the silence of her choosing from the few videos in the place. In some respects, she *was* a carbon copy of her mother, although she was not yet so bitter and horrible, surely? She didn't want ever to be bitter.

And what about her father, who spoke of him? The genes, well, he had been an alcoholic and a depressive. His spirit had never troubled her, he had faded out long ago somehow, after his death to be built up into some miracle of manhood by Clarinda: "They don't make men like that these days." History. Was there no way to transcend it?

She was glad to be drawn into a video, a Jodorowski she had watched dozens of times over the years. Her mother would have neither understood nor approved of it, which also applied to most of Clare's pursuits, likes, and possessions. There was something, a great deal, in Clare that was a carbon copy of nobody. "So sucks boo to you, Ma!'' Clarinda had used to say that, to *her* mother.

On the screen, the tall and beautiful girl, dressed in black cowboy gear, circled a man with slow, shamanistic steps, intoning, ''Nothing, nothing, nothing.'' The next scene would be the rape, and Clare, suddenly bored, switched it off. As she did so, all the lights fused. Well, that could wait until morning, she was very tired after all. She blundered over to the sofa and collapsed into something like sleep.

The doorbell rang insistently in the pitch dark. Clare knew she must answer it, must at least peer through the etched glass to see who was there. It was dangerous to answer the door in the middle of the night, but she must see. No electricity, damn, of course. She floundered over a cushion on the floor, the ringing continuing as she opened her inner door. Thank God for a hallway between herself and whoever—two doors was better than one.

Out there in the hallway was a blaze of unearthly brilliant light and a dank chill more cold than dawn, and nobody at the door, no shadow except the pattern of branches from a wayward wisteria, which now seemed like a questing hand.

She hurried back into her flat, locked the door again, and stood in a cold sweat in the dark, half believing. Light, and cold. Bright. And the electrics all fused? Different circuit? Why so cold? It was no good looking for explanations, Clare knew; something quite *different* had happened.

Were those soft footsteps, of a naked old woman, just outside? No, there was an empty hush. Inanely, Clare called, ''Who's there?'' and there came the reply: ''I am, you fool. I am. Who else? It's cold here, I have nothing, nothing, nobody is looking after me, it should be your responsibility, you are a bad girl, I always said so!'' Clare wept, knowing that the words were from inside her own head, and yet hearing that they were not. She stood there in the dark, her wet face buried in the

coat hanging by the door. A carbon copy. In some ways,
Clarinda had not looked after her mother, either. Clare's
granma had been put into a home; none of her eight
children wanted the responsibility of a very difficult and
strange woman. She had been somewhat psychic, too—
perhaps this came down through genes, strange visita-
tions, dreams? Madness. Her granma had often woken
in the night to hear voices, one a family joke, a voice
commanding, "Persevere." Percy Vere the ghost. And
more than once she had been heard talking in her sleep
in a strange language.

And is it too late to put things right, can genes be
changed? Will my children, whom I rarely see these
days, put me away when I am blithering and old? Probably. Better than being a nuisance and intruding upon
their lives. Clare stood until the light filtered in through
the curtains; then she mended the fuses, began the day
slowly, exhausted. Something must be done about all
this, she thought; I am cracking up.

As often when in distress, she left her work and went
shopping, avoiding the department stores and concentrating on junk shops, where she could often find something
for her collection. She found a lovely little statuette of
Kum Yin, and bought her for rather too much money,
thinking, Well, it is one step up from spending a fortune
with a credit card, as many lonely women do. She had
seen them often, taking tea with parcels crackling
around their feet, in the false bliss of a spree. Clarinda
had once bought two pairs of shoes in one day, and
been thoroughly nice to everyone for a few days afterward. Clare had seen the expat wives in Hong Kong,
bored out of their minds, spending and spending. One
little goddess did not make a wasteful consolation. She
bore home her trophy and washed away the grime from
the delicate porcelain. The phone rang.

"Hi! It's me, you'll be delighted to learn." Phil, oh
dear. Oh, hello.

"I've got theatre tickets for Friday, a Tom Stoppard,
do you like his stuff?"

"Actually, yes, most of them. . . ."

"I've heard it's a good production, do say you'll come. Dinner after?"

"I don't know, I've rather a lot of work. . . ."

"You aren't going to go out with that pratt Kingsley? I saw him chatting you up at my do, he won't do you any good."

"I'm not going out with anybody, and nobody will do me any good, especially a male nobody, thanks. I don't like Kingsley, if that's the name of only one of the pratts who chatted me up, and I don't like men anymore." She was laughing, but he could not have missed her seriousness.

"Bullshit, you like me. I'll pick you up at six, huge cocktails first. And you needn't think I'm after your body only, I'm after your mind, too. But more than that, I just can't bear to go to the theatre without a beautiful companion, okay?"

"What!?" He had hung up on her. She laughed aloud. Cheeky sod! Beautiful! Her? She looked in the mirror over the mantel, and then picked up one of her little Hong Kong *feng shui* demon-scaring mirrors to have a closer peer by the window. All she could see was an aging face with a less than perfect jawline. And a few mustache hairs that had escaped her ritual attentions. Clarinda, there was no denying the likeness. She turned more into the fading light, looking and looking at all the details that were herself alone. And then suddenly got the shivers from the cold by the big old window, and put the mirror back in haste. The fire had not drawn up yet and October was proving chilly. October already— she must write to Anne, who would be very interested to hear about Phil. Although there was not much to tell, he had not even kissed her yet. Good.

She sat by the struggling flames, dithering between reading the latest Anita Brookner, and listening to Tom Waits, but a sudden insight as to elements in both put her off either. She picked up her new Kum Yin and rubbed it on her shirt to polish off smears, and found it warmed up immediately, almost hot. She replaced it on her little Indian coffee table, seeing the figurine smile in the firelight.

"Why are you getting excited, Kum Yin?" she asked, and thought, Jesus, is this how madness starts, talking to *statues?* Of course not; she'd talked to plants for years and got good results. It was only when your tradescantia started making threatening statements that there might be just cause for alarm.

She hastened out to the little kitchen to toast crumpets and make tea, and returned with her tray, which also held a bottle of wine and a glass.

She woke in the night from a unpleasant dream encounter with Clarinda. The room was cold, the remainder of her wine warm. Her second night not spent in bed—heck, she would look a fright if she went out with Phil; her reflection now looked exhumed and flaccid. She suddenly knew what she must do; it had been apparent just below the surface of her mind for some time. But it had seemed crazy. She gently stirred the ashes and found a glow. A fire was a symbol of love, all the warmth that a family must provide. She fed little pieces of fuel to the embers and crouched watching, recalling her dream.

Clarinda had been naked, as never seen by Clare in life, and weeping, as Clare had seen only once. Just once, at Christmas. They had all been seated before the special food, wearing paper hats, pulling crackers, all the silly traditions that the adult Clare secretly loathed, but which she provided for her children so they would not feel deprived. There had been no Christmas of any significance in Clare's childhood. Clare had looked up from serving blazing pudding to see tears rolling down her mother's powdery cheeks. She had gently taken her into the drawing room, pulled the curtains, made her a cup of tea, and then put an arm around the thin shoulders in a stiff gesture. Clarinda had apologised: "I've always been too tough, that is my trouble. But then,

I've had to be.'' She had sternly pulled herself together and drunk her tea and rejoined the party, by then sprawled in front of *The Wizard of Oz*. Clare had felt totally inadequate faced with a weakened Clarinda; she had been able to offer nothing more sustaining than ''There, there, cheer up,'' those words most dreaded by the seriously depressed. The words that bewildered husbands offered distraught wives. It had been an opportunity missed for some kind of late reconciliation; they could have somehow perhaps opened up areas of mutual forgiveness. Maybe.

Clare hoped that during her last visit before her mother's death, some understanding had taken place, while she was drawing and performing those very minimal tasks. Clarinda had been past speech, but Clare had uttered some few very real words, and taken the look in the eyes for the end of loathing. Perhaps it had been mere emptiness.

Now she fetched her collection of cutouts and knelt on the hearthrug, suppressing feelings of silliness.

''Mother, here you are. Presents. I'm sending you lots of lovely things.'' A smart coat of pure wool turned to ash in a moment, followed by a good black dress, two pairs of shoes, a crocodile handbag with gold fittings and a silk lining, leather gloves, a string of pearls, discreet lacy underwear (bias-cut pure silk), the grapes, highly coloured illustrations of traditional English food, a bottle of whisky, cigarettes, scent, cosmetics, a cashmere jumper.

''Here you are, really expensive and luxurious things.'' The ash floated around in the updraught, the smoke curled. Clare sat back glowing, her heart beating.

''It's true I neglected you, but it is in the family, isn't it? You didn't look after Granma, you never wrote to my Aunty May, we were not a close family. I'm sorry, Clarinda, forgive me. Have these things, you always liked nice things.'' She incinerated a picture of her mother's favourite chocolates. Kum Yin smiled. Clare felt a weight lift from her spirits, and, also smiling, took herself off to bed at last.

But sleep did not come. The experience of propitiation had disturbed something deep. She wondered, Is this what the Chinese women at the temple feel, burning their dead-clothes? A lifting of the spirits, as if a cloud had gone? I feel as if I have really done something for my mother, given some sustenance, but how can this be? Could the spirit of a cashmere jumper fly up in changed molecules to clothe the spirit of a dead woman? It was not that, of course. It was a change of heart, some inner forgiveness in herself that changed.

Then she smelled smoke. She was back in the sitting room in a moment, choking on thick clouds. The hearthrug was on fire. She stared, paralysed. Impossible. The fire had been out, she had replaced the spark-guard. Had she? Then she saw. Suddenly fiercely angry, she began smothering the Turkestan rug with the sofa cushions, ran for a pail of water, shouting.

"You bitch, you absolute bloody bitch, you always were greedy and ungrateful, not content with trying to set fire to your own house out of sheer spite you now start on mine. Well, you are dead, remember? You can't do this to me. Just go away, go away. I've had enough of you, making *me* feel guilty because *you* were a bloody awful woman. Nobody could have put up with you, the way you acted. I know, I know, you had a hard life, my father died, everything went wrong for you, I know, God do I know." In her frenzy, Clare knocked Kum Yin flying into the hearth, where she broke in two. "Damn you, damn you, now look! Stop it, you evil old woman, go away from me. Your misery is not my fault, never was. Lay off, go, forever!"

The fire had not really been very bad, but the rug was ruined and everywhere seemed grimy or wet. Perhaps a section of the valuable rug might cover a footstool or make a small cushion. Wreckage, always rescuing things from wreckage. Wrecked life, but not, no, not her own. She would be different. She was.

Wearily clearing up, she resisted an impulse to call Phil. She could cope with this alone. For a moment, she thought it would make an amusing story over dinner on Friday, but of course that was stupid. Having cleared up most of the turmoil, she turned from it to return to her bed. As she switched off the light, she thought she heard the contemptuous sound of an old woman spitting.

Afterword

To find oneself slowly turning into a monster must surely be good material for a horror story. To suspect that perhaps one is going insane is also a rather rich field to explore, not that either of these themes is original, more classic, I would say. And to travel across the world in search of inner harmony only to get in deeper contact with a ghost that haunts one, the contact being an image from an alien religion, that too has been written about often enough. To be honest, until the very time of writing this note, I had not realised that I had interwoven these three ideas into "The Ancestress," not being given much to literary analysis. I am surprised how easy it is to find patterns in what I had thought of as an autobiographical story, exploring the theme of how powerful genetic influence is, and how hard it is to throw off what is inborn—indeed, it is impossible; it has to be transformed somehow. And when I say "autobiographical," I should point out that this story is also fiction, very much so. I do not collect porcelain nor pick up rich and powerful men on aeroplanes, perhaps alas. But no—even these two last are true, if not exactly hobbies.

What is fiction is the way the separate elements have been combined, made sense of, quite differently from the way the events originally happened. I have made connections that were not there in real life. Another way to put it would be to say I had discovered connections through the medium of fiction, but I must add that the process was far from therapeutic, a process that should in any case be divorced from writing. Quite the reverse; the more I write and think about the deepest current of all in this story, the favourite spiritual indulgence of women, guilt, the more haunted I become. I look at my hands, my face, hear the things I sometimes say, and think, My God, it is happening, in spite of everything. There is nothing to be done. Perhaps, reader passing a peaceful hour, it is happening to you also, a haunting from the realms within, whole universes of time and events compressed into miniature time bombs called genes. What is free will when faced with a determinism such as that? If you have a mark on you, which says you will become what you once most loathed, can it ever be erased? That is a question for you to answer, or perhaps the subject for another story.

Josephine Saxton

GETTING AWAY FROM IT ALL

Ann Walsh

The rats came the first night. She had seen their signs in the cabin when she unlocked the door, and, trying to hide her own revulsion, had persuaded the children to sweep up the droppings and tufts of cotton pulled from the upholstered couch. By the time she had, according to the real estate lady's instructions, activated the propane appliances, pumped up the cistern that supplied running water, and disposed of the two full saucers of rat poison, the girls had finished their attempt at sweeping. It was clean enough for now, she thought. Tomorrow she would sweep again, and mop the floor with a strong bleach solution. Exhausted by the long drive and the search for the isolated cabin she had rented for the summer, she tucked the two girls firmly into their sleeping bags in one bedroom, settled herself in the other, and fell into a deep, dreamless sleep.

She should have realized, she told herself the next morning, she should have realized that the rats would come back. The groceries she had left stacked on the kitchen counter were scattered on the floor, loose macaroni mixing with rice, sugar, and corn flakes. Every box, every bag, every item she had so carefully packed had been damaged in some way. Even less edible items— soap, pepper, paper towels—had been savaged, and fresh black droppings lay over everything like a satanic snowfall.

She cleaned up and, by the time the children woke, the kitchen showed no sign of the invasion. Everything was stored in the oven, the fridge, or sealer jars she had found in a cupboard, and she had discovered a large box of rat poison and refilled the saucers.

The cabin had been abandoned for several years, which was why the rent was within her single-parent budget. A faded FOR SALE sign hung crookedly on a tree outside, mutely pleading for new owners. It was not far from a small town, but the access road, eleven miles of deeply rutted, treacherous trail, had probably discouraged buyers.

Around the cabin the weeds were waist-high, and she had to carry the four-year-old as they struggled down to the beach. A patch of scorched earth marked a firepit, and a picnic table stood nearby, almost hidden in a thick stand of purple fireweed.

"Mummy?" Jenny's voice, usually strident with first-grade exuberance, was soft, timid. "Do we *have* to stay in this place? I don't think I like it here."

"Nonsense, Jen. It's just overgrown, lonely. No one has taken care of it for a long time. We'll clear a nice path down to the beach—see, there *is* a bit of a path under the weeds—then it will be easier for you to walk. We can build a campfire tonight and have hot dogs and marshmallows. It will be *fun!*" She smiled at the child, wondering why her own voice had sounded so loud and harsh.

The beach was beautiful, sandy and shallow for a long way out and nestled in a small cove that kept the water calm and warm. While the children splashed and searched for frogs, she began clearing the trail with a rusty but still serviceable sickle she found near the picnic table.

Once, stopping work to wipe the sweat from her eyes and to check on the children, she glanced up at the hillside behind her and saw, almost hidden among tall cedars, the dark bulk of another, larger cabin.

Curious, for no one had mentioned a second place close by, she called to the girls to stay out of the water until she came back, and pushed through the deep undergrowth on the hillside toward the hidden cabin.

It was large, built of gray-weathered logs, and surrounded by a wooden porch with a low railing. As she got closer, she could see that it was obviously deserted, and had been for a long time. The windows were boarded over with plywood, the steps to the front porch were pushed askew by saplings that nudged the foundation, and two solid planks were nailed, crosslike, over the front door. Oddly disappointed, she turned and began the downward climb. As she walked, she realized why the large cabin had been built so far away from the water. The view was spectacular. She could see far across the lake, around a bend in the shore, to where a solitary mountain, still snowcapped in July, reared distantly through the heat haze. Below her the lake threw off slices of sunlight, and she could see her children digging intently in the sand. Of her own cabin, she glimpsed only the roof and her bedroom window through the trees.

In the evening, sunburned and exhausted, the girls again crawled into bed early. She made herself a cup of tea and with it walked down the now-cleared path to the beach, admiring her handiwork. She stayed until the sun began to set, watching the coloured rays slant off the water; then, tired herself, she made her way back up the trail.

When she reached the cabin, both children were crying. She ran to their room, stopping abruptly as a large gray rat sitting between the two beds slowly turned, stared at her for a moment with basalt eyes, then scurried between her legs and out the door.

She reassured the children, set out yet another saucer

of poison, and went to bed. That night she dreamed that she heard music.

Slowly, the cabin became home. The rats stayed away, although the poisoned bait seemed untouched. The sickle and an old push mower revealed a tiny lawn, and the appearance of pansies alerted her to the presence of a flower bed edged with white-painted rocks. She took out several years' growth of weeds and discovered other perennials—pinks, daylilies, and a clump of flowering poppies. Someone had once spent a great deal of time in this place, she thought. The propane stove, fridge, and water heater, the fully operational bathroom and ingenious water supply, the flower beds, and the pleasant, solid furniture, all suggested a home rather than just a summer cabin. A home that someone had loved, but left. Why? she wondered, but quickly pushed the thought aside. Now it was her home, at least for a while. The girls were happy, their bodies becoming tanned, their hair sun-streaked. The treasures of lake and forest, new to city children—minnows, frogs, chipmunks, and the small kayak they had found—were keeping them cheerfully occupied. She was happy, too, she realized. Content. At peace.

But by the end of the first week in the cabin, she was no longer sleeping well. The music that she heard in her dreams became louder, more persistent. There were party sounds, too—the clink of glasses, distant bursts of laughter, sudden spatterings of conversation that she couldn't quite understand. Her dreams were always the same: she was lying in her narrow cot in the cabin and angrily listening to the sounds of a party to which she was not invited.

Then one night she realized that she *wasn't* asleep, *wasn't* dreaming! She sat up, fully awake, and listened. The music still played, the faint voices laughed. She went to the bedroom window, pushed aside the curtain, and stared out into the night. The big cabin on the hill glowed with light. It streamed through the large front windows, over the porch, touching the cedars with colour. Shadows moved against the windows, and the music seemed louder.

Puzzled, she let the curtain fall back into place and went into the kitchen. She lit the lamps, made tea, and tried to laugh at herself and her sudden fear. The owners of the large cabin had come back and she, being so involved with the children, the lake, the flowers, hadn't noticed them arriving—that was all. But wouldn't she or the children have heard a car? Several cars, in fact? And there *was* no road up the hill to the big cabin. Well, maybe there was another road, one she hadn't noticed. They could have come that way, perhaps.

But—the plywood had been removed from the windows, the front door was open, unbarred. Surely she would have heard hammering, shouts, the noises of opening a house that has been abandoned for a long time.

She stayed there in the bright kitchen until the dawn came, listening to the sounds, which faded with the growing light. When the sun dimmed the propane lights and tentatively reached across the room, she stood up and went outside. Uneasily, but with a growing sense of anticipation, she made her way through the long, early-morning shadows, up the hill, toward the large, now silent cabin.

Nothing had changed since she was last up here. The boarded-over windows and doors, the saplings and weeds pushing against the porch and stairs, and the thick, undisturbed underbrush on all sides were just as she had first seen them.

After that, she didn't try to sleep, but spent all her nights in the kitchen, turning the pages of a book, drinking tea, trying not to listen to the voices she knew she could not be hearing. The twelfth night, she heard them call her name.

The tourists were American, elderly, and kind. They pulled their big car onto the shoulder of the country road and spoke to the two bedraggled children who stood there, holding hands and trying not to cry.

"Mummy went away," said the oldest, rubbing at her eyes with a scratched, sunburned hand. "For two whole days. We got scared, so we walked to the road."

"We got losted," said the small one. "And see, a big rat in the cabin bit me. But I didn't cry."

She held out her arm proudly. The tourists looked at each other, their eyes wide with some unspeakable thought, then bundled the children into the car, turned around, and drove hurriedly back to the town they had just passed.

For on the child's arm was the perfect imprint of a vicious bite—two deep half-circles, the unmistakable mark left only by human teeth.

Afterword

In the early 1980s, I became obsessed with the idea of purchasing a summer retreat, a small cabin on a secluded lake where I could "get away from it all." For a long two months one summer, I dragged my children from one cottage to another, never finding the place that I knew was the right one. One day in August, a cloudy day with a hint of early frost, we bumped our way over ten miles of bush road to a deserted cabin on the shore of a lake that was as secluded as anyone could desire.

That cabin had been deserted by humans, but not by the rats. They had been everywhere; the furniture was shredded, droppings crusted the floor, and the air was thick with their smell. My children announced that this place was haunted and retreated hurriedly to the car. I stayed longer in that cabin, but not much longer. Into the room that had once belonged to children, into the room where the walls still bore pictures of smiling suns over crayon-blue lakes, the rats had not ventured. The quilts on the bunk beds lay smooth and whole, no black droppings covered the bright orange dresser or the beach ball that huddled in one corner, flat and airless. Some unseen barrier had halted the rodents on the threshold of that open door, and the childrens' room remained untouched. Untouched and permeated with a sense of waiting, waiting with ready-made beds and a beach ball that might still prove useful, waiting for those unknown children to return.

I drove as rapidly as I could back to the main highway, the children unusually quiet in the backseat of the car. I never did tell them that I, too, had caught the strangeness of that empty cabin, had sensed the presence of the ghosts that lived there with the rats, waiting.

This story, "Getting Away from It All," is how I laid those ghosts to rest, for what I had seen and sensed in that infested cabin haunted my dreams for many months.

I did, eventually, buy my small cabin, on another lake. I write there through summer nights, my old manual typewriter thumping, gently shaking the oil lamps that shed a golden light across the table. I listen to the lonely call of the loons, the licking of wavelets on the shore, and the whispering of the tall pines that surround me. I listen to the night sounds, and I watch the moon slanting silver across the water. The ghosts of that other cabin have been well laid to rest, for no rat has ever come near.

Ann Walsh

LOOPHOLE

Terry McGarry

She woke from a deep sleep as if from general anesthesia. There was the sudden awareness that time had passed and events had occurred and she had not been present, and the additional realization that things had happened to *her*. Then there was pain, gradually increasing as she probed downward from her brain to her heart and her gut and her crotch, each of which hurt in its own unique and nonphysical way. The wounds were emotional; but they were inflicted in her sleep while she lay helpless, and no malpractice suit could be filed against her mind.

She wondered what had been removed this time.

After the dunes had gone, she watched his descent through the still, dark air, a throb of it around him coalescing into a mist. Under his glittering black eyes, his heart-shaped mouth on her throat was a needle-bright sting of white teeth ringed by a sensuous suction. She felt weak and light-headed, and reached for him, but grasped only mist. The damp squeezed through her as desolate tears, and she surfaced crying into the pillow. The dry, unsatisfying dream tears gave no relief to her body's strained ache, but it could have been worse; it had been a different dream this time, with minimal violence. The room was chilly and she reached for the comforter, more awake now, depressed but alert. She turned over against a warm bulk, and froze.

Larger than the cat, it breathed and therefore could be neither a tangled blanket nor her giant teddy bear. It felt like none of her old lovers, and there were no current ones.

And it moved.

"Who are you and what do you want?" she asked in a flat voice.

"You wouldn't believe me if I told you," came the soft reply from just behind her head. It had an odd hint of amusement in it, and desperation, and a brittle timbre like the echo off a picket fence.

He did not touch her, or speak further; almost unobtrusive, he left her afloat in a passive paralysis. Would he strike if she moved? Would he constrict her with that giggling male enjoyment of strength, would he—

"Who the fuck *are* you?" she demanded, the old bitterness welling into rage that thrust her from him into the black air—toward the door, the light switch, her robe—while the skin of her back convulsed with the expectation of a blow.

"If you turn on the light, you will recognize me," he offered pleasantly, but the warning in it stopped her hand halfway to the switch. For a moment her fingers poised in the shadows, and then her palm slammed down fiercely on the jutting plastic.

There was no one in the room.

And then the phone rang.

She woke bleary and drained to dawn and a sour cigarette, coffee and the subways. As the residual fear and disgust stopped bubbling in her stomach, she stopped in a deli for a take-out breakfast. On line, she primped briefly in front of her compact, mildly irritated at a new crack in the glass that bisected her reflection grotesquely. She ran a hand through her thick, dark hair and added more blue liner to her eyes to offset the webs of red veins. She would be pretty again if she ever got some rest.

As she entered the cool lobby of her office building, she felt revived by the clear glass and smooth, indifferent marble. A dark, pin-striped executive stepped into the elevator behind her, and pressed the button for the floor above hers; as she passed him getting out, he glanced up from his paper, and his eyes seemed to draw all the warmth from her face. Shaken, she headed straight for her cubicle; the phone was ringing, and she fumbled it a little so that a metallic voice was speaking by the time she had it to her ear. ". . . said, is this the legal aid people?"

"Yes," she whispered, her hand tightening on the cold plastic.

"You want to counsel me, baby?" the voice buzzed, distorted by some electronic device. She slammed the receiver down, but the cold, inhuman tones had a horribly familiar inflection that stayed in her ears, teasing her, for the rest of the day.

She usually smiled a little, covertly, as eyes followed her entrance to the bar; she still took adolescent pleasure in turning heads. But this was her customary retreat, and any one of the men in the small crowd could be her obscene phone caller. It was a comfort to see Dave the bartender's amiable face; she slid up on her favorite corner bar stool and was soon pondering the amber depths of a drink, watching the imminent release of a bubble from a melting ice cube.

Where the hell did he get my home number? she thought. When this had started six months ago, she'd had it changed to an unlisted one to thwart him, although that still left her vulnerable at the office. Until the phone company started offering the call-tracing option she'd read about, there was no point in contacting the police again, and to report the really disturbing part, about the man in her bed, would be asking for a trip to the shrink; hell, she couldn't even explain it to herself. Had it been one of those double-jeopardy nightmares where you dream you've woken only to be threatened again in your own distorted room? The memory was already slipping away, defying her attempts to rationalize it. She resolved to buy an answering machine the next day so she could screen her calls; perhaps that would make her feel more in control of things again.

When Dave told her a gentleman near the door had bought her a drink, she glanced curiously over her shoulder, intending to routinely decline the offer and the hassle. But something about the man he pointed out made her shiver involuntarily, and to cover it she turned back with a shrug of acceptance. Dave, who had been especially protective these last months, set the glass down and hovered unobtrusively as the torn stool cushion beside her whooshed air under a new weight.

"Thank you for this," she said, looking up at last and raising her glass in the suggestion of a toast. "Maybe I can return the gesture."

"That won't be necessary." He leaned into the light, his porcelain face sliding into a smile as she met his eyes. They were black, and she thought for a moment she could see through them to the shadows beyond, so little light did they reflect. She felt suddenly unable to breathe.

"Are you all right?"

She murmured an automatic yes-I'm-fine. Then she banged the glass down on the bar. "No, I'm not. I've had a lousy day. Hell, I've had a lousy goddamn year. Now, you look really familiar to me, and it bugs me. So tell me: Do I know you?"

"Not particularly well."

She squinted at him for a moment. "Okay, that was a bizarre answer, but maybe it was the way I asked you." She sipped her rye. "Have we met before?"

"That's a difficult question, from someone who doesn't know my name and hasn't volunteered her own."

"I'm Alex. Why did you buy me this drink?"

"You're very attractive. I wanted to strike up a conversation."

"Why?"

"I just told you."

Exasperated, she dug a cigarette from her purse. "Fine. Pardon my paranoia. Do you come here often?"

"No."

"Do you work around here?"

"No."

"Have you considered going to a dialogue coach?"

He smiled again, but his eyes did not crinkle, and he seemed to be evaluating her. She took the look for a warning, but as she got up to leave his expression changed entirely and he restrained her with a light, electric touch. "I'm sorry," he said, very quietly. "As I've told you before, you would not believe the truth, and I hesitate to frighten you more than you already have been."

His suddenly sad, desperate face buffered the statement, so she sat down again and waved Dave away with a reassuring nod. "Go on, then."

He seemed to collect himself. "It's so easy in daydreams, isn't it? You meet someone, you talk for a while, you go off together; in reality you have to be on guard for perverts and exploiters. I thought I could intrigue you with mystery, but I nearly drove you away."

His expression had changed almost down to the features themselves, as if the bones in his face were malleable. She was fascinated, trying to distinguish this nose from the last one, to identify the precise change in the mouth, and she lost the next few sentences.

". . . have met before. In the elevator—"

"And in my apartment. So that was you. Is this a big

joke, or what? Did Eddie hire you or something?" *This guy must be the caller,* she thought; *what do I do now?*

"No, and no." He smiled again. "To answer your other questions, I have come here several times—when you dreamed that this building had burned down, and when you fantasized that Dave seduced you. And I do work in this area, when you do; I've been at your desk when you half-dozed after a big lunch, and I've accompanied you as you slept on the train home.

"I come from your dreams, Alexis, and I'm asking you to help me."

She fumbled for the lights in the apartment, afraid of the dark, afraid of her fear. She turned on the radio, closed the blinds, pulled the phone cord out of the jack, and wrapped herself in her robe, cocooned in sound and light. She thought of the "Twilight Zone" episode where a man believes a dream woman stalks him, and of "Mission: Impossible," where elaborate setups fooled executives and dictators; but she wasn't crazy yet, and she wasn't worth a scam like this. She rummaged for a box of No-Doz left over from college until she remembered that sleep deprivation causes hallucinations. She paced the floor, avoiding the cat, then flopped onto the couch and thought of the hideous, half-familiar buzz on the telephone, tried in vain to match it to the stranger's odd face.

She expected him to appear, to finish the conversation she had run out on. But he did not, and when the DJ announced 3 AM and several attempted diversions had failed, she gave up and went to bed, flinging herself at whatever sleep might bring.

The beach was familiar, red and warped, the dune she stood on stretching hundreds of yards down to the ocean. Broken things cracked away from the nearby cliff face, splashing into the water, and she was afraid to try the descent lest the same thing happen to her. But she knew the wave was coming, because it always did, and she stood undecided whether to dive through it, to where Eddie was, or to run for higher ground. It was too late; the wall of water towered over her, and she turned and ran up the dune—reached the crest—could just see the small town below when the wave broke silently over her. She waited for the water to rush back and away, for the dream to be over, but Eddie dragged her out of the foam and then pushed her back down under it. "I was safe!" she cried out angrily; "I had made it! I was safe!"

It became her father's voice, shouting. There were no words, just rage, and her name over and over again, her full name, a girl's name, his name distorted to fit his disappointing firstborn. Her little, bigger brothers were playing army outside. They wanted her to be a nurse, but she demanded to be an officer, and they broke all her toy soldiers and laughed as her father threw away the pieces. Eddie came to take them, but she had hidden the garbage bag in her room, and when he found it Eddie's rings flashed in a convex arc toward her face, again and again, until she knew no one would ever recognize the boneless pulp again. "SO YOU THINK YOU CAN OUTSMART ME HUH OUTSMART ME HUH—"

She woke screaming her frustration, in a cracked squeak, that the dream had ended the *same way,* swearing to her damned Catholic God anything if only she could break the infinite loop of events, go back to that moment and—

And what? she thought, awake now. Kill Eddie? Get revenge for bones that had healed, retrieve her drowned pride? Those were the real dreams. I should have gone to the cops when I had the chance, she berated herself for the thousandth time; I was an asshole to try to protect him. But blaming herself would do no good; relationships did not come with no-fault insurance, and whatever the complex motives, the fact was that he had beaten her severely a year ago and she had left him and it was over. If it weren't for some weirdo harassing her on the phone, she would be fine by now. *He* certainly was, from what she had heard; he had hung up on her when she called to get back her keys (costing her new locks), and one of her coworkers had seen him with another woman several times. Perhaps, she thought, he had never loved her at all. So for the thousandth time she put it out of her mind, as she had boxed up all his things and dumped them down the trash chute, as she had hocked the ring for a ludicrous price, venting her aggression, she thought, on every physical reminder of him. She had kept only the teddy bear that lay beside her now, and she dug her nails into its arm, about to hurl it at the wall; then she remembered the arcade, Eddie's dancing eyes and tousled curls and wacko grin as he conned the girl into fixing the game so he could win Alex the impossible prize. It was the only good memory she had left, and she hugged the giant silky thing against her and sobbed carefully away from it into the pillow until dawn.

She left work early the next day, unable to keep her eyes open, resenting her clients' problems, knowing she looked a little drugged or hung over. She wanted to cry out for help, wondered what they would think if she ran shrieking down the hallway, knew there would be no point. She had been down before, and something inside her always pulled her out of it. She decided to have a few drinks while she was waiting.

At Dave's, the stranger sat in the dark corner by the men's room. She wasn't sure it was him, since he looked shorter, more swarthy; but she was too tired to play guessing games and brought her drink right over to his table. This, at least, she could straighten out.

"Well, I'm back," she said. "Sorry about running out last night. But what you said did sound pretty off-the-wall."

"It was the truth," he replied calmly, and the dry voice confirmed his identity. "But you had every right to be skeptical. *I* don't even know quite how I became conscious, only that I did, trapped in a nightmare that turned out to be yours. I had to get out. It's rather unnerving to wake up into the middle of a dream.''

"Sure." She tossed back her shot of rye, savoring the slow burn in her throat. "But, giving you the benefit of the doubt, I should have seen you in my apartment again. Or in my sleep.''

"I have no intention of going back into your head, not in its present state. And after you rejected me here last night, I knew it would do me no good to alienate you further. I respect your privacy.''

"How courteous.''

"Purely self-serving. I told you my life depends on you. And I know you want to help me. In fact, I know parts of you that you can never sanely confront. And I trust you anyway.''

She thought of how she had listened to his story and then walked out, only to wait outside, stalling, smoking three cigarettes, watching for him to come out. He never did, and when she peered back inside he was not there. She looked up, but it was hard to focus on him. She wanted to cry again.

"The other night," she began slowly, addressing her drink, "I was dreaming of a vampire, and there you were. You're a parasite, feeding on me, using me to make you real.''

His voice was patient, and deeper than before although it retained that strange bone-dryness. "But look at what I offer you. I can be any man you desire, for as long as you like—your whole life, if you wish— or a different one every day. . . .''

His teasing hurt. "You're a prostitute, then.''

"I told you how badly I want to live.''

"So convince me, if you know me so well. Find just the words that will sway me, dig them out of the back of my mind.''

"Arguments are logical." He smiled. "Dreams are not.''

"But they seem to be while they're happening. You're

a failure even as a dream.'' She regretted the words immediately, but it was too late to retrieve them, so she looked up and forced her eyes to stay on his face. She was not as startled this time by the change: The dark stranger had vanished, and his eyes were a slit blue under tawny hair. ''Look. Can't you be yourself? Do you have a self to be?''

''Only yours.''

''Then you're out of luck.'' She put her head in her hands and squeezed her hair tightly, painfully away from her scalp. The drink and the string of nights seemed collected behind her eyelids in a sticky, heavy scum. *Shame on you, Alex.* You're trained to know the difference between helping and being used. But her mind had caught on something—a puzzle, a challenge. She stared suddenly up at him. ''You look like the movie star— Brett Davis.''

''So I do.''

She shook her head, annoyed. ''No. Brett Davis would never say that. First of all, he has a touch of a Southern Accent, and yours is classic mid-Atlantic. I was right about the dialogue coach; you'll need one. People don't talk the same in reality as in dreams. Plus you'll have to stop being all these different characters. Even if I did go for a little wish-fulfillment in my sex life—and I've had it with romance for now, you should know that, Sigmund—in public you'll have to settle for one face if you want to be really real. In fact, there are a lot of practical considerations here. What are you going to do for money, and identification, and clothes, and so on? Can you pull those out of my head?''

His big hand closed over one of hers and drew it to his face. His cheek was warm with a hint of beard; she could feel the swell of the jawbone, the fleshy pouch of jowl, the muscles contracting as he smiled again. ''You're very good at your job,'' he said softly as her limp hand fell away. She felt dizzy again, unfocused, as if her contact lenses were slipping, but she continued to stare stubbornly at him, determined to see this through.

He filled out as if taking a deep breath; his hair curled slightly, reddened along with his pallor, and after what seemed like a long while she blinked hard because she was looking at Eddie.

"Now, that's not fair, you jerk," she snapped, her heart beating very fast. "You're trying to distract me—"

"But I didn't initiate the change. You did. And you're certainly addressing me as you would Eddie."

The waitress appeared and wanted to know what this gentleman was drinking. Alex frowned—the waitress had already served him one drink—then realized that this was the girl who spent her time in the bathroom and her wages paying for skipped-on tabs, and of course, this was not the same gentleman. "I wouldn't know," she said, and gave the girl a ten. "This is for me and my friend who left." She fumbled a little as she snapped her purse shut hard, waiting for the girl to go. Then she rose to leave. "The last thing I need is old wounds reopened. Christ." She glared into the corner where he had leaned back out of the light, not caring that she couldn't see his face, not caring whose face it was. "I'm going home to get some rest, and you can take that opportunity to vacate my alpha or delta or whatever the hell waves they are. And if I get any more calls or see you again, I'll have you arrested, I swear to God."

"Alexis?"

"What?"

"You might want to sit back down."

"Now, why in the hell would I want to do that?"

"Because Eddie just walked in."

Before she could demand to know what new trick this was or quell the surge of fear, she heard a voice she thought she had forgotten, the one thing the stranger couldn't duplicate.

"Well, speak of the devil."

Eddie smiled that lopsided grin full of teeth that seemed to have been sliced off at an angle so he had to cock his jaw to compensate. His merry eyes flicked to the table behind her and registered the two glasses. He loosened his tie, tossed his jacket onto a chair, and turned it around to straddle it, with a scrape of leg on floor.

"So, Ally, did I tell you that AT&T made me the fucking most unbeatable offer?" Eddie said, as if continuing a conversation. She almost responded, from habit, before the intervening silent months rushed back; she shoved trembling hands into her pockets and tried not to look at the cordial, crooked smile that blurred into the memory of a mouth twisted with irrational rage. "Took 'em long enough; they finally figured since I'm their biggest threat right now they'd be smart to get me on their team. . . ." He hadn't even looked into the corner or acknowledged another presence. He'd assumed his dominant role like an old coat, and she knew that in her passivity she had all but put it on his shoulders. Her mind began to spin, around and around his babble of ego, as if trying to weave a web so tight it would choke the words off, and all the while another part of her shouting *Say something, do something, shut him up, make him stop*, her bones still aching from the time she'd tried. Around and around . . .

"Hello, Ed," the brittle voice broke in, preceding him from the dark corner as he leaned forward into the sphere of light from the fake antique hanging lamp. He extended a freckled hand. Eddie's hand.

She heard herself laugh. "Eddie Lester. Meet Eddie Lester."

Ed looked from the hand to the face. "Is this a joke?"

"I don't think so. Don't you want to shake hands?"

"What, are you fucking plastic surgeons now?"

The loop closed around her again. She managed to move her body around the table on which the proffered hand rested lightly, and tugged on the sleeve. She had to get him out of here before Eddie got out of control. "Come on, let's go. A joke is a joke, right? We'll go somewhere and finish our conversation—"

"Wait up, Ally. I want to talk to this guy. How the hell did you swing this? Christ, you look just like me."

LOOPHOLE

She liked the baffled look on Eddie's face: She had tried so often for at least that look in lieu of acceptance, love, anything but smug superiority. But escape was all she wanted now, escape from her own paralysis, and she winced as the stranger began to talk, because Ed's big, bewildered eyes were narrowing, and she had seen them do that one too many times before.

". . . understand your confusion, because I understand you." His arm slid away from the insistent pressure of her fingers. "I know how you fell in love with Alexis over the telephone when she was a receptionist for the phone company you were a sales rep for. She was in college then and you loved to play the big shot. But she graduated and got a prestigious job, and you had to work harder and harder to stay on top, to play on her fear that she wasn't good enough for the big boys' league, to get her to pay attention to you and not the hardcases she worked with."

Ed's hands were spread, his mouth open in disbelief. "What is this bullshit? What have you been telling this nut, Ally?"

"She finally felt smothered by you, unappreciated, put down by your drinking companions. So she began dating men who made her feel loved. That's when you beat her. But when she left you, it was as if she'd had the last word—so you started making phone calls."

Ed was across the table in one fluid movement, his hands full of lapel and collar. "She fucked everybody in sight. She was a whore, she's lucky I offered to take her back. You want to talk violence here?"

Alex felt as if she'd remembered something that had been on the tip of her tongue, something obvious that had eluded her. "Eddie—those phone calls—"

Ed's green eyes turned cunning. He shoved his look-alike against the wall and dropped one hand away. "What phone calls? How does this guy know about phone calls unless he's makin' them, huh?"

"If you're innocent, why are you about to hit me?" said the stranger's voice.

Alex looked from one Ed to the other and felt herself constrict—throat and bowels and tear ducts—until the tension seemed to ripple down her arms, scream through her tendons, each neuron locked in the ancient replay of shout and punch and flinch and grunt from which emerged Ed's voice, the voice she hadn't heard in months, except, of course, on the telephone. She saw Ed's arm come back, fist clenched, rings glittering, a year ago and now, but now she had her hand in his mass of curly hair before this punch could connect, yanking him away with all the force of a year of pent memories so the arm swung harmlessly this time through the air; and before she knew she'd struck, he'd hit the floor, nose spurting blood, and her hand fell limp and numb back to her side. She wondered if her college ring would leave a mark, like the Phantom's, in his face.

Dave was shouting by then, moving in to stop the fight that was already over, the lamp swinging crazily, its rocking shadow concealing the stranger's fade-out. Alex barely saw him go; she was shouting at Eddie who was shouting at her, but she was laughing inside, exulting, knowing she would never be trapped again.

"All *right*." Dave slammed his fist down on the table, which someone had conveniently righted. "Where's the other guy, the guy who started it?"

"Ed started it," she said truthfully.

"Where's the guy who decked be?" Eddie demanded through a bloody handkerchief. "Fuckid coward busta rud off."

She realized he was embarrassed to admit it had been her, little Ally who never fought back, and since Dave knew how Eddie had treated her and was on her side—was probably angry now because he had failed to protect her this time—she decided to play it out. "What guy?"

"What do you bead, 'what guy'? Your boyfred, Ally—"

"Did anyone here see a man run out?" Alex asked the circle of gawking customers. It murmured no and I-don't-know, including the waitress, who had probably been in the bathroom anyway.

"Well, what did he look like?" Dave asked Eddie.

Eddie stared at Alex for a long moment, then swore. "You set be up for this, you bitch."

"Well, someone knocked you over, I saw that much," a man said; Alex knew they'd all been at the front end of the bar watching the Mets game, but the brittle smack of fist on flesh and the meaty wooden sound of Eddie's fall must have been self-explanatory.

"I did it, Dave," she said, grinning openly now, raising her red knuckles as proof. "And you know those obscene phone calls I've been getting?"

Dave nodded.

"Well, the caller's gonna have to bend the receiver around the bandage on his dose."

When she got home he was there, petting the cat; he stood up, ever the gentleman, as she entered. He was quite ordinary-looking this time, brown hair and eyes, about her height, dressed casually. He reminded her of someone, but she couldn't place it and didn't try. "Well, that's one hell of a year wrapped up," she said by way of greeting. "Eddie admitted about the phone calls as soon as I accused him of getting my unlisted number through his new job. It was pretty stupid of him to come looking for me to brag about the job in the first place, since that's how I made the connection, as it were. But he was always that way. I told him I had tapes of all those calls in a safe-deposit box and that I would give them to the police if he bothered me anymore, let their electronics people decode his voice. I don't, really—"

"I know."

She paused. "Yeah. You know a lot of things. Things I never managed to put into words. I really owe you one." She sat down next to him on the couch. "In fact, you're the first man who ever got close to me without dominating me, too. My mom died when I was five, and my dad—never mind, I can see you know all this already, too. Okay, well, what do you want in return for your help?"

"I've gotten what I wanted."

"No, seriously, can I help you get started, can I put you up while you look for a job? I thought you were the parasite, but now I feel like it's the other way round. Dammit, will you say something, *please?*"

He raised his eyes, and she found it easy now to meet his calm gaze. He ran a hand through his thick, dark hair, looking tired, and human. She reached out to him and touched his cheek again, and he smiled. "All I can really say is good-bye."

"What? Where are you going?"

"Back where I came from."

"Into my dreams?"

"More or less."

She huffed, exasperated. "Then why on earth did you bother coming out?"

"Because you needed me."

"But you said *you* needed—" She stopped and shook her head. "Look, I don't give a damn anymore where you came from, but you can't just *leave,* not before I even get to really know you. . . . Hell, do you like baseball, do you like olives? What kind of books do you read?"

"Yes, no, and Westerns."

"Same as me. That's three points in our favor. We could make a very good couple." That sounded superficial to her, so she added, "I love you," but that sounded just as flat and odd, and she collapsed into silence.

"Of course you love me," he said gently. "You always did, through the fear and awkwardness. I admit I didn't care for you when we first met face to face; I enjoyed scaring you, spitefully. But I care now. That's the important thing. That and getting back where I belong."

She began to see, slowly, why he looked so familiar. "Everything will be all right then, huh? When you go— come—back?"

He nodded. "You do understand."

"I guess. There is one thing, though. . . ."

"Yes?"

"You never told me your name. I mean, do you even have one? Or do I have to say good-bye to 'hey, you'?"

"That won't be necessary," he said, his voice very low, the voice she heard when she read or verbalized thoughts—his distinctive voice, her voice. " 'Hey, me' will do."

Afterword

My interest in fantasy, dark or otherwise, seems to be genetic, inherited from my mother, Lee, who was reading science fiction back in the forties (when it was not considered ladylike to do so), and who fed me a steady diet of fantasy books as bedtime stories. Later on, after I had discovered the work of Shirley Jackson and learned that the most terrible monsters are those of the mind, my mother told me about a recurring nightmare she used to have. She would dream that she had woken into her own room, and wandered out of it and down the hallway of her house with a growing feeling of foreboding. In the living room she would glimpse a grotesque, hulking, shadowy creature, and she would stand paralyzed with terror until she really woke up. The dream continued to plague her until she found the courage to go into the living room, to walk up to the creature, and to look it in the face, whereupon she woke crying with pity at the pain and loneliness she found there, and never had the dream again. While "Loophole" is not necessarily her story, or mine, it is intended to be the story of a woman's struggle to look part of herself in the face. For helping her do that, I owe a thank-you to Shawna McCarthy and the members of her writing workshop at the New School in New York; and in order to credit the other half of my genetic makeup, who loved fantasy more than any of us, "Loophole" is dedicated to the memory of my father, Pat.

Terry McGarry

THE COMPANION

Joan Aiken

The ugliness of her rented cottage was a constant source of perverse satisfaction to Mrs. Clyrard. To have traveled, in the course of her seventy-odd years, over most of the civilized world, to have lived in several of its most elegant capitals, and finally to have come to roost in Number Three, Vascoe's Cottages, had an incongruity that pleased her tart, ironic spirit. Mrs. Clyrard indulged in a constant battle against life's unreasonableness and inequities. Her private hobby was finding fault—with the British government, the world's so-called leaders, with her bank, with her friends, with the young, the old, the stupid, the BBC Third Programme, the weather, and the cakes from the village shop. It gave her intense, not wholly masochistic gratification to survey her hideous rented furniture, to go into her dark little unfunctional kitchen and discover that the gas pilot had gone out again, that before putting a kettle on to boil she must laboriously poke a long-stemmed match into the dirty interstices of the stove, turn, at the same time, a small, gritty, and inconveniently placed wheel, and wait for the resulting muffled explosion; this ritual, which often had to be enacted several times a day due to the fluctuations of gas pressure, filled her with a dour amusement, confirming, as it did, all her most pessimistic feelings about the world. The aged, recalcitrant plastic ice trays, which were more likely to split in half under pressure of an angry thumb than to eject a single cube of ice, the front gate that refused to latch properly, the wayward taps turning in improbable directions, emitting a thin thread of lukewarm water, the varying levels of the cottage, which had steps up or steps down between all its rooms, even one in the middle of the bathroom—these things fulfilled her expectation that life was intended to be a series of cynical booby traps.

Nevertheless, Mrs. Clyrard could have lived in comfort if she had chosen. She was rich, had been married, had had a successful career as a painter, had had children even, now satisfactorily grown and disposed of; she was a handsome, intelligent, and cultivated woman; death had removed her husband, it was true, but otherwise she need have had little to complain about; yet all possible amenities had been, it seemed, wantonly jettisoned in favour of retreat into the exile of a Cornish village. Not even romantic exile, for Talland was far from picturesque: it was a small, random conglomeration of ill-assorted, mostly granite buildings, established on a treeless hillside as if they had been dropped there.

Vascoe's Cottages, of which Mrs. Clyrard occupied Number Three, had been a nineteenth-century addition, two pairs of plain red-brick semidetached labourers' dwellings, which some hopeful later landlord's hand had embellished with heavy chalet-type ornamental woodwork, thereby further darkening the already inadequately lit interiors.

"Oh, that will do for me very nicely," Mrs. Clyrard had remarked with her usual brief smile, on first observing Number Three over its stout enclosing privet hedge.

"Are you certain?" her friend and prospective landlady Mrs. Helena Soames doubtfully inquired. "Are you sure it will be big enough for you—*light* enough? The furniture is rather a job lot, I'm afraid—I could have it taken out, if you would like to put in your own things—"

"No, no, let them stay in store. I can't be bothered with them. This is admirable. And the furniture will last my time."

Mrs. Clyrard was in excellent health, but she always spoke and acted as if in expectation of imminent death.

She moved herself into the cottage with a minimum of fuss or added impedimenta (a typewriter, some books); quickly learned the names and ways of the local trades-people; and had soon established herself on terms of remarkable cordiality with all her neighbours, the terms being that she listened to—indeed, drew out by some unique osmosis of her own—all their dissatisfactions and complaints, meanwhile herself maintaining a considerable reticence. Complaint is addictive; people came back eagerly, again and again, for more; Mrs. Clyrard had all the company she could have wished for. She listened, she made her own dry comments and never disbursed advice; this was the secret of her popularity. She never offered information about herself, or divulged her own feelings. If asked what she did with herself all day—for it was plain that she was neither house-proud nor a dedicated gardener—she replied:

"I am writing my memoirs. I have known any number of famous people"—and it was true, she had—"and plenty of reputations will have the rug pulled from under them if I don't die before I have finished."

Although she frequently and drily referred to her possible death, she manifested no anxiety about the prospect, and seemed not particularly troubled as to whether she finished her memoirs first or not. Very few things appeared to trouble Mrs. Clyrard particularly; she found a sour pleasure in her occupations. Meanwhile the years rolled by, bestowing on her no signs of age or infirmity;

nor did she manifest any disposition to seek more comfortable quarters than Number Three, Vascoe's.

"I don't know how you can endure the poky little
place," Miss Morgan frequently remarked when she
dropped in to complain about Mrs. Soames. "It's so
dark and cold. When I was living here with the old lady,
I thought I should go mad with the inconvenience. It
must be the most awkward house in the world. Even
with that lift installed—"

The old lady had been Helena Soames's mother, Mrs.
Musgrave. For ten years prior to her death from heart
disease she had occupied Number Three, Vascoe's, and
Miss Morgan had been her companion. The lift had been
installed for Mrs. Musgrave's benefit; it consisted of a
metal chair with a counterbalance in the stairwell, oper-
ated by a small electric motor. Mrs. Musgrave's son, an
engineer, had installed it himself. The old lady had sat
herself in the chair, been buckled in with a seat belt;
then she pressed a button and was conveyed slowly up
or slowly down. The lift, with its ugly metalwork, still
remained; but Mrs. Clyrard, who had a rooted mistrust
of all machinery, saw no occasion to make use of it.

After ten years Mrs. Musgrave had died, and Miss
Morgan, lacking a function, was removed to the manor
to housekeep for the daughter, Mrs. Soames—an
arrangement that gave little satisfaction to either party.

Almost every day at teatime, Miss Morgan called in
on Mrs. Clyrard with some grievance to relate about
Mrs. Soames's fault-finding, heartlessness, inconsis-
tency, or sarcasm, to which Mrs. Clyrard listened with
her usual acute impassivity.

"I do wish *you* would have me for your companion,
dear Mrs. Clyrard," Miss Morgan, who had a slight
stammer, often sighed out. "I am s-sure we should get
on so well! I would be so h-happy to look after everything for you while you wrote your memoirs, and would
not dream of asking for a s-salary; all I want is a home."

"My dear woman, what possible use would I have for

a companion in this tiny box of a house? I am almost too much company for myself.''

Wispy, myopic little Miss Morgan would take herself off, pleading, ''Think it over, dear Mrs. Clyrard—do think it over!''

In the evenings Mrs. Clyrard often heard the other side of the case: her friend Helena generally dropped in for a glass of sherry and a grumble about Miss Morgan's self-pity, inefficiency, forgetfulness, untidiness, tendency to martyrdom, and general inadequacy. Mrs. Clyrard made no comment on that, either. Nor did she see fit to intervene when Mrs. Soames's patience finally ran out and she dismissed the unsatisfactory housekeeper, who, being far too old by now to secure another post, went lamenting away to live with her married sister in Lanlivery, after a final and unavailing plea to Mrs. Clyrard to take her in.

More time went by. Mrs. Clyrard lent a noncommittal ear to the outpourings of other neighbours: of harassed parents who could not deal with their young; of rebellious teenagers who could not endure their parents; of betrayed husbands; of frustrated wives; and of disillusioned friends who had fallen out. Her own private life remained as apparently tranquil as ever; her excellently coiffed iron-gray hair turned a shade paler, her hawklike profile was unchanged; she wrote a few pages a day at the desk in her upstairs study, cooked light meals for herself, waged her usual guerrilla war against the inconveniences of her house, and continued in her customary state of sardonic composure.

But presently—and how it happened, Mrs. Clyrard was not precisely aware, for the change came by such gradual degrees—her equable daily routine became disrupted; not seriously, but just enough to be noticeable.

The form taken by the disturbance was this: Mrs. Clyrard, seated upstairs in a state of recollected tranquillity at her typewriter, would suddenly find her concentration broken by an odd urge to go below and perform some slight, unnecessary task in the kitchen. Sometimes her more rational self was able to withstand the trivial impulse; but sometimes it was not, and almost before she was aware of the process she would find herself at the kitchen sink washing tea cloths, or cleaning the leaded-glass panes in the front door (which made no difference to the light, for the untrimmed privet hedge grew within six feet of it), or polishing shoes, or defrosting the refrigerator.

This was very annoying, but Mrs. Clyrard had no intention of submitting to it. She was a woman of total practicality. If she felt a twinge in a tooth, she consulted her dentist; if she detected a rattle in her car, she referred it to the garage. Possible psychic phenomena weighed no more and no less in her estimation than failures in the electrical system or mice in the pantry: as she would call in an electrician or a cat for the latter inconveniences, for the former she had recourse to an exorcist. Fortunately, she was acquainted with one: an old friend of hers, a rural Dean living in semiretirement in Bath, still took an active interest in paranormal occurrences, and occasionally officiated at a ceremony to remove some unwelcome or disturbed spirit.

Mrs. Clyrard wrote and invited him for a visit, arranging to have him accommodated at a nearby guesthouse, since she detested having people staying in the cottage.

When he arrived, she lost no time explaining the nuisance to him.

"Somebody is trying to occupy my mind—or my house," she said matter-of-factly, though with a considerable degree of irritation. "I should be very much obliged if you could deal with it for me, Roger."

The Dean, delighted with the odd problem, promised to see what he could do. To assist him, he fetched over a medium from Bath—a city much plagued by psychic phenomena, possibly due to its enclosed, low-lying, and damp situation.

The medium, Mrs. Hannah Huxley, a portly, blind lady, acquiesced with the Dean in taking the problem as a most serious challenge. They turned back the carpets, they inscribed formulae and diagrams repellent to invading spirits on the floors of all the rooms, they recited incantations, they lit candles and sprinkled water, they performed various rituals involving the doors, the windows, the curtains, the mirrors, the stairs, the fireplace, the lights. At one point during the proceedings, which were long, and to Mrs. Clyrard somewhat tediously repetitious, Mrs. Huxley went into a trance.

"Did your husband," she suddenly inquired, emerging from this condition as abruptly as she had gone into it, "did your husband die of a head injury, Mrs. Clyrard?"

"Certainly not," said Mrs. Clyrard with asperity, startled and not best pleased at this intrusion into her private affairs. "He died of intestinal carcinoma."

"That's odd. I have distinct evidence of a presence quite close to you who has at some time suffered from a head injury. Are you quite sure that you can think of no such person?"

Mrs. Clyrard moved a step or two aside, distastefully, before replying again, "Absolutely not."

Her faith by now somewhat diminished, she watched in ironic silence as the Dean and Mrs. Huxley came to the conclusion of their ritual, having now apparently located the intrusive entity.

Kindly, cajoling, uttering mellifluous Latin phrases formed for the purpose of coaxing such undesired visitants from their lodgings, the Dean walked slowly backward, beckoning, to the front door, opened it, waited, and recited a final prohibiting admonition before closing the door and returning to the fireside.

"There, it's gone!" he said with a beaming smile. "It can't come back inside now."

It? thought Mrs. Clyrard, on an impulse of strong protest; how could that vague, unhappy, intrusive, indefinable emanation be compressed into and pinned down by such a brusque, particular little monosyllable as *it?*

"Poor thing, it simply hated to leave," the Dean went

on. "No, I'm afraid it didn't want to go in the very least. Did you hear it whimpering?"

Mrs. Clyrard had not.

Stifling her scepticism, however, she civilly thanked the Dean and his colleague, refreshed them after their exertions with tea and cakes from the village shop, conversed for a polite hour, and finally, with relief, saw them to the door and said good-bye. Still sceptical, but in a cool spirit of scientific investigation, she went upstairs for an experimental hour's writing. And the Dean had been completely right, perfectly justified in his confidence: there was nothing to disturb her concentration; she found she could work in untroubled peace for the whole hour. Not a single thought of the tea things waiting unwashed downstairs so much as slipped over the edge of her consciousness.

When Helena Soames presently arrived for a glass of sherry, at half past six, Mrs. Clyrard was in a highly self-congratulatory state of mind and, contrary to her usual reticent habit, related the story.

"But I still can't imagine who the person suffering from a head injury can be," she concluded.

"Oh, can't you?" said Mrs. Soames, who had listened with the greatest interest. "But it's perfectly obvious, my dear. It must be poor Miss Morgan."

"Miss *Morgan?* Did she have a head injury? I never knew of it."

"It was over before you came to the village, of course. In fact, it happened while Miss Morgan was looking after my mother in this cottage, after Edward had installed the chair lift. Miss Morgan had strapped Mother in and then—stupid woman—stuck her head over the banister to say 'Is there anything you want me to bring you, Mrs. Musgrave?' Of course, the counterbalance came down, hit her on the head, and knocked her silly. She was never quite the same after that, but then she hadn't been too bright to start with. Luckily, Mother died not long afterward."

"Miss Morgan—yes, of course," said Mrs. Clyrard

reflectively, remembering the doleful little woman's plea to be allowed to return to the inconveniences of Number Three, Vascoe's: "I'd be so happy to look after the house for you while you wrote your memoirs. I wouldn't *dream* of asking for a salary. All I want is a home."

"It simply hated to leave," Roger had said. "It didn't want to go in the very least."

Looked at through those eyes, the dark and poky sitting room with its Tottenham Court Road furnishings momentarily took on the appearance of a warm and happy haven.

"Miss Morgan," Mrs. Clyrard said again. "What became of her?"

"Oh, she went to live with that married sister in Lanlivery. The sister had always despised her. Miss Morgan didn't want to go, but what could she do? At her age, she couldn't get another job. Anyway, evidently it was a disastrous arrangement, for about six months later I heard that she drowned herself in a brook. All for the best, really; as I said, she'd never been quite with it after that accident. Well, *you* must have noticed it—she used to come wailing round to you often enough."

"Yes. So she did," Mrs. Clyrard said in the same thoughtful manner.

Miss Morgan: that melancholy, ineffectual little woman; ineffectual in death as in life, apparently.

Or was she?

Seeing Helena to the door half an hour later, closing it briskly behind her, Mrs. Clyrard was aware for the first time that the previous trivial though irritating mental distractions that had assailed her might have been exchanged for something even more unaccustomed: a sensation of discomposure, disquiet; perhaps even—to analyse it closely—fear?

For although the Dean and Mrs. Huxley had led the whimpering, reluctant whatever-it-was along to the front door and out of the house, that was *all* they had done; they did not claim to have annihilated it, or driven it any farther than the threshold.

Mrs. Clyrard allowed herself an uneasy glance at the door that framed its glass-paned square of dark.

Might not her visitor—out there in the little privet-enclosed garden—out there behind the glass-paned door in the rainy night—might it not feel now, perhaps, a certain degree of *resentment* at its exclusion?

Mrs. Clyrard heard the garden gate—which as usual had failed to latch properly—begin to creak and clatter as it swung to and fro in the rising wind.

She knew that she ought to go and fasten the gate before the hinges were damaged. And yet she lingered in the dreary little hallway, strangely reluctant to set foot outside the security of her house.

Afterword

"The Companion" is a true story. I have only changed the names, in case any of the people mentioned are still alive. The main character, "Mrs. Clyrard," was an old friend of my father, who settled, in old age and widow-hood, not far from where I live, and of whom I was very fond. She lived all her life on the fringes of the literary world, had known poets, analysts, and composers; her chief desire was to figure, herself, in some literary work. "Why don't you write a story about *me?*" she used to say, and so, when she told me the basic elements of "The Companion," and I turned it into a short story and had it published, she was delighted. My father had also written a story about her called "Spider, Spider," but I never dared inquire if she was aware that this was a portrait of her. Toward the end of her life she began to tease my sister and me by threatening to appoint one or the other of us as her literary executor. She had always announced her intention of producing some great book of memoirs. "All the diaries I've kept, all the people, the scandals I have known—it will be your job—the job of *one* of you—to sort them out." My sister and I regarded this prospect with mixed terror and exhilaration. We had seen the papers, all right; we knew they were there in the little haunted cottage—piles and boxes of them. What might we not find? But what a task! And we had plenty of our own writing to get on with.

In the event, after our friend's death in her nineties, a granddaughter arrived from America, briskly crated up all the books (several of which were on loan from us), and, when we asked what she had done with the papers, said, "Oh, I burned them." *"Burned them?* All those papers?" If we had known, she said darkly, what an old *fiend* her grandmother had been when she was growing up, we'd agree that burning was the best, the safest thing to do with those papers. Shocked, stunned, nonetheless, at the loss of our poor friend's immortality, we had no reply to make; after all, the papers were gone, there was nothing to be done. But it did occur to me to wonder if this ruthless act might have been committed by the granddaughter acting, unwittingly, as the agent of another; if this might have been poor Miss Morgan's final revenge.

Joan Aiken

MR. ELPHINSTONE'S HANDS

Lisa Tuttle

Mr. Elphinstone's hands were cold and slightly damp. This unpleasant physical detail was Eustacia Wallace's first impression of the medium, and even after she had a good look at him in the light—the large, deep-set eyes, the graying beard, the high forehead—even after she had heard him speak in a well-modulated, educated voice, Eustacia could think only of how much she had disliked the touch of his hands.

She glanced at her sister and saw that, like the others in the stuffy, overcrowded parlor, Lydia Wallace Steen was completely enraptured. She found herself rubbing the palms of her hands on her skirt, and forced herself to stop. If she had been wearing gloves, like any properly brought-up young lady—if she hadn't been such a hoyden as to lose her last pair and too careless to borrow from her sister—if she had been dressed as the other ladies, dressed as she should be, she would have known nothing of the condition of Mr. Elphinstone's flesh.

Lydia would be horrified—quite rightly—if she knew her younger sister's thoughts. Eustacia struggled, as she had struggled so often before, to lift them to a higher plane. Mr. Elphinstone was talking about Heavenly Rapture, Life Eternal, and the Love Which Passeth All Understanding. Eustacia found it hard to concentrate. It wasn't that she preferred to think about Mr. Elphinstone's hands, or about the unpleasant warmth of the room, or the fact that she hadn't had enough to eat at dinner, only . . . all these things, things that belonged to the real world, had a power that abstract ideas, for all their beauty, lacked. What chance had Perfect Love against a joint of beef or a cold, moist human hand?

"We imagine the dead, our loved dead, as being like us; as being, still, the people we knew—our children, parents, siblings, friends, sweethearts. We think of them wearing the same bodies, with no difference, only passed beyond our ken. But, my dear, dear brothers and sisters," Mr. Elphinstone went on, lowering his voice dramatically, "this is *not so*. Death is a transformation much greater than the birth to which it is sometimes compared. The soul leaves the body at death, achieving a new and wonderful existence. Mortality is burnt away with the flesh. There are no bodies in the afterlife, no flesh in heaven. Do you understand me?"

Heads nodded around the room. Eustacia nodded, too, wondering if there would be refreshments later.

"They are different, the dead. We cannot comprehend how different; we will know that only when we join them. The wisest course is to accept our ignorance, to accept that they are gone from us, God's will has been done and all is well. . . . But, of course, it is the nature of the living to question and to mourn—*not* to accept, but to want, always, to know more. Isn't that why you're here?"

He stopped, apparently expecting an answer. There were uneasy shiftings from his listeners, and Eustacia took advantage of this to scoot her chair a little farther away from the fire. A thin, elderly woman in rusty black silk cleared her throat gently, and Mr. Elphinstone let his dark eyes rest on her. "Yes, Mrs. Marcus? Tell us why you have come."

"You know."

"Yes, I know, but tell us."

"It's my son, Nathanael. He died at Bull Run. He was only eighteen. My only boy . . . I never knew the moment of his passing; I waited a long time before I heard of his death, and even then I couldn't be certain. For years I— But finally . . . I thought I had accepted it. Two years ago my husband passed on. And since then I have thought more and more about our Nathanael . . . worrying about him. Waking up nights fearing he was cold, or hungry, or hurting. Mr. Marcus could always take care of himself, and I was beside him at the end. But Nathanael was only a boy, and he died on a battle-field—I'll never really know *how* he died. I keep think-ing, if only I could have been with him at the end, to mop his brow or hold his hand, to give him some little comfort. . . . If only I could see him once more, to know that he's not in pain and he's not unhappy. Just to see him once more . . . just to have a message from him would make such a difference."

"Ah, yes," said Mr. Elphinstone softly. "Yes, of course. Touch and sight and hearing are all so important to us, the living. We cannot communicate without our senses; without them, we cannot even *believe*. And the dead, who have passed beyond that, still feel our needs and attempt to give us what we want . . . they attempt to touch us, speak to us, communicate. Yet how can they communicate without a body? How can they speak, how can they touch without flesh?"

Mr. Elphinstone's burning eyes fixed upon Eustacia. She went hot and cold. What did he want from her? Everyone was waiting for her to answer. There was no escape. She opened her mouth and out popped: "Ghosts."

"Ghosts?" He smiled gravely. "But what are ghosts? Of what are they formed? The dead have no material substance. They do not block the light. *They cannot be seen.* And if they are to communicate with us in some way, in any way, physical substance is required. Where is it to come from? Nothing comes from nothing, as the poet said. And they must have something if we are to know them. Whence does it come? Why, dear people, dear, dear friends: It comes from me." His smile became positively beatific; his face seemed to shine. "I am uniquely gifted to give our dearly departed a brief, a transitory, yet not entirely unsatisfactory, semblance of life. Certain mediums are gifted in this way with the ability to produce a substance known as *ectoplasm*, an emanation from my very flesh that clothes the fleshless spirits and allows them, however briefly, to live and speak to their loved ones. It is not God's will that they should be returned to *this* life, when he has lifted them to a greater one, but neither is it God's will that those they have left behind should suffer unduly, or doubt His promise of eternal life. It has been said, truly, 'Seek and ye shall find; ask and it shall be given.' So now, dear friends, dear seekers, I ask you to watch and wait as I offer myself unselfishly for the use of any spirits hovering near."

The lamps were extinguished as he spoke, and the room was lit only by firelight. Lydia touched Eustacia's arm and whispered: "Watch *him.*"

Mr. Elphinstone's eyes were closed. He sat like a statue. The others, having been here before, knew what to look for, so they were aware of what was happening before Eustacia noticed anything unusual. It was only by their rustlings and murmurings, and by Lydia's clutching hand, that she understood it was not a trick of her eyes in the dim light: There was a whitish vapor issuing forth from the region of Mr. Elphinstone's knees, upon which his hands rested.

But it wasn't only a vapor. It seemed to have more mass and solidity than that. Now he raised his hands to chest level, and it was obvious that this amorphous, shifting, cloudy-white stuff adhered in some way to his hands, grew out of them, perhaps. To the sound of gasps and moans and sighs from the assembly, the shining cloud between Mr. Elphinstone's unmoving hands began to shape itself, to take on form. A human form, although small. A head, a neck, shoulders, arms . . . that was a face, surely? Eustacia wasn't sure if there were facial features to be discerned in the flickering light, or if she was unconsciously making pictures, as one did when watching clouds.

Suddenly Lydia cried out. "That's my baby! Oh, sweet George!"

Then she tumbled off her chair in a dead faint.

The seance was brought to an abrupt halt by the need to help Lydia. In all the turmoil of fetching smelling salts and water and relighting the lamps, Eustacia did not see what happened to the ghostly baby, but it was gone. Mr. Elphinstone, pale and worn-looking, remained aloof and said nothing as the women fussed about poor Lydia.

But poor Lydia was ecstatic. A trifle shaky, but, she assured everyone, the shock had been a joyful one, and she had not felt so well, so uplifted, in years.

"He was smiling," said Lydia. "I never thought I'd see my baby smile again! Taken from me at three months, but he's happy in heaven. He'll always be happy now, smiling forever. Such a comfort, to see him again and know he's happy."

It was for this Lydia had come to see Mr. Elphinstone, of course. Eustacia felt ashamed of herself for not realizing. She had thought at first this evening's outing was one of Lydia's ways of introducing her younger sister to society and, therefore, to more eligible young men. Then she had thought the séance simply another of Lydia's larks, like going to hear the speakers for woman suffrage. She hadn't realized it was personal; indeed, she tended to forget that her sister had ever known the brief, bitter blessing of motherhood. The babe had not lived long, had died three years ago; and in that time there had not come another to fill his cradle. And yet it had not occurred to her that Lydia might still be mourning. Usually Eustacia envied her sister the freedom granted her by marriage, but now she felt only pity.

For days afterward, back at home on the farm, the excitements of visiting her sister left behind, Eustacia was plagued by something wrong with her hands. She couldn't seem to get them warm, not even by chafing them in front of the fire, which she was seldom allowed to do. For there was work to be done—there was always work to be done—and the best way to keep warm, said her sister Mildred, was to keep busy. It wasn't worth arguing. And it wasn't really the temperature of her fingers that bothered her but something else that seemed at odds with it: Although they felt chilly, her hands perspired profusely and constantly. She wiped them whenever she could, on her apron or a towel, but it did no good. Her hands were always cold and damp.

Just like Mr. Elphinstone's hands.

She tried not to think of it. It was too silly. What could his hands possibly have to do with hers? Was there such a thing as a cold in the hands that she might have caught from him? She had never heard of such a thing—a cold in the head, a cold in the chest, but not the hands—but that didn't mean it wasn't possible. A doctor would know . . . but doctors were expensive. Her father, seeing her perfectly healthy, would not countenance a visit to a doctor. If she tried to explain to her father, she was certain his idea of a "cure" would be the same as Mildred's: more hard work, less idle dreaming. She didn't try to tell him, or anyone. Embarrassed by this odd problem, she washed her hands often, and kept a ready supply of pocket handkerchiefs.

One afternoon as she helped her sister shake out and fold clean linen from the drying line, Mildred suddenly screwed up her face and said sharply, "Eustacia! Have you a runny nose?"

"No, sister." She felt her face get hot.

"Where do you suppose this came from?" There on the stiff, freshly washed whiteness of the sheet glistened four little blobs of mucus. On the other side, Eustacia had no doubt, would be found a fifth, the imprint left by her thumb. She stood mute, blushing.

"Have you lost your pocket handkerchief? 'Tis a filthy, childish habit, Eustacia, to blow your nose into your fingers; something I would not have expected from you, careless though you often are in your personal habits. And so unhealthy! You should think of others."

"I didn't! My nose isn't—! I didn't, Mildred, honestly!"

Mildred might have believed her since Eustacia, for all her faults, was no liar, but she couldn't stop, was scarcely aware of, the little furtive gestures by which she attempted to dry and hide her hands.

Mildred's eyes narrowed. "Show me your hands."

There was a kind of relief in being caught; in being forced, at last, to share her dirty secret. Despite her having just wiped them, her hands were already moist again. Welling up from the ball of each finger, pooling in the palms, was something thicker, stickier, and less liquid than the perspiration she had, for several days, believed—or wished—it to be.

Face twisting in disgust, Mildred held her sister's hands and examined them. Something nasty. But it had to be as obvious to Mildred as it was to Eustacia herself that the substance had not been blown or wiped onto the hands but was being produced—excreted—through the skin of the hands themselves.

"I don't know what it is," Eustacia said. "It's been happening . . . several days now. I told you my hands were cold. You can feel that. At first it was only the cold; then, they seemed to be wet . . . and now . . . this. I don't know what it is; I don't know how to make it stop." She burst into tears.

Tears were always the wrong tactic with Mildred. Scowling, she flung Eustacia's hands back at her, and wiped her own harshly in her apron. "Stop bawling, girl, it doesn't pain you, does it?"

Still sobbing, Eustacia shook her head.

"Well, then. It's nothing. No more'n a runny nose. Go wash yourself. Wash your hands *well*, mind. And keep them warm and dry. Maybe you should rest. That's it. Lie down and keep warm. You can have a fire in your room. Rest and keep warm and you'll be as right as rain by tomorrow."

Eustacia stopped crying, pleased to know she would have the luxury of a fire in her room, and the still greater luxury of being allowed to do nothing at all.

In a family of hard workers, Eustacia was the lazy one. Lydia, too, had disliked the labor required of daughters in a house without servants, but Lydia was never idle. She enjoyed sewing, particularly embroidery and fine needlework, loved music, and was often to be found reading improving books. Whatever time she could steal from chores she invested in her own artistic and intellectual pursuits. Eustacia, on the other hand, enjoyed conversation and reading novels, but was happiest doing nothing. She liked to sleep, she liked to dream, she liked to muse and build castles in the air, sitting by the fire in the winter or beneath a shady tree in the summer.

Although Mildred and Constance often castigated Eustacia for laziness, Lydia had formed an alliance with her, believing her younger sister was, like herself, of an artistic temperament. She encouraged Eustacia to forget her present woes by thinking of the happiness that would be hers in a few years, once she was married and the mistress of her own household. Lydia, after all, had married well: a man who gave her a piano as a birthday present and paid for private lessons. Their house in town was staffed by a cook, two maids, and a manservant, and there was a boy who came to do the garden twice a week. Lydia's husband was not rich, but he was, as they said, "comfortable," as well as being very much in love with his wife. Lydia was not so vulgar as to propose that Eustacia "marry money," but her husband knew a number of young men who were up and coming in the business world, men who would soon be able to afford a wife. It was to give Eustacia a chance of meeting an appropriate mate that Lydia often invited her to stay and took her out to concerts, soirees, balls, and other social gatherings.

Eustacia went along with Lydia wherever and whenever she was asked, but wasn't sure she believed marriage was the answer. She was not beautiful; more fatally, she lacked the personal charm that made men dote on Lydia. She might find a husband, but surely not romance. And even if she managed to marry a man who loved her, who was not a farmer, not poor, and not a petty tyrant like her father, her fate might still be that of her mother: to bear ten live children in twelve years and die of exhaustion. She was not eager to exchange one form of servitude for another.

In the bedroom she had once shared with Lydia and Constance but now had to herself, Eustacia laid a fire in the hearth. The clear, sticky muck on her hands transferred itself to the logs and paper, but they burned with no apparent ill effect. When the fire was drawing nicely, she undressed and put on her nightgown. By that time she was yawning mightily, and as soon as she had crawled into bed she felt herself slipping deliciously into sleep.

When she woke the next morning her eyes were sticky, the lashes so gummed together that it was a struggle to open them; and it was not only her eyes that were affected. All over her face, her head, her hands, her upper body, she could feel the tight, sticky pull of dried mucus. It was there like spiderwebs, or a welter of snail tracks, crisscrossing her face, looping around her neck, her arms, and dried stiffly in her hair. She felt a myriad of cracks open as her face convulsed in disgust. A tortured moan escaped her lips as she scrambled out of bed. The water in the pitcher was icy cold, but for once she didn't mind, scarcely even noticed, as she splashed it onto hands and face and neck and chest, splashing it everywhere in a panic to get the slimy stuff off. It was not cold but revulsion that made her shiver.

Eustacia was not the excessively sensitive, refined creature contemporary manners held that women should be. The daughter of a working farmer could not afford a weak stomach, but Eustacia knew that she was not so fastidious, not so "nice," as her sisters, and this was a matter of some shame to her. Sometimes it made her angry. It wasn't fair. Men didn't have to pretend they were made of porcelain, so why should women? Perfection was unnatural. The body was a messy thing.

But not like *this*. This mess was not natural. Thank God, it proved to be easily washed away. Calming now that face and neck and hands were clean, Eustacia poured the last of the water into the bowl and tried to judge if there was enough to wash her hair.

There was a knock at the door, and before she could say anything to stop her, Mildred had entered.

"Are you feeling better this morning? Ah!" Her sharp eyes saw something and the hidden worry on her face was transformed in an instant to something else, to understanding. "It's your sick time, of course."

"No—" But before she could protest, Eustacia realized what she had been too preoccupied and frightened to notice earlier. She felt the wetness between her legs, twisted around and saw what Mildred had seen: the bloodstain on her gown, the unmistakable badge of her condition.

"But what are you doing up? You'll only make yourself ill. You want to keep warm. I'll fetch some clean towels. Now, into bed with you. I'll tell Pa you're feeling poorly and won't be down today. I'll bring you up some toast and tea, and build up the fire in here. Well? What are you waiting for?"

She made a gesture below her waist. "I . . . have to clean myself."

"All right. But be quick about it, don't be standing about in the cold. You know a woman's constitution is at its weakest at these times."

Left alone, Eustacia realized that Mildred had decided there was nothing seriously wrong with her. The strangeness of hands exuding mucus had been redefined as a side effect of menstruation. No matter how odd and unpleasant, because it was happening now, when she was bleeding, it was to be accepted as yet another symptom of the female sickness.

She fashioned a toweling diaper for herself, put on a fresh nightgown, and got into bed. There was blood on the sheets, but it had dried. Why change them now, when she would surely soil them again? With five sisters, she had seen how differently Eve's curse afflicted different women, even women with the same parents and upbringing. She wondered: Could Mildred be right?

But Mildred didn't know what she knew—that her hands had been cold and damp, sweating this strange substance not for just a day or two, but for more than week.

A hand went to her head as she remembered. Tentative at first, then frowning with surprise, she combed her fingers through clean hair: not clotted, not matted, not sticky, not stiff. Clean.

She got up to find the hand mirror, to let her eyes confirm what her fingers told her. She picked her dress off the chair where she had hung it the previous night and examined the skirt. But although she remembered how often she had wiped her wet, sticky hands there, now she could neither see nor feel any trace of foreign matter. Her pocket handkerchief, too, was clean, although she could remember quite vividly the horrid slimy ball she'd made of it.

All gone now. Gone to nothing. Was it over?

She pressed her fingertips against her cheeks and brushed them against her lips. They felt cold and ever so slightly damp.

So quickly it had become a habit to wipe her hands whenever she felt them becoming wet. Now, half reclining in bed, propped up on pillows, she decided to do nothing and see what happened.

Her hands rested on top of the blanket at chest level. She felt a tingling sensation in the fingertips, and then she saw the stuff oozing out in faint, wispy tendrils.

Her skin crawled at the sight, and a horrible thought occurred to her. What if those slimy tendrils were now emerging not only from her fingertips, but all over her body. Those prickling feelings . . . She gasped for breath and held herself rigidly still, fighting down the urge to leap up and rip off her gown. She would wait and see.

The shining tendrils thickened and grew more solid. They took on the appearance of ghostly fingers. They *were* fingers. They were hands.

She thought of Mr. Elphinstone's hands, and of the ghostly form that had appeared between them, had appeared to grow out of them. Meanwhile, the hands attached to her own grew larger still, and then began to elongate, to grow away from her into arms. She stared in wonder. So she could do it, too! Mr. Elphinstone wasn't so special, after all.

But these hands and arms were not those of a baby. They were much too big for any baby. And there was something unpleasantly familiar about them as they grew into the chest and shoulders of a man. The head was still unformed, but Eustacia suddenly knew who it was.

It was Mr. Elphinstone, of course. He had done this to her. It was his wicked plan to come to her secretly in this nasty, ghostlike manner. In a moment his head would grow out of that neck, his face would form and eyes would open, and he would look down on her and smile in triumph, his hands closing firmly over hers, his lips . . .

No. It was impossible. She would not have it. She refused.

Growling incoherently, she rubbed her hands fiercely against the blanket. The half-finished, cloudy likeness of a man still hung in the air, a face beginning to form. Once it had formed, once his eyes had opened and looked down at her, it might be too late. She might never escape his clutches. Feeling sick and furious, concentrating all her mind on denying his power, she swung both hands at it. She had imagined dispersing it, but although its appearance was cloudy, it was not made of smoke. Her hands sank into something horribly cold and slimy. It was thick and soupy, not entirely liquid, but not solid, either; something like clotted milk or half-set cheese, but worse, indescribably worse. It was something that should have been dead but was alive; something that looked alive and yet was dead. And it was cold—she'd never felt such a cold. Not a clean cold like ice or snow. This cold had the quality of a bad smell.

The feel of it made her gag. It made her head swim. But she persisted. Her fingers grasped and tore until she had pulled it to pieces; until she had completely destroyed the unnatural, unwanted effigy.

Then she got out of bed and tottered across the floor on weak legs and threw up in the washbowl. Her head ached fiercely. She rested a moment, then opened the window. It was a cold and windy day, and she was grateful for that. The wind would rush into the room and sweep out the nasty smells of sickness: the smells of blood and vomit, and something much worse.

I've won, she thought, weary but triumphant. You haven't got me. I'm *free*.

Mildred came in and found her leaning on the windowsill, head half out the window, shivering with the cold but still sucking in deep, invigorating breaths of the pure winter air.

"What on earth are you doing? Do you want to catch your death?" Mildred's hands, firm and controlling, grasped her arms. Eustacia resisted, refusing to be steered back to bed, afraid of the horrible remains she had left quivering and clotted on the blanket. "I felt sick . . ."

"Yes, I see. You must get back into bed, you must keep warm."

Every muscle, every bone, every ounce of flesh still

resisted—until she saw the bed, clean and dry and empty, not a trace of the horror left.

She collapsed with relief and let Mildred tuck her into bed where, utterly exhausted, she fell asleep immediately.

When she woke, her hands were warm and dry.

Her body's only discharge came from between her legs, and that would pass after a few days. She was back to normal. She had won. She made a face at the Mr. Elphinstone in her mind, his image fading fast, and almost laughed out loud. She was happy, with four days ahead in which she would not be expected to work at all, time in which she could sleep and dream and read and think. Despite the mess and bother of it, Eustacia never minded her monthly visitor; on the contrary, she was grateful for the regular holiday it brought. She knew she was quite capable of working throughout her sick time, but she certainly wasn't going to argue with Mildred about it. Mildred thought permanent damage could be done to a woman who overstrained her constitution at such times. And a menstruating woman (not that such a word ever passed her lips) could do harm to others as well: Milk would turn and bread not rise in her presence, and the scent of her would drive domestic animals wild. Modesty forbade a woman displaying herself when the curse was upon her, which meant she must keep to herself and the company of women. Eustacia thought Mildred was overnice in regard to their father—after all, he had been married and shared a bed with his wife for years—but she was happy enough to avoid her brothers, and even more men to whom she was not related. The thought that they might notice something wrong with her was humiliating. She was happy to keep to her room and rest.

It was not until late that evening, after Mildred had taken away her supper dishes and left her an empty chamber pot and a bundle of clean towels, that she felt the tingling in her fingers again. She realized then that they were cold, and, as she tucked them into her armpits to warm them, she felt the dampness.

She stared at her hands and saw the mucus blobs swelling and stretching from her fingertips, elongating and thickening into fingers as she watched—

"No!"

Long fingers, hands, bony wrists—hands she recognized.

"No!"

Denial was of no use. It was in her, and it had to come out. She thought she could feel it seeping out of the flesh beneath her breasts and behind her knees, and there was a tickling sensation on the soles of her feet. She couldn't keep it in. It had to come out.

It had to, but *he* didn't. She stared at the hands and willed them to break off at the wrists. Two disembodied hands floated free, but more of the whitish matter gushed out, forming new hands.

Ectoplasm, Mr. Elphinstone had called it. The stuff produced by the bodies of the living to provide the dead with temporary flesh.

There were his hands, his arms . . . But why his? Dead or alive, she had no wish to communicate with him. If she was to provide a habitation for spirits, they should at least be ones of her own choosing.

She thought about her mother. Her mother had had lovely hands, even though roughened by toil: slender fingers, graceful, shapely hands. As she thought of them, creating them in her mind, they were recreated before her. Cloudy, milky shapes, but recognizably *not* Mr. Elphinstone's hands. They were a woman's hands. Her mother's hands.

She gazed at them with feelings of awe and accomplishment, unsure whether this was her own work, or if she had her mother's spirit to thank for routing Mr. Elphinstone. She tried to join arms on to the hands, wanting to see more of her mother, but, as she struggled, she fell asleep.

Her hands stayed dry through the night, but this time

she did not expect that condition to last. Indeed, her fingers were dripping like infected sores before midday.

She knew that meant Mr. Elphinstone was trying to get out. She didn't know exactly why, but she could guess: she had read enough novels. This was not the usual way that men attempted to overpower young women, but that didn't mean it was any less dangerous. Probably, she thought, he had been planning this from the start, from the very first moment when his damp, chilly flesh had pressed hers. She didn't know how his ghost could harm her, or even if it could, but she certainly would not give it the chance to try.

During the next four days Eustacia successfully fought off his every attempt to return. She couldn't stop the ectoplasm, but she could control the forms it took. It was hard work, but she enjoyed it. She came to think of it as a new kind of art, a sort of mental modeling, as if the ectoplasm had been clay and she was using the fingers of her mind to push and smooth and mold it into the shapes of her choice.

At first, it was her mother she concentrated on, for her mother was the only person who had passed over whom Eustacia knew well or had any real desire to see again. But it was difficult, and not really very satisfying. Whole bodies were out of the question, requiring more ectoplasm than her body could produce at one time, so she concentrated either on hands (which were easiest) or on heads. Her mother's head was never quite right, and the more often she tried to produce it, the harder she found it to recall what her mother had really looked like. She was not limited to the dead, so she also created likenesses of Lydia and Mildred. But even the form of Mildred, whom she saw every day, was not really very like. The faces she made were just as clumsy and unfinished as they might have been if she had been working, untutored, in clay or stone. She knew who they were because she knew what she intended. She was not sure anyone else would have recognized them.

Unsatisfying as it was, it was also the most amazingly

tiring work. More exhausting than milking the cows or laundry day. After less than an hour working on another ghost of Lydia, sleep would catch her up, inescapable, and she would slumber heavily for several hours.

Yet the energy spent was worth it. Not only did her efforts ward off Mr. Elphinstone, but they temporarily exhausted her supply of ectoplasm, winning sometimes a whole day of normal life and dry hands.

If she did that every evening, if she spent an hour willing ectoplasmic shapes into existence before falling to sleep, Eustacia figured, she could keep her peculiar condition secret and under control. But it wasn't so easy. Perhaps it was laziness—she imagined Mildred would think so—but there were many nights when she was simply too tired to do anything but put herself to bed. She enjoyed playing with the ectoplasm, making faces and hands, but it was hard work all the same. It took reserves of energy she did not always have, especially by the time she was ready for bed.

Fortunately, she didn't have to share her bed with anyone. She didn't mind—now that she knew the stuff could be washed off or, if left, would soon dry to nothing—the morning stickiness of the sheets or the mess on her body. Her hands were not the only source, if they had ever been. Like perspiration, the slime oozed from all the pores of her skin: from her legs, her feet, under her arms, her chest and back, even (and most horribly, because most visible) her face. Afraid that someone might notice, Eustacia took more care, forcing herself to stay awake past her usual bedtime, or waking early, or escaping to the privacy of her room on one pretense or another for long enough to do something with the excess ectoplasm.

But despite her best intentions, her body leaked, and one suppertime Mildred noticed. When everyone else had left the table, she stopped her sister with a look and said: "You must be more careful."

"I wiped my hands—and I did wash them before I came to table—"

"It's not only your hands, now, is it? You've left a trail—no, don't look, I cleaned it up. Father didn't notice, nor did Conrad, but what if they should? Next time, I think you'd best take supper in your room."

"What? But why? How can I? Every night? Never eat with the family?"

"Of course not every night. But while you're—during your—" She nodded meaningfully, unable to pronounce the euphemism.

"But it's not like that. I'm not—"

"Your face," Mildred muttered with a look of revulsion. She made small brushing gestures at her own forehead, and Eustacia became aware of the by-now familiar, chilly, tingling sensation from three different spots along her hairline. Both her handkerchiefs were already saturated, but she raised one, balled in her hand, and wiped away the offensive trickles.

"Go to your room," Mildred said. "Clean yourself. I'll tell the others you're feeling poorly—"

"But I'm not! I'm not feeling poorly. This is something else. I don't know what it is, but it's not connected to—to *that*—at all. And it's not like a cold, something that clears up or goes away after a few days . . . it's never gone away at all, not wholly, not since it started. It's a part of me now. Sometimes I can control it a bit, but I can't make it stop—I can't make it go away." Mildred had never been her favorite sister; indeed, had they not been related, Eustacia was not certain she could have loved her. But that look on her face, even had it been the face of a stranger—a look of horror, of loathing, barely controlled—for that look to have been caused by her, it was unbearable.

Eustacia burst into tears.

"Oh, stop that! Stop that at once. Crying never helps."

"Why are you so angry?"

"Because you're being silly."

"But why do you look at me like that? As if . . . as if it's *my fault*. You can't blame me—I didn't make this happen, I never wanted it. If I were bleeding, you wouldn't tell me to stop, you couldn't expect me just to stop; you'd clean my wound and bind it and perhaps send for the doctor—''

''I shall send for the doctor. Not now, but in the morning. I would have done so sooner if I had realized—but I can't think there's any urgency, if this has been going on all month, and you still walking around as if it were nothing. . . . Now, will you go to your room, before you make any more mess? You're dripping.''

''It's not my fault.'' Her tone was belligerent, but what she wanted was reassurance. Acceptance.

''We don't choose our afflictions,'' Mildred said coldly, looking away, ''but we shouldn't be proud of them.''

Alone in her room, Eustacia wept again. She had been very young when her mother died, and was seldom aware of missing her. But she missed her now. Mildred might have taken Mother's role as the female head of the family, but Mildred was not her mother. Her real mother would not have been horrified by the changes taking place in Eustacia, no matter what they were. Her real mother would have embraced and comforted her, wept with her, not kept Mildred's chilly distance.

A pale, semi-opaque tendril was snaking out of her wrist when a fat teardrop fell, disintegrating it. Saltwater—or maybe it was only tears?—seemed to work more efficiently than plain water. Eustacia was so fascinated by this discovery that she forgot to cry.

After some time, she lit the lamp and sat down to write to Lydia. Downstairs, she suspected, Mildred would be writing a letter to be despatched to Dr. Purves in the morning. Well, she would send a letter, too, on the same topic but from a different perspective, and to someone who would probably be of more use than a doctor. Lydia, after all, had seen for herself what Mr. Elphinstone could do. Lydia would be in sympathy, and she might know someone who could help. Not Mr. Elphinstone, but there must be other mediums—perhaps even a lady medium? Lydia, with her wide social circle, was bound to know someone who knew someone. . . . If absolutely necessary, some third party might even approach Mr. Elphinstone in a roundabout way. He must have realized by now that his plan to take control of her had not worked, so perhaps he could be persuaded to lift his curse.

Composing the letter was difficult. When put into words, what had happened to her sounded horrible, and Eustacia didn't want Lydia thinking that. She didn't want her favorite sister horrified or revulsed, as Mildred was. She had to choose her words carefully. She couldn't say too much. She was mysterious. She evoked the spirit of the séance. Lydia must come and see for herself. When she was here, Eustacia would be able to make her understand.

Until the doctor arrived, Eustacia was made to keep to her room as if she were contagious. She usually didn't mind solitude and was grateful for any excuse to avoid work, but what once would have felt like freedom was now an imposition. She was being punished for something that was not her fault.

Alone in her room, cut off from her family, she concentrated on extruding ectoplasm and forming it into shapes. She created shaky likenesses of Mildred and Lydia. She worked herself to exhaustion and beyond, determined to clear her system of the ghost-matter, to give the doctor when he came nothing to find. Let him think he had been called all the way out here for some fantasy of Mildred's.

But it was no use. Perhaps she had been overconfident about the laws of cause and effect and in believing she had some control over what her body produced and when, for despite her labors, she woke the next morning lying in a puddle of something half liquid, half matter. And when Dr. Purves arrived in the afternoon, mucus dripped from her fingertips, her clothes clung stickily to her damp flesh, and she felt trails of drool beside her mouth, on her brow, and beneath her ears.

"Hmmm!" said Dr. Purves, and "Well, well!" and "What's this?" He didn't look revolted, horrified, or even astonished. There was, on his face, a carefully schooled, nonjudgmental look of mild interest. "Feeling a bit hot, are we?"

He thought it was perspiration. "No," said Eustacia hopelessly.

"Ah, do you mind if I . . . ?"

She gave him her hand, and felt the surprise he did not allow to register on his face. He looked at her hand, touched the stuff, waited, watching it well up again. "Hmmm. And how long has this been going on?"

She told him. He asked questions and she answered them truthfully. He did not ask her what she thought was happening to her or why, so she did not tell him about Mr. Elphinstone or the matter produced by the bodies of mediums for the use of those who had passed over. She didn't tell him that she could, with her thoughts, increase the flow and cause it to shape itself into images. Dr. Purves was a man of science; she knew he would not believe her, and she didn't believe he could help her. Undoubtedly Mildred hoped the doctor would be able to give a name to Eustacia's disease and also provide the cure, but she knew otherwise. She knew now, watching him watch her, that he had never seen the like of this before, and that he didn't like it.

He asked her to undress. He examined her. He told her he was taking a sample for testing. She watched him scoop a tendril of ectoplasm from her armpit into a small glass bottle and cap it firmly. The piece he had captured was the size of a garden snail without the shell. She watched him put the bottle safely away in his bag. By the time he got home, perhaps even by the time he left this house, that bottle would be empty. Would he come back for more, or would he decide it had never existed, preferring not to know anything that might contradict his rational view of the universe?

While she was dressing, he washed his hands very thoroughly. She wondered if soap and water were a protection, or if she had now infected him. But perhaps the doctor, skeptical of spiritualism, would be protected by science and his own unbelief. She wondered how he would explain it, and what he would do, if his body began leaking ectoplasm.

"Now, you're not to worry," he said. "Rest, don't exert yourself. Keep yourself warm. And clean. Wash and, er, change your sheets as often as you feel the need."

"What's wrong with me?"

"There's nothing wrong. You mustn't think that. Didn't I say you weren't to worry? Just keep warm and rest and you'll soon be as right as rain. I'll have a word with your sister before I go, about your diet. I'll tell her everything she needs to know." He made his escape before she could ask again.

She slumped back in her bed with a grim smile. She hadn't expected an intelligent reply. She knew he didn't know what was wrong with her, and no amount of thinking, no amount of study, no amount of second opinions from his learned colleagues would change that. Even if he locked her up in a hospital somewhere and watched her day and night, he'd be none the wiser, because what had happened to her belonged to another realm, not of scientific medicine but of mysticism.

She suddenly saw herself in a hospital somewhere, locked in an underfurnished room in a building where lunatics screamed and raged, watched by men in white coats through a hole in the door, and she went cold with dread. She burrowed under the sheets and pulled the blankets up to her nose with hands that were cold but, for once, miraculously dry. That must not happen . . . surely Mildred wouldn't let that happen to her? But of course, Mildred didn't understand, and she might well trust a doctor who promised a cure. Eustacia wished the doctor had never come. She knew he would never cure her, no matter what he tried, and she did not want to be studied by him. If he decided she was an interesting case . . . Eustacia clenched her teeth to stop them chattering. She wouldn't let it happen. Mildred wouldn't let it happen. Lydia wouldn't let it happen. Lydia was coming soon. Lydia would understand; Lydia would save her.

Lydia arrived four days later. Sitting in her chair by the window, well wrapped in shawls and blankets, with nothing to do but watch and wait, Eustacia thought she'd never been so glad to see another person. It was life Lydia brought into her room—the sickroom, her prison—life and a taste of the world she had grown hungry for.

"Whatever is the matter with Mildred?" Lydia asked as she swept in. "A face as long as a wet Sunday when she said you were poorly, but—oh!" The cheerful prattle ended, the exclamation shocked out of her when, as she bent to kiss her sister, her lips encountered not the familiar warm, soft texture of her cheek, but flesh slippery with a chill and slimy coating.

"I'm not ill," Eustacia said, looking urgently into her sister's eyes. To her relief, she saw neither horror nor disgust reflected there, only a puzzled concern. "No matter what Mildred thinks, or the doctor. It is odd, though . . . hard to understand . . . hard to write about in a letter. That's why I wanted to see you . . . I wanted you to see me. Because I am all right. I am still *me.*"

"Of course you are! Still my own dear sister. Is this some new ploy to escape doing chores? Or is that what Mildred thinks? I had thought, from the way she spoke, that it was your time."

She shook her head. "Do sit down, Lydia. I'll have to show you." She was excited and scared. There was a tingling inside, a nervous reaction to match the purely physical, localized tingle in her hands. The feeling of something that had to come out. And now, a new excitement because there was meaning and new purpose to what she was about to do. For the first time, she had an audience. Was she good enough for her audience? Lydia's response was all-important.

"You remember . . . Mr. Elphinstone?"

"Yes, of course."

"And what he did that evening, and what he showed us? The ectoplasm? He did something else that same evening, to me. When he touched me. I don't understand how or why, but he gave it to me somehow." She paused, aware of gathering her power, of concentrating it all in her hands, which she held now before her, just above her lap. Lydia said nothing, and there was nothing in her look but waiting and wonder.

"Watch," said Eustacia, and stared at her own hands as the thick, wavering white steam poured out of them, her fingers become fountains. Ten separate streams merged and grew into one almost-solid form: head, neck, shoulders, chest . . . until it was a baby floating there, its features somewhat vague and undefined but still and undeniably a baby. There.

Eustacia felt a little dizzy and had the familiar sensation of having been drained. But she also felt triumphant, and as she looked up from her creation she was smiling happily. "There—see? It's your baby."

Lydia's face had gone an unhealthy yellowish color. She shook her head slowly. "No," she said, sounding tortured. "That's not my baby—it's not!" She clapped her hands to her mouth, retching, and staggered to her feet, knocking the chair over with the heavy sideways sweep of her skirts. She managed to get to the basin before she threw up.

Eustacia closed her eyes, but the noise and smell made her stomach churn in terrible sympathy. She kept her gorge down with great effort. "I'm sorry," she said, when Lydia's crisis seemed to have passed. "I know it must be a shock to see your baby—"

"No! That's not my baby! How can you?"

Eustacia struggled to rise, reaching for her sister.

Lydia shrieked, "Don't touch me! You monster!"

"But . . . but you were so happy when Mr. Elphinstone did it. This is the same—don't you see? I can do the same thing—"

"It's not the same! It's not the same!" Lydia glared at her, and this look was much worse than the look Mildred had given her, for there was not merely horror in it, but hate. "How could you? What are you trying to do, make me miscarry?"

Eustacia's mouth hung open. "I didn't know . . ."

"Monster! Monster!"

The door opened then—Mildred, attracted by the noise. Weeping, Lydia rushed to the safety of her older sister's embrace. They went out of the room together, and the door closed, shutting Eustacia in alone with the thing she had made.

She looked at her creation, the baby bobbing and floating in the air like something unborn. Like something dead. But it had never been alive. It wasn't real, not a real baby. But neither was the thing Mr. Elphinstone had made, although, in the dim and flickering firelight, it had seemed real enough to eyes that wanted it to be. She understood that the situation was different here and now. But she hadn't meant any harm. She thought of getting up and going downstairs, going after Lydia and explaining, making her understand. But she had not the energy for it. It was impossible. She could scarcely even think. All she could do was fall back in her chair and fall asleep.

When she woke, with a throbbing head competing for attention with a painfully empty stomach, it was much later in the day and the room was thick with shadows. The baby had vanished back into the nothing from which it had been conjured. She rose from her chair and stretched aching muscles, feeling as if she had become an old woman while she slept. Certainly she felt like a different person from the hopeful girl who had waited impatiently for her sister that morning. She hoped that the passing of the hours had calmed Lydia. Maybe she would be ready to listen now; and surely if she listened, she would understand. Eustacia still felt Lydia was the one person in the world who *could* understand.

But when she reached the door, she could not open

it. She thought at first it was her own weakness, and continued twisting the handle to no avail. Her wits were still so slow after her sleep that it took her some time to realize that the door to her room had been locked from the outside.

They had locked her in.

It had to be a mistake. She went back to her chair, turned it so she could look out the window, and sat down. She did not want to find out that it had not been a mistake, so she would not pound on the door and make demands that could be refused. Mildred would come up and unlock it later. It must have been locked on account of Lydia's fright. Once she was allowed to explain, there would be no more need for locked doors.

By the time Mildred came up with her dinner on a tray, Eustacia was almost ready to weep with hunger and worry.

"Mildred, I have to see Lydia, I have to explain—"

"She's gone home."

"I didn't mean to upset her; I have to tell her—"

"Oh, I know. It's not your fault." A sneer was not Mildred's usual expression. She would not meet her sister's eyes as she spoke.

"It's *not* my fault—I can't help it. I didn't mean it— oh, please—"

"*I* know. You're ill." She snorted. "I saw the doctor. I rode with Lydia into town, and I had a consultation with him. Do you know what he said? There's nothing wrong with you at all, not physically. He says it's all in your head. You know what I say? I say it's evil. Not sickness—evil. Not in your head, but your heart. Evil in your heart. And that is your fault. You'd better admit it, missy, and pray to God to take it away. There's your dinner."

"Please!"

But Mildred was already out of the room without a backward look. And then came the sound of the key turning in the lock.

Eustacia ate her dinner. What else was there to do?

After she had eaten she could think more clearly, but the thoughts were not pleasant ones. It was obvious Lydia would be of no help; she had been too badly frightened. If only she had been more cautious . . . if only she had led Lydia on a bit more carefully. . . . She thought of Mr. Elphinstone's pompous speech; they way he had elicited responses from his audience; the extinguishing of the lamps. By firelight, my baby would have looked more real, she thought. But it was too late to think of that now. Lydia would not help her. The doctor had, literally, washed his hands of her, declaring her either a fake or mad. And Mildred was of no use, either, having decided she was bad. Worse than that, Mildred was her jailer, and represented her whole family.

Who was there who could help her?

She remembered the cold, damp touch of Mr. Elphinstone's hands, and the way his eyes had pierced into hers. He had marked her then, that evening; he had made her his, although she had tried to deny it. To give in now, to go to him despite her revulsion . . . she would be trading one sort of imprisonment for another. But at least it would be different. Not the life she would have chosen freely, but still a life. And she would learn to use her talent. It would *be* a talent then, and not a loathsome illness.

But how could she go to him when she couldn't leave this room? She might write a letter, but anything she sent out would have to go through Mildred. She imagined Mildred reading it and throwing it on the fire. And even if she managed to bypass Mildred, she realized with despair that she had no address for Mr. Elphinstone.

Hopeless.

There was a tingling in her fingertips.

No, not hopeless.

She remembered how the form of Mr. Elphinstone had first emerged from her body . . . the struggle, and how terrified she had been. He was still there, still waiting to come out. She no longer feared him, at least not

162

in the same way. There were other, greater fears. She was ready now to welcome him and his plans for her.

She put out her hands and let the solid, smoky stuff stream out; watched as it formed into fingers touching her own at the tips. A man's fingers, a man's large hands, bony wrists lengthening into skinny arms, naked shoulders, and naked chest. She was trembling now and starting to feel faint, but she held her hands as steady as she could and let it go on happening, thinking all the while of Mr. Elphinstone, remembering him as he had been, and as he was. Now the neck and head. The shifting clouds of his face roiled and finally solidified into bearded chin and mouth, long thin nose, high brow, and the eyes . . . the eyes were closed.

She stared and waited for them to open; waited to have those blazing orbs fixed on her, and to see the lips move, and to hear him speak. He was finished now, at least, as much of him as she could make. She could do no more. It was up to him to take over. But Mr. Elphinstone looked dead, like the baby, hanging motionless in the air.

Lydia had said that at most seances, when ghosts appeared they spoke, answering questions and making cryptic remarks. Her baby, of course, had been too young.

"Talk to me," said Eustacia. "Tell me what to do."

Her breath disturbed the figure, making it bob slightly. A bit of one arm disintegrated, leaving a hole the size of a baby's fist just above the right elbow. She cried out again, and her fingers closed on cold, dead matter. When she pulled away, sickened, she saw she had destroyed parts of both lower arms, and the hands floated free, detached from the arms. One of the hands floated up toward the ceiling, becoming more insubstantial as it rose.

Mr. Elphinstone could not speak to her, for Mr. Elphinstone was not here. She had created something that looked like Mr. Elphinstone—or like her memory of Mr. Elphinstone—and that was all. It did not live. It never had and never would. It was inhabited by no ghosts. There were no ghosts. She could not blame Mr. Elphinstone for that, nor for the fact that he could neither enslave nor save her.

She was alone in her room as she watched her dream disintegrate. She was alone with her disease, her curse, her madness, her strange, useless talent.

Afterword

You don't hear much about ectoplasm these days, but to Victorian-era spiritualists it was the explanation for the disembodied hands and ghostly faces that appeared during séances, as well as for the transparent figures sometimes captured on film when photographs were taken of mediums. How could purely spiritual creatures be made visible? The answer was: through the medium, an individual capable of exuding a mysterious substance called ectoplasm.

I became interested, about fifteen years ago, in the history of spiritualism and attempts to communicate with the dead, and through my reading was particularly struck by the concept of ectoplasm. It sounded like the purest pseudoscience, and had the appeal of much logical nonsense. I wondered what ectoplasm had looked like, felt like; I didn't want to believe it had been purely a hoax, something made up to fool the credulous. There were plenty of frauds in spiritualists circles, but many mediums were genuine and believed in what they were doing. Were there any who "really" produced ectoplasm? What would it be like to believe your own body capable of producing ghostly forms?

At around the same time that I discovered ectoplasm, I read an article about a New England family of Tuttles, who had been farming the same piece of land for generations. Although they were not related to me, the coincidence of surname caught my attention. I have forgotten most of the details, but can never forget the one Miss Tuttle from an earlier century who became pregnant without benefit of husband. Her family did not turn her out; what they did, I think, was worse. They kept her physically, even as they rejected her. She continued to live in the family home, but to the end of her life no one spoke to her directly again. She became a nonperson for her sin, a kind of living ghost. And yet she did not—could not?—ever leave.

Someday, I knew, I would write about her, just as someday I would write a story featuring ectoplasm. Over the years those two ideas (and who knows how many more) were mulched together in the compost heap of memory, and one day the first line, about Mr. Elphinstone's hands, came into my head. And there was the story, emerging not unlike some ectoplasmic creature from my head as it was born into words.

Lisa Tuttle

SERENA SEES

G. K. Sprinkle

Barbara inhaled deeply, awareness seeping through the trance. If only she could come back from her meditations to those who wanted her, instead of also facing station politics and skeptics. Snatches of sound emanated from the headphones around her neck. She opened her eyes, scanning the studio equipment. One phone line was blinking. The CRT showed all four lines open, three breaks before eleven.

"The new guy's on this hour," the producer said through her desk speaker. "I'll be back before midnight."

She looked up through the glass separating radio studio from control room. "No."

"It's okay, I've briefed him," he said. "Seen those ratings? We're number one this time slot." He held his right thumb up. "Checked your abort/delay switch?"

She smiled and nodded. He left. They were a great team. She entertained; he promoted. She brought her lips to the microphone: "Testing, one . . . two . . . three." She looked into the control room. The new tech nodded, and flashed ten fingers twice. "Go ahead, use the desk speaker," she told him. She put the headphones on. Perfect timing. The eerie music the producer liked ended.

"There are things beyond sight. Things beyond sound. Things in the dark reaches of the mind that few can see." Barbara hated the deep bass voice-over. "She lights the way . . . Serena." The music crescendoed; cymbals crashed.

"Good evening," Barbara said. "Welcome to 'SerenaSees.' Your questions answered Monday through Friday from ten until one. All phone lines are open, 387-KNTE. Your problems, your questions; I want to help. Call 387-KNTE." She looked at the CRT—no Dave, Ed, or Al, thank God, but he did keep changing his name—Mary on the first line. She pushed it. "Hello, Mary. You're on the air with Serena. Can I help?"

"Hello, Serena. It's so good to talk with you. I listen all the time. You're wonderful."

"Thank you, Mary. Let me help you." Good, a talker. Should be easy.

"Oh, I'm praying you can. Will my husband find a job?"

Barbara sighed. These calls tore her apart—people wanting advice instead of fun. "He's been out of work a while," she tried.

"Yes. Six months. They say he's too old."

God, he'd probably never get another job. "I see a job in his future, but not soon. I feel he'll be starting a business of his own."

"But he was a telephone lineman."

That was a toughie. "He's always wanted to do something else."

"Yes. How did you know he wanted to raise chickens?"

"Serena sees. Thank you for calling. Our lines are open for your questions, 387-KNTE. Hello, Jack, you're on with 'Serena Sees.' Your question." Please, not him, she thought.

"Yes. I wonder about my future."

Someone new, good. "The future is cloudy, the more I know the better." That should bring him out.

"Will my girl take me back?"

"I see pain, harsh words between you."

"Yes."

He was a clam, but maybe . . . "She wants to get married; you don't."

"No."

"She's worried about money." Please. Talk.

"I thought so. Fraud."

Oops. She pushed the abort/delay switch. "We don't say things like that on 'Serena Sees,' " she said. Thank God for delays; no one would know what he'd said. "More of 'Serena Sees' after these messages. Our lines are open; 387-KNTE."

Barbara sipped water as the commericals droned in her ears. Her hands shook slightly. Why did it bother her so much this time? She gave people what they wanted; nothing wrong with that. No, it wasn't the last caller. It was the other one with the cold, quiet voice. That Dave or Ed or Al, or whatever his name was. What did he want? Why did he call?

"Five seconds," the new tech whispered through the desk speaker.

"Speak louder," she said. "It's okay." Barbara leaned toward the microphone. The commercial ended. "It's so good to be back. Our lines are open for you—387-KNTE. Hello, Don, you're on with 'Serena Sees.' Your question."

"What do you see in *your* future, Barbara?"

No, not that voice, four nights in a row. She didn't see the new guy in the booth. She pushed the abort switch. How did that caller get through?

He laughed. "Don't know, do you, psychic? You told Cindy I was wrong for her, and you know nothing about us."

The call didn't disconnect. Barbara jiggled the headphones—dead. He was talking through the desk speaker. She plugged her headphones into another jack. The ten-thirty news tape was running. She pushed a phone line and dialed 911. Nothing happened. The lights went off. She felt a cold draft as the door to the hall opened behind her.

Afterword

Much of my view of Texas is what I see driving between Austin and other cities like Dallas or Houston—an endless flat strip of highway between here and there. On those days when I travel 400 or 340 miles, I'm the captive of my AM radio. Several stations think fun entertainment includes a psychic reading people's futures and finding their lost trinkets. In "Serena Sees," I imagined someone who didn't agree.

G. K. Sprinkle

TRICK OR TREAT

Pauline E. Dungate

It was the morning after All Hallow's Eve that Claire almost tripped over the large, soggy cardboard box that someone had placed on her step. She thought it might have been left by the children who had knocked on her door the previous night demanding, "Trick or treat." Her first instinct was to cram the unsightly thing into the dustbin. As she bent to pick it up, it squeaked. She shuddered at the thought that there might be a rat inside. Fetching her leather gardening gloves and holding a broom at arm's-length, Claire lifted back the flaps. Nothing jumped out, but something began to cry. She edged closer.

Inside were four very bedraggled bundles of fur. One raised an overlarge head and waved it unsteadily on a scrawny neck. Blind eyes searched for her. It mewled again.

She hated cats, but no creature should have to suffer unnecessarily, so she made the kitten a nest of some old rags and fed it warm milk from an eyedropper before disposing of the bodies of its three siblings and leaving for work.

Her antipathy for cats had been there from childhood.

Claire's most vivid memories of her school days were of tiptoeing round her mother's darkened bedroom bearing cups of milky tea. Claudia Gredzinski always seemed to be suffering from a migraine headache or recovering from an asthma attack, and the girl was never allowed pets in case their hair affected her mother's chest. Claudia would even cross the road to avoid meeting animals such as cats, and friends who acquired them were no longer welcomed.

It was Claire who had to do what cleaning was permitted, but never when her mother was in the house, as the dust aggravated Claudia's condition. And Claire who had to sprinkle pepper round the garden to keep out the neighbourhood cats. Her father had taken a ship back to Poland when she was five; Claire often wished she could do the same.

Claudia remained dependent upon her daughter until she died. Claire was thirty-eight then, and the first thing she did was to clean every corner that had been forbidden to her before and redecorate so that the house became a bright, pleasant place to live in. Never having been allowed a boyfriend, such was Claudia's domination of her, Claire didn't suddenly expect to find one now, so she lavished her affection on a large tank of tropical fish and bought herself a parrot. The bird's previous owner had taught it an uncouth vocabulary, but Claire took satisfaction in knowing that Claudia would not have approved.

She did, even two years after her mother's death, still scatter pepper in the garden to deter the cats.

Much to her surprise, the kitten was still alive when she returned. It sucked her fingers feebly as she fed it again. When it was a little stronger, she decided, she would deliver it to the Cat Protection League.

She never got round to it, and Charles the parrot learned some new words.

In colouring, Freddy, as Claire called him, was mostly white. He had irregular black patches on both flanks, and black forefeet. A mask of darkness covered one side of his face, and from the moment his legs were strong enough, he followed Claire about the house, his tail pointed rigidly upward as if attached to the ceiling by an invisible wire.

Gradually, Claire got used to having a cat about the house, though his sharp claws caught and snagged the fabric of the chair covers as he flexed them in play. Her hands, too, suffered. He would pat at them, his pads soft against her palms, then, excited by the game, rake her skin with extended talons. When she swore at the sudden pain, he gazed at her solemnly with large green eyes.

Freddy wasn't the only change in her life.

Max Shelton was at least ten years older than she was and worked in the accounts department of the same Birmingham store where she was a floor manager. They had met very occasionally but never stopped to talk. She'd heard that his wife had left him after nearly thirty years of marriage and was a little surprised when he asked if she would like to go for a drink with him when the store closed on Christmas Eve. She felt sorry for him, knowing what it was like to spend Christmas alone, so hesitated only a moment before she said yes.

Max dropped her off at her gate afterward. She felt light-headed from the single Martini and lemonade as she fumbled with her key. She turned and waved to Max as he drove away.

Freddy wound himself round her legs the moment she closed the door and purred loudly. The sound had a harshness to it that she hadn't noticed before.

"I know, Freddy," she said. "I'm late. And you're hungry. Did you think I'd forgotten you?"

She prattled on as she opened a tin and spooned the meat into the cat's bowl. Freddy gave her a reproachful look before attacking it. She made herself a sandwich and carried it through into the next room. Charles sidled up his perch toward her, cackling.

"Who's a pretty bugger, then?" he said.

"Charles is," Claire said with a smile.

As there was nothing worth watching on TV, Claire slipped a music cassette into the player. She settled in an armchair to watch her fish and subconsciously counted them while she nibbled her sandwich. One of the bright orange swordtails was missing. It was probably hiding amongst the weeds, which had grown to dominate the tank. That was unusual, as both fish tended to display themselves prominently near the surface of the water. Claire decided to fetch a towel and trim back the overgrown plants.

An hour later, the tank looked neater and a heap of limp fronds lay in a bowl on the table beside the tank. There was no sign of the swordtail. A thorough search had failed to reveal it—alive or dead—within the vegetation. Freddy sat beside the bowl, watching intently. A pink tongue flicked out to lick his nose; his expression was almost smug.

Claire reprimanded herself. She must beware of giving human attributes to her pets. It was an old-maidish thing to do and she was not yet prepared to call herself that. Besides, there was no way Freddy could have got at the fish; she was sure the splash covers had been in place. She scratched the cat behind his ears, and he purred with the rasp of sandpaper on old wood.

The January sales were almost as overwhelming as the pre-Christmas rush, but by the end of the month the store had calmed down to its more usual sedate pace. Max asked Claire to dinner, and she invited him in for coffee at the end of the evening.

"Would you like a brandy to go with it?" Claire asked.

Max draped his coat over the back of the sofa. "Not as I'm driving," he said, "but you go ahead."

She hesitated. They had drunk a bottle of wine between them during the meal. She felt more relaxed than at the beginning of the evening, but she was still nervous. It was difficult to know what the right thing to do was, especially when she'd never entertained a man alone before. She didn't want to appear naive or gauche. She compromised and poured a small one, sipping it before setting the glass on the table and going to fetch the coffee.

She pushed the door open with her foot, carrying the tray carefully and trying to avoid stepping on Freddy, who entwined himself affectionately about her ankles. Max was standing next to Charles's cage, lifting the cover.

"What a magnificent bird," he said. "Why do you keep him covered?"

"His language is also magnificent, and not very polite." Claire set the tray down on an occasional table.

"Fuck off, Freddy," Charles said obligingly.

Max laughed. "I see what you mean."

Claire flushed, relieved that Max didn't appear offended. "I don't normally use sugar," she said. "I hope these little packets are all right."

She handed Max a cup with a couple of sachets in the saucer and took her own. Freddy stalked around the room, pausing for a moment to gaze up at Charles, who screamed at him, then leapt for the table by the fish tank. Claire's forgotten brandy glass toppled. Freddy began to lap at the spilled liquid. Claire set down her cup, grabbed a handful of tissues from a box on the shelf above the aquarium, and dumped the cat unceremoniously on the floor.

"You'll make yourself ill if you drink that," she told him.

"Can I help at all?" Max asked.

Claire shook her head. "I don't think there's any damage," she said, and tossed the damp tissues in the wastepaper bin.

She had barely settled down again before there was a choking sound from behind the sofa. Freddy had been sick. She hauled him out by the scruff of the neck and took him into the kitchen, fetching a roll of paper towels and a damp cloth to clear up the mess. She used the paper to gather up as much as she could. As she scrubbed at the patch, she pricked her finger: A fine bone protruded through the towel. Claire glanced at the tank. There was no sign of her favourite—the angelfish. She looked down at the bone again, feeling tears beginning to form. Gathering the cleaning things, she fled to the kitchen.

"I'm sorry," Claire said. She had wiped her eyes, given her nose a good blow, and applied an extra dab of powder to her cheeks before returning to the sitting room. "It's been such a good evening and I've spoiled it."

"No, you haven't." Max gave her hand a squeeze. "Can I see you next week?"

"If you want to."

"Yes, I do. I'll give you a ring and fix it." He gathered his coat and shrugged into it. "Good-bye, Charles," he called.

"Up yours," said the parrot, and produced a shrill wolf whistle.

Next time, Claire resolved, Freddy would stay in the kitchen or, if he continued to be a nuisance, go into the garden when she had visitors. Which was where he would go right now if she could find him. But the animal stayed hidden. Claire banged about in the sink washing the coffee cups. Then she returned to the sitting room and knelt in front of the aquarium. It looked empty without the angel. The marbled fish had been the first one she'd bought.

"Damn you, Freddy," she said quietly. "Damn you."

By the end of the weekend, the cat had inveigled its way back into her affections. On Sunday she had kept him shut in the kitchen until two pots of geraniums hit the floor. She put him outside despite the fact that it was raining, and only permitted him back—in a very bedraggled state—at feeding time. She banged the bowl down before him and left him to it. By Monday evening, her day off in lieu of Saturday, he was curled in her lap purring contentedly.

Tuesday was a working day. As usual, Claire fed the animals before fetching in the milk and preparing her own breakfast. As she stooped to pick up the bottle, Freddy shot past her, disappearing into the bushes. Normally, while she was out, the cat remained in the kitchen, supplied with plenty of water and a litter tray. The occasions when he got through into the rest of the house she put down to her carelessness in not closing the kitchen door properly.

She left the front door ajar while she got ready for work and waited as long as she dared before setting off for the bus stop. She called and rattled his dish, a ploy that usually worked, but he didn't reappear. Finally, Claire locked up and left, though not without a last look round the front garden. She only just caught the bus. She threw herself into the first available seat as it jerked into motion. From the window, she saw a black and white shape sitting on the wall, watching her.

In the evening, Freddy strolled up nonchalantly as she let herself into the house.

It was the beginning of a pattern. At first she would only catch a glimpse of Freddy as the bus pulled away or she alighted after work. Then he began stalking her— a shadow moving stealthily in the hedges or lurking on the other side of a front wall. By the end of two weeks he was openly following her, not just to the bus stop but shopping as well. And he was always there when she came back, even if she caught a different bus. Did he sit at the stop all day, she wondered, or did he somehow know when she would return?

Occasionally, when she was reading or sewing, she would look up to find him staring at her from his place in front of the fire. She shivered, seeing something sinister in his hypnotic gaze, and she had an inkling of how a mouse must feel. She chided herself at being so foolish. The rest of the time he was an ordinary, affectionate young cat.

The fact that Freddy seemed to have taken a great dislike to Max, Claire put down to his early kittenhood. The only other person Freddy had met was the vet who had injected him against cat flu. It might explain why a nervous cat would scratch a hand that tried to rub behind his ears in friendship, or urinate into a lap after he had warily consented to sit there. What Claire didn't like was Freddy's expression of triumph when he did those things. Or the way that he contrived to pull down Max's coat from where she had hung it in the hall and defecate over it.

The next time Max took her out, he declined her offer of coffee.

"I'm sorry, Claire," he said. "I like you very much. I'd like to know you a lot better."

Claire looked away from him and out of the car window, unable to meet his eyes. She could guess what he was thinking. Freddy sat in the centre of her path, watching. It was the way she expected he would look at prey.

"It sounds silly, but I think that cat's jealous of me," Max said.

It's him or me, Claire thought, that's what you're saying.

"Thanks for a lovely evening," she said aloud, unfastening the seat belt and reaching for the door handle.

"Claire." His hand on her arm stopped her. Max leaned over and kissed her on the mouth, the first time he had ever done so.

Moments later, she was standing on the pavement watching the car recede. Tears blurred her vision. "I'm doing a lot of crying these days," she thought.

Something brushed her legs. She flinched and looked down at Freddy. "At least *he* has given me a choice," she told the cat.

The crash woke Claire. Her heart was beating faster than normal as she tried to decide whether it came from outside, downstairs, or if the chimney had dropped bricks through the roof. Then she heard Charles screaming.

Throwing back the bedcovers, she groped for her slippers, flinging her arms into her dressing gown as she hurried downstairs.

She touched the light switch. Charles's cage had been knocked over. The parrot climbed rapidly up the side of the armchair. Freddy paused in a half-crouch, one paw raised. He turned his head to scowl at her, tail lashing. Charles launched himself clumsily into the air. Freddy leapt. Charles squawked. They connected.

Bird and cat hit the carpet; Freddy gracefully, Charles a bag of feathers.

Claire flung herself at Freddy, batting the animal with her hands. She screamed the words Charles had taught her. She stuffed the cat into the empty parrot cage. Her hands were lacerated where he bit and scratched at her. She used the belt of her dressing gown to tie the cage shut. She sat back. She was trembling with rage.

Tuesday evening, Claire phoned Max.

"He's gone," she said.

"Who's gone?"

"Freddy."

There was silence at the other end. She wondered if she had misunderstood him. Perhaps he had been using Freddy as an excuse to get rid of her.

"Will you meet me somewhere?" Max asked. "Can you get to the Bull's Head? At the end of Highfield Road?"

"I think so."

"In about an hour? I'll meet you in the lounge."

Max had the drinks ready on the table when she arrived—an alcohol-free lager and a Martini and lemonade. He took her hand as she slipped onto the bench seat beside him.

"Tell me," he said.

"He killed Charles."

"I'm sorry. I liked that bird." Max's fingers squeezed hers.

"I took him to London. Yesterday. On my day off. I found a Cat Protection League place and left him there. Said I was moving into a flat and couldn't keep him."

Max took a sip of his drink. "Claire," he said. "It may not be the right time to ask, but will you come away with me? For the weekend?"

Claire spluttered. A mouthful of Martini went down the wrong way. Max slapped her between the shoulder blades as she started choking. Her eyes watered.

"I told you I wanted to know you better," Max said. "What better way than a holiday together? Separate bedrooms, if you prefer."

"When?"

"Easter. How do you fancy York when the daffodils are out?"

Claire liked it very much. The sun shone for them both days. She regretted that she had never been before, but when her mother was alive she wouldn't have dared suggest it. It would probably have brought on one of Claudia's attacks. Since then, it hadn't occurred to her.

"It's a pity we have to go back," she said.

Max gave her a quick smile before turning his attention back to the road. "We can do it again," he said. "Lincoln, perhaps, or Durham."

"I'd like that."

They drove in a companionable silence, Max concentrating on navigation onto the motorway, Claire taking in the changing environment.

As the junctions flicked past and it began to get dark, Max said, "Would you get the AA book out of my bag? I don't want to miss the turnoff."

The zip shoulder-bag was stowed behind the driver's seat. Claire reached behind.

"Ouch." She withdrew the hand sharply.

"What's the matter?" Max asked.

"I caught my hand on something sharp." She twisted

in her seat, pulling the belt out of the reel to give herself more mobility. She peered round to gauge the position of the bag. Two green eyes reflected back the light of a passing car. She jerked back and sat very still.

"Max. I think there's a cat in the car. I saw its eyes."

"It's your imagination, love. Something catching the light."

Claire stared at the line of red beads welling from the graze on her hand. So like the scratches Freddy used to make. She glanced down. A black and white paw appeared between the seats, dabbing at the gear stick.

"There's no way a cat could've got into the car, is there?" Claire's voice was tight, her mouth dry, and she could detect a touch of hysteria in it.

"Of course not."

The imaginary cat squeezed between the seat-belt stalks. Freddy looked up at her. His claws snagged into her skirt as he climbed onto her lap. Claire didn't dare to move. Max was right. It was her imagination. Her guilt at having abandoned the animal. She couldn't really feel his weight across her thighs. Or the warmth of his body. His purring was actually the hum of the car engine. In a moment Max would look her way. Reassure her that nothing was there.

Freddy's tail flicked backward and forward at the edge of her vision. He tensed. About to spring.

I must grab him, she thought. I must grab him.

Freddy leapt. Max released the wheel. The spitting furball clawed at his face. Max clawed at the cat. At her. The car swerved. The lorry loomed close.

Claire screamed. She heard the screech of metal on metal. And the scrunch of glass. And the squeal of burning rubber.

And silence.

They let her out of Leicester Royal Infirmary after three days, when they were sure there were no hidden injuries. She hadn't seen Max. She had been afraid to ask, afraid he would blame her for the accident. He hadn't asked to see her, either.

The journey back to Birmingham was nightmarish. Every time she glanced through the train window, she could see a cat. It was as though the whole of feline kind were checking on her progress. When she closed her eyes, there was a pair of green ones burnt into the undersides of her lids. Trying to focus anywhere else brought her attention back to her broken nails. Had she tried to dig her way out?

And there had been no sign of a cat in the car. She had asked that. Insisted. It had taken the fire brigade two hours to cut them out. But there was no cat. She became hysterical when they denied it. She needed to know it was not her imagination.

The train decanted her into the the city centre during the dead time between rush hour and the evening crowds, and she stood for what seemed a long while, waiting for a bus to take her home. Her thoughts kept returning to the crash and the missing cat, hoping it had been real—a stray that had slipped in unnoticed, looking for shelter. It could have escaped into the darkness; she had no clear idea of how long it had taken the ambulance to reach them.

But underneath lurked the idea that it had been Freddy the changeling who had succeeded in robbing her of everything: the fish, then Charles, and now Max. All she had cared for.

The road was deserted as she walked quickly along it to her gate, her head swinging from side to side as she searched, expecting each moment to see him, crouched on a wall. Or skulking under the hedges. Shadowing her, as he used to do.

Claire groped in her bag for the front door key. Though the light from the street shone directly on it, she had difficulty fitting the key into the lock. She pushed the door open.

The first thing she noticed was the smell. It had been in the house when she left, but she was so used to it that she hardly noticed. But now, even after several weeks, the odour of cat urine was still strong and unpleasant. Almost as though it were fresh. Her chest constricted. It was hard to breathe. She pulled at her clothing.

Was this how Claudia felt, she wondered, at the beginning of an asthma attack?

She lurched forward, suddenly dizzy as blood squeezed behind her eyes. She clung to the stair rail, her lungs heaving against the paralysis of her diaphragm. She sank to her knees.

Light from the streetlamp spilled past her. From the stairs, a pair of green eyes reflected it back to her.

Afterword

There can't be many little girls who have handed back their Sunday School prize on the grounds that it was about soppy ballet dancers. The boys were all being given Biggles books and I wanted one, too. So at the age of about eleven I was already reading in genres that too many regard as male preserves

That hasn't changed much, but I do prefer to read the kind of horror that doesn't have to rely on vast quantities of blood and entrails to achieve its effects. I find a story far more satisfying if it makes me look over my shoulder and feel that it could happen to me tomorrow, or be happening now, somewhere not too distant. The stories I write reflect, I hope, the kinds of things I like to read.

For some people the boundary between a phobia and madness is very narrow. So it that between a genuine fear and a belief that something supernatural is haunting you. In "Trick or Treat," I also wanted to explore how a phobia originates. Perhaps it is the memory of an event from childhood; the initial terror is long past, but the mind associates an object with an effect. Or perhaps it is the subconscious absorption of another's fears. In this story, I wanted Claire to think that perhaps she was being irrational and that her distrust of cats was acquired from her mother. Yet I don't believe that a phobia can be cured that easily, and I wanted the reader to wonder whether Freddy was behaving according to his natural instincts or was something more sinister.

To add to that doubt, the date he was dumped on Claire's doorstep was important. All Hallow's Eve was traditionally the night when the Little People stole unbaptised children and substituted changelings for them.

Often when I write, I find that subconsciously I have included elements I was unaware of. Freddy was named after a Swedish farmhouse cat that I met one summer. He adored flies and would devour as many as could be caught for him. It was only when I was halfway through writing this story that I realised that Freddy is also the name given to the monster in the *Nightmare on Elm Street* films.

Other scenes have also been drawn from life: I have often watched my husband pruning surplus weed from his tank of tropical fish, and have seen a friend's cat sitting close to her aquarium, apparently admiring the spectacle of lunch, moving.

Pauline E. Dungate

TICANAU'S CHILD

Sherry Coldsmith

I parked my Chevy in the dusty lot near the pavilion. My family called it the "pavilion" because of the wire-mesh net that joined the tin roofs of the two facing bungalows. Leafy vines covered the net, shading the few picnic tables that served as a dining room. Sprinklers whirled on top of the buildings, but I knew the water would do little to cool the sweltering interiors. Beyond the pavilion was a grassy meadow, and beyond that I could see the live oaks that grew by the banks of the Guadalupe River. I couldn't afford this weekend away from work, but it was good to be back at the pavilion, a holiday camp that was more like a home to me than any of the Texas towns I had lived in as a kid.

Mother was sitting in her car, staring into space. She had phoned me a couple of hours ago, whining that my dad was flirting with some woman who had double-booked the bungalows. It was unlikely there was anything to her story, but it seemed the only way I could pacify her was to come down to the pavilion myself. If I didn't drive down to see Mother, I knew that she'd want to stay at my place for a few days, and there was no way I was going to let that happen. She'd soon realize that Tom had left me, and then she'd demand to know why our marriage had been so brief. I just wasn't ready to have that scene.

I walked over to her. "Mom? Hey, Mom," I said. She looked up at me with bloodshot eyes.

"Do you want to go somewhere and talk?" I asked. I'd never been very good at playing a social worker role, but I could at least give her moral support.

"No, not now. Please go tell your dad I'm out here."

The hot drive had made me irritable. "Mother, I just dropped my dissertation so that I could come down here, and the first thing you do is tell me to buzz off and get Daddy. You don't even thank me for coming."

"I'm sorry, Karen, I know your studies are important to you." She dabbed at her eyes with a hankie. "It's just that your dad's hardly noticed me this past week. The whole gang's carrying on as if nothing has happened. No one's noticed what a rotten time I'm having."

She was obviously feeling miserable, though it wouldn't be the first time that one of my dad's misdemeanors was an excuse for melodrama. "Okay, I shouldn't have griped at you, either. If you tell me where Dad is, I'll go get him."

"He's down by the river, fishing," she said bitterly.

"Should I tell him you want to talk to him?"

"No. Just tell him where I am."

"If you want Dad to come and talk things over," I said, trying to keep an even tone of voice, "then you've got to say so. Don't play games with yourself."

"I haven't done anything wrong. Why are you picking on me?"

She began to cry. I walked away from the car, wishing I could change the last few days of my mother's life. And failing that, I'd like to change her. She never could deal with people in a straightforward way.

I started down the half-mile path to the river, grateful

that I was getting a chance to cool my temper. Mother never missed a chance to pity herself, and it always infuriated me, even though I knew why she felt so insecure. My real father had left us for another woman. Vance had disappeared before I turned three, and though I couldn't remember anything about him, I could still hear Mom saying, "Daddy's gone and left us." And after that I remember a hurt—a big hurt. Now that I was single again, I was finding more and more reasons to brood over Vance's desertion. Why hadn't I been pretty enough, or charming enough, to keep my real dad?

I reached the banks of the Guadalupe. The water was a deeper green than I'd ever seen it and the river was wider than it should be. In the dry months of summer, the Guadalupe was often more like a large creek than a river, but not this year. Now she was a sated panther, lumbering to the gulf, arrogantly proclaiming that she had thwarted the seasons. It made me feel uncomfortable, somehow. I had been coming here every year of my life, and I thought I knew all of the river's moods.

I started walking upstream, in the direction of Dad's favorite fishing hole. Perhaps I should tell him about the divorce and then he could tell Mother. But would the reasons sound any more convincing to him than they would to her? In their world, a woman should do anything to please her husband, even if it meant doing something that scared the life out of her. Sex scared me. It wasn't the act itself I dreaded so much as the nightmares that followed. "Postcoital trauma," the shrink had said.

I never brought Tom to the pavilion. Our relationship had not lived to see even one summer. The nightmares weren't too bad at first, and Tom had been very understanding in bed, very patient. After making love, he would whisper reassurances until drowsiness garbled his speech. When the nightmares got worse, I'd lie awake, terrified of falling asleep, while a postcoital grin spread over Tom's face. I put a stop to our lovemaking. Tom hung on for a while longer, until I started forgetting my appointments with the shrink. I was too easily side-tracked by my research, too prone to forget things that were not relevant to my work. One night, Tom collected his toothbrush and comb and drove off without a word. Packing his things a few days later, he told me the score in his best English professor voice: He would not live "like a sexually importunate beggar." That was a month ago.

I heard voices upstream, shouting my name. My dad's friends were floating in the water, each man sitting in an inner tube and trying to keep a steady position in the lazy current. There was a double six-pack of beer cans tethered to one of the tubes. The men welcomed me and pointed to my dad. He was sitting on the bank, a fishing rod in his hands, apparently oblivious to the shouts of his friends. His fair hair was neatly combed back and he was wearing a pair of swimming trunks that revealed his plump, white legs. As I approached, I was struck, for the first time in years, by how obvious it was that we were not blood kin. It didn't matter to me, though. I still thought of him as "Daddy."

"What a nice surprise, baby girl," he said when he finally noticed me. "I didn't think you were coming this time."

"That's what I thought, too," I replied, taking a seat beside him, "until a very distraught woman called me this morning."

"Oh. Have you seen your mother yet?"

"Hi, Bob." A young woman wearing sandals and loose-fitting shorts had walked up behind us. "Who is this pretty girl you're talking to?" She sat on the grass while Dad introduced her as Yvonne. She looked relaxed and cool in the dire heat—not glamorous or cheap as I had expected. And she was exceedingly hand-some: a little taller than me, with dark hair and skin. If I could make myself over, keeping my best features and changing my least attractive ones, I'd look a lot like her. Maybe that's why she seemed so familiar.

"Dad, I think you ought to go talk to Mother. She

was sitting in her car when I drove up." I'd hoped to quiz Dad on his version of the story before Mom started forcing me to take sides. Now it would have to wait.

"Yeah, Bob," Yvonne said, "she seemed pretty upset last night. Your daughter and I will do a little girl-talking while you're gone."

Dad reeled in his tackle and ambled away from the bank. He was a big man, and he always moved as though he were uncertain about which direction to plod in. For the life of me, I couldn't believe that someone as attractive as Yvonne was interested in him.

She leaned back against her hands, extending well-muscled legs before her.

"Did your mother tell you about last night?"

"No, she hasn't said anything specific at all. She told me that Dad was behaving like an old fool with some woman who was at the pavilion." Yvonne took out a cigarette and tapped it twice on one end and twice on the other. I recognized that gesture in someone I knew, but I couldn't say who it reminded me of.

"Well, your dad and I stayed up late last night, just shooting the breeze. We were talking about you, mainly. I was even saying how much I'd like to meet you. I guess we should have gone to bed when everyone else did, but we just lost all track of time. Your mother came out and accused us of indecent behavior but I told her we didn't get up to anything. Your dad's very nice, but he's not my style at all."

I giggled at that. I couldn't imagine Dad being anybody's style—not even my mother's.

"And besides," Yvonne continued, "what did your mother think we'd do? We were in the middle of the pavilion with people snoring all around us."

I bummed a cigarette off Yvonne and tried to look noncommittal. What indeed could they have done? They might have scribbled torrid messages to each other, I suppose, but it seemed unlikely. And it was true that Mother had more hang-ups about sex than a Christian art gallery.

"Where's my mother's friends?" I asked.

"Down at the hot springs, drinking beer and laughing, I imagine. I've been having a good time with those gals."

I got up, intending to walk to the hot springs. If Dad had been indiscreet, then Mother's friends would be delighted to talk about it. Yvonne stood up, too, an eager smile on her face. We started down the path to the hot springs and I realized I was glad to have her company. Without someone to talk to, I'd only start brooding again.

"How did you find out about the pavilion, Yvonne?"

"Oh, a friend of mine in Houston told me about it." There was stress in her voice, as if she was trying hard to sound casual.

"Are you here on your own?"

"Yeah. I quit my job a few months ago, so I'm on a long vacation."

I asked the usual questions: whether she had a steady boyfriend and what kind of work she did. She was nothing like my colleagues at the university, of course, but I'm pretty adaptable to my parents' *amigos*.

She stopped to point out a large bull snake, hugging the branches of a mountain laurel.

"I read that Indians used to believe animals were messengers, sent by our ancestors," she said.

"That's not quite true," I replied, "but close enough. My dissertation is on the folklore of the Plains Indians. I'm afraid I've overspecialized, though. I don't know much about the Coahiltecans who lived around here."

Yvonne gave me a knowing smile. It was almost patronizing, as if she knew everything about the subject and found my PhD topic a bit quaint. "Your dad told me about your interests. Why did you choose to study Indians?"

"Oh, I could give you a lot of reasons. I could tell you what a fascinating and intriguing subject it is. I could tell you why we should preserve Indian artifacts and oral traditions. Those reasons are valid, of course. But the fact is that my natural father was half-Indian. I guess I went into the field to spite Mother. The only time she'd talk about my real dad was when she wanted to say how worthless he was."

Mother said that Vance didn't want the responsibility of raising a family, so he ran off with someone else, leaving everything behind, including us. I never doubted her explanation, but I still resented her secrecy about Vance. She wouldn't even describe him to me. Grandmother had said I was the spitting image of him.

"I dry fresh food the Indian way," said Yvonne, "and I pick my own herbs and use Indian remedies when I'm sick. There was a *curandera* in my hometown and she could change the weather and summon coyotes. So while you college kids 'preserve' Indian customs, some of us live them!"

"A lot of younger people these days are trying to live like Indians," I said noncommittally. Yvonne's picture of Indian life was naive, but I no longer scoffed at the preposterous notions of my parents' friends. Let them go on thinking that UFOs might give us a cure for cancer, or that horoscopes could fight heart disease. The nightmares of my marriage had taught me to respect irrational fears.

And Yvonne's enthusiasm *did* remind me of the thrill I used to get from my studies. Perhaps my reasons for going into the field had been feeble, but I found my studies all-consuming once I started them. Instead of dating and socializing like other students, I had holed up with my books until I met Tom, another academic who I hoped would make few demands on my time.

We walked around a bend in the river and found my mother's three best friends sunning themselves on big beach towels. Grace, Joy, and Irma were chatting idly in the hot sun. Each woman's dyed hair clung to her forehead, a sign that they'd all been bathing in the hot springs.

"Well, hi, girl!" Grace exclaimed. Each woman insisted on a big hug.

"I'd love to stay and chat," said Yvonne as I sat down on a spare corner of Grace's towel, "but I ought to get lunch started."

Grace and Irma looked relieved. I had to give Yvonne credit for knowing when her presence was not wanted.

"I'll come with you," Joy Nolan said. "It's too much cooking for just one gal."

When the two of them were well out of earshot, I blurted out my question: "Can you guys tell me what my mother's so upset about?"

Irma was the first to jump in. "Well, this girl said that she had the place booked the same time as us and we tried to check it out with the owners but—"

"Only they weren't answering the phone," Grace interrupted. "And before anyone knew it, Joy was asking Yvonne to share the cabins with us."

"Which was very nice of Joy, I thought," said Irma.

"This is all very interesting, guys," I said, "but what about my mother?"

"Well," Irma continued, "your mother thinks that Yvonne's been a little friendlier to your dad than to the other men."

"Too friendly!" Grace was indignant. "She's trotting after Bob every time I look up. But I do think that your mother's overreacting, Karen. I didn't see any flirting going on. In fact, they were talking about you most of the time."

I asked what they were saying about me and got an earful of my dad's pride in my academic career. For a moment, I wondered who Mother was really jealous of, me or Yvonne.

"And Yvonne seemed so impressed by everything he said that he just couldn't stay quiet about you," said Irma.

Grace uncapped a bottle of suntan lotion. "But they *were* spending a lot of time around each other." She was determined to hold the floor. "And your dad knows better than anyone how jealous your mother can get." That was certainly true, I thought. Yvonne should have noticed it as well. Maybe Yvonne was deliberately taunting my mother, though I couldn't imagine why.

"So what really happened last night?" I asked, wishing they'd give me some useful information.

"What? Did something happen?" Irma asked, ever alert to the possibility of gossip.

"Yvonne told me that she and Dad stayed up talking and that my mother accused them of fooling around. Did Mom actually find them doing anything? Were they . . . compromising themselves?" I asked, terrified that I'd accidentally say the word "fuck." Mother would kill me if I said that in front of her friends.

They both cackled. "Why, honey"—Grace scooted over and put an arm around my shoulders—"your daddy may act like a fool half the time, but he's no playboy."

I laughed at the very idea of Dad the playboy. He was every bit the man I had hoped Tom would be: someone safe, solid, and predictable. Dad was anything but the Don Juan type. His only crime was that he could be cloddish and insensitive sometimes.

"Your mom's awful touchy about other women," Irma said. "I guess that losing her first husband made her paranoid about keeping her second."

Grace put the lid back on the unused lotion and stood up to leave. "Come on, Irma, let's go help the others with lunch."

After the women departed, I mulled over what they had said about my parents. It looked as if Mother was irked that Dad had ignored her and she had called me out here hoping to use me as a weapon against him. And I'd thought Mother wanted a friend to lean on. There had been times when she seemed not to like me very much. She'd always been a little cold toward me, treating me as if I were just a sideshow to her happy marriage. While I lived at home, she tried everything she could think of to make me get out of the house and meet other kids. But I was always a loner, and a pretty contented one, too.

I tasted salt on my lip, a reminder that I was dripping

with sweat. I got up and followed the path to the huge
live oak that sheltered the hot springs and the bank
above them. I ducked beneath the branches of the oak
and found the shrine that faithful Catholics had kept
there for decades. Mother once told me that a beautiful
statue had stood beneath the tree. Now there was a
sorry plaster Madonna, anchored to a slab of concrete.
Over the years, the statue's vivid paint had flaked away.
Only the thorns that gripped her pale heart had any
color. Their green pigment had become more intense
over the years, or so I imagined, and now they were the
same color as the river moss. My research had included
a study of myths that fused Indian earth spirits with the
Madonna figure, but I was too sluggish to recall the
name of the spirit that was supposed to preside over
this stretch of the Guadalupe.

I climbed down the high bank using the exposed roots
as footholds, and stepped onto a muddy rock ledge at
water level. I slipped off my cutoffs and T-shirt and then
stepped into the bubbles. The dark, mossy stones on the
bottom made the pool look unknowably deep, but the
water was only waist-high; it lapped against my belly, a
little warmer than blood heat—perfect. Men hated the
springs for being so hot, but Mother and I, and my grandmother before she died, loved the waters. The bubbles
soothed all knots in the muscles, all pains in the womb.

I floated on my back and closed my eyes, wishing I
was buoyant enough to fall asleep. Since Tom had left,
taking the nightmares with him, I had begun to nap frequently, catching up on the rest I had lost during my
brief marriage. I could never remember anything tangi-
ble about the nightmares. Fear stayed with me, though,
and the faintest trace of something allusive and familiar,
something like the smell of Grandad's pipe or the tinkling of a jewelry-box lullaby. But the harder I tried
to remember the dreams, the further they receded into
sleep.

My shrink tried hard to make me relive my nightmares. "If you can't remember them," she had asked

in her well-modulated tones, "then how do you know they are anything to fear?" Just the evidence of my flesh, doctor dear. I told her how raw I sometimes felt after the dreams, as if I'd been manhandled or violated. The quack had then quizzed me about Dad. I could tell what she was thinking when I told her he wasn't my real father. "He's a decent man!" I swore. He certainly never would have touched me in the way she was implying. If anything, there had been a lack of physical affection in my family. Dad was very loving in his words and deeds, but he and Mom had never given me more than a peck on the cheek. It had not really bothered me as a kid, but I did notice that other children seemed to get more hugs than I did.

I opened my eyes and gazed at the play of light between the leaves and branches of the tree. The water coiled around my limbs. I could stay in here forever, I thought, and let my watery flesh dissolve away; let the essence of Karen mingle with the snow-fed broth of the river—the river warmed by hot springs and the runoff from our grasslands. Our Lady of the Guadalupe. Ah, I remembered her old name now. It was Ticanau. She was not as kind as other spirits. She was jealous and grasping. Perhaps the Catholic shrine had been intended to make Ticanau behave.

I felt a nibble at my toes and I yelped, startled. Some fish would chew anything that stayed still long enough.

"Hello? Karen? Is that you?"

It sounded like Yvonne, calling from somewhere beyond the branches. How long had she been nearby?

"Mind if I join you?" she asked as she climbed down the bank. She draped a towel on a gnarled root.

"Is it time for lunch?" I asked. I was floating upright now, resting comfortably in the water, which almost reached my chin.

"No. It'll be a good hour before the men are back from shopping." She pulled her baggy shirt over her head, then slipped off shorts and briefs in one motion.

"Shopping? The only thing they'd go shopping for is more beer."

"And that's exactly what they've gone to get," she said. She waded into the springs and stood beside me, the water coming up to her hips. "Did you talk to Irma and Grace about me?"

"Yes," I replied, feeling awkward. I realized that I was staring at her. Her naked body was perfectly formed and, as far as I could tell, unblemished.

"Do you believe now that your dad and I didn't get up to anything?"

"Well, I'd still like to talk to my dad, but I guess I do believe you. I have to admit that Mother can sometimes be hysterical when it comes to sex."

"Well, I'm glad she asked you to come here, Karen."

I smiled at that, pleased that Yvonne liked me. "Whatever happened, I'm sure Mother will get over it before too long. I may as well fuck off home sometime today."

"What did you say?" Yvonne asked. She looked as if I'd said something shocking.

"Sorry," I said, apologizing before I was even certain what I had done wrong. "You being my age, I didn't think I'd have to watch my language."

She bent down and grabbed my face, forcing my lips to pucker. "Someone should wash your mouth out with soap, little girl. And to think you were once your daddy's sweetest baby girl." She let go of me and waded to the bank. She hadn't even bathed in the springs.

I wanted to burst out laughing at such a display, but I was cringing like a child instead. "Sorry, Yvonne—honest," I found myself pleading. I didn't believe she was really offended by the word "fuck," but I couldn't stop apologizing for having made her scold me. I followed her to the bank, where she was drying herself with the towel.

"I'll forget all about it," she said, "if you promise me you'll stay a few more days." She gave me a smile so gorgeous it almost took my breath away. I smiled back, and she began to rub me dry with the towel. She gestured for me to turn around, and then she rubbed vigorously, giving me a light massage when she was finished.

We strolled back to the pavilion and before I knew it, I was telling her about Tom and the bad dreams. She promised me that I'd forget all about him. Familiar words, I suppose, but she said them with such conviction that I felt more confident than I had in many weeks.

I ate a big lunch of chili, cornbread, and beer. My parents were nowhere to be found, a fact that their friends politely avoided mentioning. Instead, they asked me about the university, about Tom and the kind of car he drove. Yvonne was charming around them, and they were delighted by her, a sign that they all thought Mother was just out to spoil the fun. By the time I flopped onto a hammock for an afternoon nap, I was convinced that Mother's distress had been an act.

When I awoke, the hammock was rocking wildly beneath me. My genitals and backside felt bruised and swollen. I ran to the toilet, where I had violent diarrhea. My old nightmares were back. And this time they had not been preceded by sexual contact. Sometimes I wondered if I poked myself during these dreams, but there were never any visible signs of assault, only pain. I cleaned myself up and then returned to the hammock, unwilling to go back to sleep but loath to leave the cocoon of soft twine.

I lay there, sweating in the heat, listening to the trickling of water from the rooftop sprinklers. For the hundredth time, I tried to think of something in my past that would explain why I had these dreams. I'd had a good home, a stable family. There were no funny uncles to diddle me and I'd never been the victim of a sexual crime, or any crime at all, for that matter. Hell, I was the only female student I knew who had never seen a flasher or caught a Peeping Tom.

I got up and walked through the kitchen to the shower cubicles, feeling queasy. I glimpsed my parents' friends through the screen windows of the bungalows. They were playing cards at a picnic table. The shower was tepid but refreshing all the same. The needles of water soothed my sore skin. And then it hit me. I had dreamed about Ticanau. It wasn't a dream about violation or a sex-crazed monster, just a fragmented story about an Indian goddess. But in my dream, the goddess of the river had been a man. I could still see him standing on a boulder, looking down at the rushing water. He was naked and held a stone knife in one hand. Then he was walking among humans, still naked, pretending to be the goddess of river and rain. But the tribe's women were laughing at him, at the thick, dark line he had painted between his legs. He had tried to join their sex by cutting off his own genitals.

By the time I finished the shower, I was feeling almost cheerful again; it was simply a bizarre, chaotic dream combining recent events in my life, as all normal dreams do. Ticanau had even resembled Yvonne. It wasn't a dream I need fear having again. I couldn't explain the bad guts, or the physical feeling of violation. Perhaps I was coming down with a bug.

I tried to separate the dream's story from the little I knew about Ticanau's legend, but it was no use. I could only recall that she was mischievous and unforgiving, a grudging guardian of the river.

I dressed in fresh clothes and wandered into the kitchen. Mother was standing over the stove, browning a huge slab of brisket.

"Hi, sweetheart, did you have a good nap?" she asked. She looked as cheerful as a new bride.

"It was okay. Have you and Dad worked things out?" There could be only one explanation for her good mood.

"Well, Karen, I feel I've been really unfair to you."

"Why? You just needed my company. How have you been unfair?"

"I just overreacted. Your dad made me see how silly I had been for thinking that he was interested in that young girl."

"Mom, don't be too hard on yourself. Yvonne said she enjoyed Dad's company." I wished that I could change the subject and talk to her about Tom, but I knew we'd only start fighting if I did that. In her book, a wife does not refuse sex with her husband; a woman should be like the Magdalen, sitting at the feet of her lord.

Mother put down the forks she was using to turn the meat. "You've been talking to her, have you?"

"Some. I can't imagine her making a pass at an old boy like Dad."

"Your father is still a very attractive man."

"To you, perhaps, but Yvonne could have anyone she wanted."

Mother wanted to dispute the idea that Yvonne was pretty, but she caught herself in time.

"And anyway," I said, "she doesn't strike me as a seductress. She's too conventional for that. When we were down at the shrine, she even told me off for my language."

There was a grimace on Mother's face. She couldn't abide swearing. "That old shrine has had a lot of use over the years. Your real dad was always down there, or so he said, praying for a new pickup, or a decent job, or freedom from temptation . . ."

Mother's voice trailed off, and for a moment she looked incurably sad. I told her I was staying for a few extra days, hoping the news would cheer her up, but she seemed not to hear me. Forget it, I told myself, you know the real reason you're staying is to please Yvonne.

That night, I ate a ton of barbecue, despite feeling sick earlier. Yvonne sat beside me and kept feeding me choice morsels from her plate. It was a wonderful banquet.

After the dishes were cleared away, I helped Dad prepare the pavilion for the dancing that would start up later, when old friends of my mother's would show up for a party she had arranged. While we waited for the guests to arrive, my dad and I sang old cowboy songs accompanied by the steady boom-chuck of Mr. Nolan's guitar. Yvonne joined in when she knew the words.

Ghetto-blasters were carried in by some of the guests, turning us singers into dancers. When I was too winded to keep grooving, I watched Yvonne do a polka with my dad, and then stepped out into the night to smoke a cigarette. A silver-dollar moon hung in the sky, bathing the twisted mesquite and live oaks in sinuous light. I took in a few deep breaths and felt—I don't know—grateful. I had my family back.

After a while, Yvonne came out to join me, suggesting we take a walk to cool off. I jumped at the offer. All afternoon, we'd been surrounded by people and hadn't had the chance to really talk. We walked through the parking lot, our sandaled feet making trails in the dust. I asked her to wait a minute while I poked around in the glove compartment of my Chevy.

"What are you looking for?" she asked.

I figured Yvonne wouldn't want to toke up with me, but I didn't think she'd scold me for smoking grass. "Don't lecture me, Yvonne, please, but I do like to loosen up with a little marijuana." I was feeling around beneath the seat. "No luck. Tom must have rescued the stash before he moved out."

"Oh, we can do much better than grass," she said, laughing. She jogged to a dense thicket about twenty yards away. Curious, I ran after her. When I caught up, I found her picking through debris on the ground.

"What are you looking for, Yvonne? I sure didn't figure you for a peyote fiend."

"Ah, here's what I need," she said. She held up some withered seeds for me to see. It was hard to tell their color in the moonlight.

"What are those?" I asked.

"Beans from the mountain laurel. You have to get the ones that have fallen on the ground. They'll have dried out some and won't be so bitter to eat."

"You just eat them?"

"You should grind them and make a tea with another powder I have here," she said, withdrawing a small canister from a pocket in her shorts.

I had read somewhere that the Coahiltecans were enamored of the laurel bean. It seemed that Yvonne did have more than a passing interest in Indian lore.

She handed me a few beans and a pinch of the powder. "It just lifts your spirits a little," she said, putting her own share in her mouth. I did likewise, hoping that I could control whatever symptoms might result. My folks would never forgive me for getting obviously high around their friends.

We stood around talking for a few minutes. I began to feel a mild euphoria—nothing I couldn't handle.

"Well, how do you feel?" Yvonne asked.

"It's pleasant," I said. She took a step toward me, her eyes bright. She lifted a hand to my cheek and traced the line of my jaw and throat and breastbone. She took another step and wrapped her arms around my waist. Her breasts almost touched mine. I wasn't sure how to respond, so I let her continue caressing me. I had never been attracted to a woman before, but for some reason I wasn't at all surprised to find that I was attracted to her.

I realized that someone had been calling my name for several seconds. "Excuse me, Yvonne," I said, pushing her away. "I think I hear Mother calling me."

"She just wants to stop us from having fun," Yvonne said, pulling me to her again. "Come on, let's go for a midnight swim in the springs. . . ."

I shook my head, but Yvonne wouldn't let go. She seemed immensely strong. "Please, Yvonne, I'm sure that Mother doesn't want anything important."

"She'll poison you against me, I know it," Yvonne said through clenched teeth.

"Look, I'll come back as soon as I've finished with her. I mean it. Whatever she might say, she can't keep me from doing what I want to do."

"Do you mean that? Do you promise you'll come back to me?"

I assured her I'd find her later, and she let me go. I walked to the parking lot, where I saw Mother sitting in her car, just as I had found her earlier that day. I realized the pavilion was not the ideal vacation spot for her; it lacked the privacy she needed to throw one of her unholy tantrums.

"Mom, are you okay?" I asked as I walked up to the car.

"No, I am not okay." Her voice cracked as she spoke. I braced myself for another round of tears.

I poked my head through the window. "Want to tell me what's wrong?" She might have seen me and Yvonne together, but we were several yards into the thicket when she called.

"It's that woman, that friend of yours."

"I thought you were over all that. You said nothing happened."

"Did you see her dancing with your father earlier? Did you see how close they got?"

"Mother," I began slowly, hoping I could pick the right words, "I haven't noticed them even speaking to each other. I know I've had a few drinks by now, but I seem to recall Yvonne has spent most of the evening with me."

"Yeah, that's kind of funny, too. I do believe she'd do anything, anywhere, with anybody. I do believe it."

"Come off your high horse, Mother. You're just attacking her because Dad's been a heel all week. It's Dad you should be confronting right now, not me or Yvonne." I straightened up and stood away from the car, wishing my head didn't feel so heavy.

"I shouldn't have to tell your dad how to behave. You can't tell me that woman is not after my husband," she said fiercely. "She didn't have to dance with him tonight, knowing how I feel."

"Oh, sure, the whole world revolves around you. Everyone's bound to know how you feel since you'd never dream of not telling them how miserable you are. You'd never miss a chance to wreck other people's good time." Yvonne's herbs had taken away all of my patience and most of my good sense.

"Why are you scolding me, Karen? I haven't done anything to hurt anyone. You're shouting at me when I'm the one who's been sinned against."

I couldn't stand the whining in her voice. "Nobody's done anything to you, Mother, except come running whenever you've called. I've had enough of your histrionics for one day."

"My, haven't we learned some big words in the college education I paid for."

"You paid for it? I think it was Daddy's name on the checks." I felt as though I'd just turned up the volume on some bad music; I couldn't stop the playback even if the switch was in my hand.

"Yes, I paid for it, daughter. Paid for it dearly. And Yvonne's going to make me pay out some more. She's trying to take *my* place in *my* family."

"Why are you so paranoid about someone who couldn't have less interest in you or your stodgy husband?" I found myself taking her seriously, even though I knew she'd say anything to make me keep miserable company with her.

"One day, Karen, you'll know what it feels like to have your husband eyeing other women." She leaned against the steering wheel and cradled her head in her arms.

"Even if that happens, Mother, I wouldn't live in fear of it for the rest of my life. Is that why my real father left you? Because he found someone who was easier to live with?" Mother sat up and turned angrily to face me. "I can almost believe it. And you've kept him from seeing me because you're a spiteful old bitch."

"You ungrateful little . . ." She was trying hard to control her tongue. "Would you really like to know why he never came back after I left him? Only because he knew I'd kill him if he ever came near you again."

"What do you mean, 'I left him'? You always said that he left you." I couldn't believe that she had lied to me about something so important.

"Karen, I left Vance because of what he was doing to you."

"What was he doing?" I felt nauseated and confused. She was going to tell me why I had the sick dreams about sex. I hugged myself in the warm night. I knew what she was going to say.

"He was molesting you."

I don't know how much time passed before I could bring myself to speak. "And you didn't leave him when you found out." It wasn't a question.

"No, I tried to stop him. I tried to be around whenever he was home." Mother reached out and grabbed my hand, but I wrenched it away. "I was working nights and we couldn't afford a sitter. I was only nineteen. I didn't know how I'd get along without him."

"This is great news, Mom. After you found out, how long did you stay with him?"

"Fourteen months. Then I met Bob and he gave me the courage to leave Vance, even though I knew I should have stuck with him. I could have kept him under control. I could have made him leave you alone, and then we'd have been happy together."

Her words hit me like the kick from an angry mule. "How could I have been happy when I've never meant anything to you? I was just a little nuisance who got in the way of your men." I kicked the car door with all the force I could muster. Let her explain the dent to her precious Bob. If the window had been rolled up, I would have put my fist through it.

"I guess you have a right to do anything you like, Karen," she said, her prim expression back on her face. "But you've got to know that I did what I thought was best for you." She turned to face the wheel as if she was going to drive off. "I thought I could keep Vance under control, but now look what he's done to you." She gave me a sidelong glance. "He scarred you so bad,

206

you can't tell wrong from right. I saw you and Yvonne off in the bushes, you know. Worse than dogs. At least they behave according to nature."

"How dare you try to excuse yourself by reproaching me! Do you know how much you've cost me, Mother? Do you?" I was shouting. "I wake up in a sweat most nights. I can't make love to a man for fear of the nightmares that might punish me later. My own husband has left me. But you've been too self-obsessed to notice that, haven't you? Haven't you?" I realized that I had opened the car door, that I was clutching the collar of her blouse. I threw her back against the seat and ran into the thicket, not knowing where I was headed, not certain of anything but my desire to get as far away from her as I could. Mesquite thorn tore at my clothes and hair, but I kept on running in the night—running as though I'd never stop.

I found myself at the river. She was a beautiful python, sleeping in the silver light. Her smell was rich with dying moss and rotting leaves. I stopped running and walked along the bank, feeling nothing.

I came to the big live oak tree and found Yvonne kneeling before the shrine. I stumbled toward her, wanting her comfort, but I stopped abruptly. The statue was different somehow. It no longer had the Madonna's feminine smile; instead, her face was frowning and mannish. A carved hand pointed to her unfettered heart—the ring of thorns was no longer there.

Yvonne stood up and approached me, but I could not take my eyes from the shrine. "The Virgin was put here to warn against Ticanau," I said.

"Yes. Put here by jealous fools. They despised Ticanau because she can bathe us in every kind of love, every kind. But I have freed her." Yvonne took my hand, her rough, calloused skin rasping on mine. "Your mother did a terrible thing, leaving her husband and taking his little beauty away."

Yvonne's soft accent had changed. Her voice was

husky with emotion. She gave me a gourd full of sweet juice that trickled down my chin as I drank. She led me into the mists that swirled above the hot springs. We splashed and played in the albuminous light, making tiny pearls of water leap in the air. Like the statue, Yvonne looked neither male nor female. She was a flawless young man-woman blurred by water and mist.

She pulled me from the river and we lay on the bank. There Yvonne began to rock me in her arms, in a warm cocoon of limbs and belly. And there I witnessed the change in her, though I could not ask her why or how she changed. I could not form a single word in my mind or in my mouth. My thoughts were frozen, like rodents staring into the headlights of oncoming cars. All I could do was babble like a baby. Her flesh was molten lava flowing around me and hardening into a new shape. Her muscles became lean and solid. I lifted my hands and smoothed her breasts away.

I babbled my delight at this flesh in my hands, this clay doll that changed shape to suit my desires. *I'm gonna give you a brand new toy.* Half-words jumbled in my mind and I moved my lips in gurgles from my own private language. *Talk properly,* said a deep voice in my head, talk properly but keep quiet. This will be our little secret.

I felt breath on my neck and a hand gripping and feeling the weight of my breasts. *You better mind me, now.* Yvonne's hands were gently amorous at first, then probing and persistent. *Be still, sit up straight, or I'll turn you over my knee.* She began to knead my flesh, to pinch my belly and buttocks. *Oh, how you've grown.* I lay staring up at Yvonne, unable to save myself, even if I wanted to. The shadows on her face had a new shape and contour—hard masculine lines. *He* knelt over me and took my hand, and made my fingers curl around something familiar but incomprehensible. Now you're gonna know what big girls do.

Go away, please. I said it in baby talk. I dragged myself a few inches up the bank and felt his nails clawing at my backside, stripping away the river mud. I can't play right now. Besides, you always go back to Mama. "Welcome me, Karen," he whispered. I remember Karen. She's a good girl, studies hard, won't have anything to do with boys. Karen won't date or stay out all night. She was as true as true until loneliness made her forget her promise.

I'm sorry, Daddy. I put my hand back between his thighs. I can be good, I promise. I'll never, ever do that again. He pulled my head down into his lap. I felt the warmth and smells of Yvonne and the new smells of the man who stroked my hair. I could hear the urging of the night, the muttering of the springs, the persuasion in his voice. I took him eagerly in my mouth, like a greedy, sucking babe, desire pounding in my skull. He held me up close to him, held me gently for a moment, like a mother. There, there now. Are you really mine forever?

I climbed on top of him. He was in me, penetrating my body, mind, and heart. I stared into his eyes, so like mine. I take after him—that's what they always said. I let myself be rocked in that cradle of perfect love. Daddy. You've come back.

I could not concentrate on the work before me, a plan for popularizing my dissertation. Instead, I gazed out the window and watched two squirrels squabbling over a piece of bread. A Siberian husky, looking miserable and defeated in the heat, ambled over to them. The squirrels ignored him until his muzzle was inches from their food, then raced up a pecan tree, leaving the dog to gaze longingly at the branches. A student came out of the building opposite my office and whistled to the husky. Seeing his owner, the dog wagged his tail and trotted after his friend.

There were few people on the concourse. I had nothing to stare at but my reflection in the window. Everyone had called it rape. My mother, who had found me alone and naked on the riverbank, had used the word without hesitation. My shrink never actually said "rape" during my year of therapy, but she had a sweetly euphonic way of saying the same thing. I didn't argue with her or with Mother. I was too lost in my own anguish to dispute their explanations.

At least the shrink got me an extension on my dissertation, and I was awarded my PhD. The public would probably adore the popularized version I was working on now, an academic's praise of Native American mysticism. But I wasn't starting this work because I wanted fame. The real reason was that I no longer had an academic's detachment. This was the only work left that I was fit to do.

And I couldn't concentrate on even this simple task. The shrink reckoned that I'd always be happier with a woman—she was certainly convinced that I'd be miserable with a man—but I couldn't imagine that anyone would measure up to my ideal. I wanted the perfect lover, the perfect mother and father, the ideal best friend, all rolled into one. I wanted a beautiful version of myself, tall and lean, someone who wouldn't abandon me the way Vance had done. The night before, I'd refused the advances of a woman colleague, realizing that I'd never let myself love again.

I gave up on the proposal and walked out to my Chevy. I headed for the city limits, planning nothing more than a therapeutic highway cruise, but I wasn't surprised when I found myself pumping gas at a convenience store five miles from the pavilion. I drove down the dusty track and parked my car in the parking lot. The grass and live oaks were wilting in the sun. The sprinklers on top of the bungalows were motionless, and the vines were dead. For once, the pavilion looked like the pair of shabby tin huts that it really was. I walked along the riverbank, noticing that the water was even deeper and broader than last year. While the grasses dried to powder, the river became more powerful, more enduring.

The old live oak was still verdant and the branches were almost touching the ground. I had to crawl on my hands and knees to enter the dome of leaves. There was a new shrine, cut from cedar, standing half a foot taller than me. His man-woman face was freshly oiled, and flowers lay at his feet. They thought my anguish was caused by rape; in truth, it was caused by his desertion. *Daddy, how could you leave me?* I knelt before the statue and kissed his scented feet. Then I stood up to hug him. I wrapped my arms around his neck and pressed my soft cheek into his hard one. I held the oiled man as tightly as I could, until I felt movement in the smooth, carved wood.

Afterword

Until I read Lisa Tuttle's *Nest of Nightmares* I thought of modern horror as an intractably male genre. This opinion was reinforced by the "splatterpunk" I had read. Though I approve of the genre's sleaziness (out of the drawing rooms and into the streets), it seems to me that male-defined sleaze constantly endorses the sex-equals-violence mythology; it's the stuff beloved of little, uncivilized boys. But here was a writer showing that horror did have more range than the juvenile gross-out or the polite ghost story would admit. Still, I wasn't quite convinced. Surely there's a better way than horror to talk about female experience, or so I thought.

And then I found myself losing control of this ordinary tale of a woman's reaction to her parents' disintegrating marriage. The plot kept skewing under the influence of something monstrous—something elusive, and indefinable. I decided that the only way to flush this demon out of the margins and onto the page was to actually put a monster into the story and then see what happened. "Monsters!" my good sense objected. I had thought science fiction was my artistic habitat, but this demon, as I vaguely recognized in the beginning, scoffs at the conceits of science and laughs at puny technology. So I took a risk and used a device from the horror genre to talk about this nameless beast who, once acknowledged, was only too glad to tell me that he was about desire and incest, and the helplessness of us all in the face of our personal histories. I have the highest opinion of the horror genre now. What better way to give material substance to the unnamed terrors in the female mind?

Sherry Coldsmith

THE DREAM

Dyan Sheldon

This is the dream. She wakes up screaming. The covers are twisted around her legs, holding her like hands. The room is lightless. There is no sound. The clock isn't ticking. Her brothers aren't whispering or snoring across the hallway. Her mother isn't hurrying up the stairs. There is only her screaming. She screams and screams. Screams and screams. But the door doesn't open. The door doesn't open, letting in the rest of the house: the lamp with the pink shade on the small table outside her room, the narrow green rug, the flowered wallpaper, the painting of a woman walking by a lake, and, downstairs, the carpet from Persia, the polished tables, the maroon sofa, the ottoman she sits on when her mother reads to her, the figurines on the mantel—the sweet-faced ballerina whose left foot is chipped and the smiling young man—her father reading in his armchair, her grandmother by the fire, talking to the shadows, the old black dog curled up at her feet. There are no sounds. No movements. Her mother doesn't come. She screams and screams.

This dream is nothing like the other bad dreams Megan sometimes has—the nightmares. Nightmares about monsters hiding under her bed, or about being stolen by gypsies or witches, or about being carried up into the sky in the claws of a gigantic vulture. Nothing like the spider dream or the tiger dream or the dream where she is lost and can't find her way back home. When she has those dreams, she really does wake up screaming, shaking and crying, holding on to the quilt. When she wakes up from those dreams, she can still see the bright red eyes of the monster or the tiger's sharp smile, feel the heat, the touch of a long rough tongue. But even though her eyes are shut and she is crying and calling out, even though, she always knows that her mother is running up the stairs, always knows that in a few seconds the door will open and the light will rush in from the hallway, and her mother will be sitting on the bed with her, taking her in her arms, saying, "There, there, darling, it's all right, it's all right, it was only a bad dream." After she's calmed down, her mother always makes her a cup of tea and stays with her until she falls back to sleep. Sometimes—after the spider dream and after the dream about getting lost—Megan's mother takes her into her bed, where even the sheets smell like her and it is possible, if Megan barely breathes, to hear her mother's heartbeat. "It was because we saw that poster about the circus," her mother will say the next morning as she's fixing the breakfast, talking over her shoulder as she works at the stove. "It was because you ate that piece of cake before bedtime, Megan," her mother will say, wiping her hands on her apron, setting Megan's bowl in front of her with a solid thump. "It was too heavy for so late." "It's the boys always teasing you, Meg. They think they're funny, your brothers. You just pay them no attention." After one of those nightmares, her mother will let her have toast and hot milk with sugar as a special treat. "It's those stories your father's always telling you," her

215

mother will say. "It's because the milkman's horse frightened you." "It's the full moon."

"All the girls in our family have bad dreams," says her grandmother, breaking her toast into her tea because of her teeth, because she doesn't have any teeth—no teeth, no meat on her bones, thin white hair. "Did I ever tell you how I used to scream the house down? Screamed it down. And my sister, Ellie, Ellie had the second sight." Megan's grandmother is a tiny doll of a woman always dressed in black or navy blue, all wrinkles and veins, her ankles swollen, her fingers misshapen. There is always something trickling (food or spittle, a milky line of tea) from the corner of her mouth. Megan has to smile when her grandmother talks about being a girl, as if she ever was, but her mother just says, "Oh, for heaven's sake, Ma, don't start scaring the child more."

She is in a room. She is in a room and she is all alone. So alone that she can hear the tap dripping in the kitchen, low voices next door, someone laughing outside. She is in the front room, but it isn't the front room, not really. If she didn't know it was the front room, she would think it was some other room, in a place she's never been. Most of the furniture is gone—her father's chair, the large china lamp and the brass one with the satin shade that her mother sits under when she knits, the pie-top tables, and the writing desk—and instead of the rug from Persia there is a faded gray carpet on the floor; instead of the lace curtains, yellowing net. The room smells of cats. In places, the dingy paper peels from the walls. The room is dark, or perhaps not dark really, not so dark that she can't see—she can see the floor, the windows, the walls, the bed in the corner where the bookshelves should be—but everything is dim, drained of colour, faded as an old photograph. She is standing at the window, looking out at the street. And the street, too, is different. Not just because the dairy across the road now has tables of vegetables outside, or because the elm tree is gone from in front of the house, but because it seems so far away. There are the houses and the shops, people walking by—jostling school-children, swaggering young men, giggling girls, busy adults with places to go and things to do—hurrying, pushing their babies or looking at their watches or carrying their groceries, stopping to talk to one another, smiling and laughing, nodding heads, shaking hands, embracing in the moment of good-bye. But she can't hear them, somehow, can't touch them, watches them as though they're in a film, up there on the screen in another world, unaware that she is standing at the window, so close her breath mists the surface. It's a dream, she tells herself in the dream. That's the way of dreams—everything the same but different, everything familiar but changed. In dreams you see people you know and they don't recognize you, you recognize people you know but they don't look the same. In dreams you are always by yourself. She stands at the window, unsure of the season or the time of day, looking at the flat sky for signs of rain. Trapped behind the glass like a ghost trapped by time.

Her brothers like to scare her. Boys will be boys, her mother always says. Her brothers think it's funny, the way she always falls for their tricks, the way she starts and drops the cup she was carrying, plops on the floor with her doll tight in her arms and tears down her cheeks. "Ooooooh, Megan Coleman," a wobbly, screechy voice will call from underneath the stairs. "Ooooooh, I'm going to get you, Megan, I'm going to get you, get you . . ." jumping out with a scream. "Watch out, Megan," one of them will say to her over supper, the others grinning at each other, passing secret looks, "I saw a monster in the garden last night, and he was looking for you. He was staring up at the windows, looking for your room," and then they laugh, choking on their food, until her father says in his quiet voice, "That's enough of that now." They leave things in her

bed—dead spiders and clumps of horsehair, wet socks—
they blindfold her and hide. But it's only a game. "It's
only a game, Megan," they say, laughing, hugging her,
picking her up in their strong, sure arms. "We're only
teasing you, you know." And then one of them will give
her a sweet, or take her to the park, or fix a broken toy,
or play with her for hours while the afternoon turns dark
outside and the smells of supper being cooked begin to
fill the house. And they watch out for her. They won't
let anyone else scare her. When she walks down the
street with her brothers she never feels frightened of
dogs, or traffic, or the rough boys who stand together
in little clumps, eyeing everybody who passes, liquor on
their breath and nothing in their eyes. When she is with
her brothers she doesn't get confused, never worries
about getting lost or being knocked over, about people
yelling at her, what are you doing? get out of the way,
what did you want? why are you here? can't you remember what you want? Not like when she's on her own.

She doesn't want to go out. She knows that she has
to go out—there is something she needs out there, something for which she must walk down the nine steps of
the front stoop and out on the pavement, something for
which she must cross at the corner. She lets the curtain
fall back in place. Maybe it isn't that she has to go out
to get something, but simply that she has to get out. Get
out of this room. She looks over her shoulder. The walls
are moving in. She sees them move. She's sure she sees
them move. An inch at a time. A half an inch. Not every
minute—but every few minutes. She turns away, turns
back quickly. Minute after minute, hour after hour, an
inch or a half an inch, maybe even less. That's why I
have to get out, she tells herself, the room is shrinking,
the walls are closing in. She looks around for the door,
but the door isn't there. Where the door should be is
only wall. There is no way out to the hall with the
frosted entrance door and the mirror and the hatstand
and the banister so polished that it shines. Where is the

door? She can't leave the room. Who could have moved the door? I'll wake up soon, she says out loud, I'll wake up soon. She looks over her shoulder. The walls move in.

Her mother says she thinks the problem is that Megan spends too much time in the house. "The boys are so much older," her mother tells her grandmother, "she's always on her own, amusing herself. I'm sure it's made her imagination overactive." Megan's grandmother takes a bit of the pastry Megan's mother is rolling and pops it in her mouth. Megan's grandmother used to make the best apple pie in the world, but now her hands hurt too much to roll the crust or peel the fruit, so she sits at the table, saying things like "I never liked it too thin," "You need a bit of lemon and a little more cinnamon, Eleanore," "I always brushed the top with cream." "All the girls in my family had a good imagination," says Megan's grandmother. "She gets it from me."

Megan and her mother go out together. If they are going to the shops, Megan's mother wears her blue coat with the silver butterfly pin and a blue hat with a single feather, and over her arm she carries the basket. If they are going visiting, Megan wears one of her best dresses and a ribbon in her hair. They walk quickly, "briskly," her mother calls it, her mother's footsteps sounding like someone counting, one two one two one two, Megan giving a little skip every few steps just to keep up, down to the end and cross at the corner, look where you're going, don't dally, don't run ahead, don't drag your feet, don't step on a crack. Her mother walks with her back straight and her head up, chatting as they go along, did you see that puppy? what's that in the window? what sort of tree is that? maybe we'll have ginger cake for tea. Her mother knows everyone. The men touch their hats, the women nod. Good morning, Mrs. Coleman. Good afternoon, Mrs. Coleman. Nice day. Fine weather. How's the family, then? I'm going your way, let me help you with your things. And Megan, they say, how you're growing, how pretty you look, I think I've got something in my pocket for you.

She is standing at the end of a long, long street. It must be their street. It must be their street, because here she stands, outside the house, holding on to the iron railing and staring at the number on the transom. It is her house, but the door has been painted red and the glass etched with flowers has been replaced with plain. There is something wrong with the road itself as well. Something she can't quite put her finger on, and some of the houses that line it have changed colour or shape, seem smaller somehow, and one or two have disappeared, the Begleys' and the Littlejohns', but there is their house, still with the knocker Uncle John brought back from Italy. She wants to go back inside. There are dogs on the street, large dogs, running free, large young men behind them, dangling chains. Go back inside, she says to herself, go back inside. Her heart is pounding. That's all she can hear—not the traffic, or the passersby, or the birds in the trees—just the pounding of her own heart. But she has to get down to the end, to the end of the street. There is some reason why it is very important that she reaches the end, gets down to the corner, but she doesn't know now what it is. Can't remember. She knew it before, though; she's sure of that, she knew it before. She tries to concentrate. She says to herself, Think, think, why did you come outside? She looks around. It is a cold day, bright and sunny, and the street is crowded. But there is no one she recognizes. Face after face. No one she knows. A colour of eye, a wave of hair, a shape of nose, a walk, a smile that makes her catch her breath, makes her look again. Isn't that? could it be? surely that's . . . But then the person turns or comes closer—and it's always someone else, always someone she doesn't know. The street is full of people, but when she raises her hand no one sees her. When she calls out, "Excuse me, excuse me," no one hears her. No one stops to tell her why she has to get to the end of the road. A voice in her head screams, *Why do I have to get to the end of the road? Just tell me that, why do I have to get to the end of the road?* Her heart pounds. There must be a hundred people on the street—two hundred eyes, not one smile. And she. They know, they must know—she knows they know—but they won't look at her, they won't tell her. No one will help her. She starts to walk. One step and then another step, one step and then another step, one step and then one step more. But when she finally stops, breathless, she is no closer to the end, it is still in the distance, so far she can't see it. One step and then another step, one step and then another, willing her feet to walk, her body to move. But when she looks up again she is still near the house. Like walking in treacle. Walking in a dream. Left foot, she thinks, right foot, left foot, right foot, everyone else hurrying by, running, shoving her out of the way, bikes flying past, just keep going, she tells herself, just keep going, one step and then another step, one step and then another step. Slow-motion dream. She must step from the kerb. Into traffic. Cars speeding, horns shouting, brakes sharp and shrill. She stands there. The road is feet beneath her. Miles. She is balanced on the edge of a cliff and the ground is miles away. She stands there. Forward? Backward? Left? Right? Voices are screaming at her. Move. Move. Move. People push past her. Move. Move. Get out of the way. And she stands there. Trembling. Stands there. Shaking. Stands there, and stands there, and stands . . .

She wakes up in her bed. Sunlight bursts through the window, making the coverlet look as white as the summer clouds that drift by outside, making the tiny pink roses on the wallpaper as bright as the roses in the garden. She is warm in the sunlight, safe in her bed, her head against the pillowcase her grandmother embroidered for her with her stiff old hands, violets and honeysuckle, her name in blue thread, her arm around her worn stuffed bear. She can hear the boys laughing across the hallway. "Last one up's a lazybones," they shout through her door. "Hurry up! Hurry up! It's the picnic today." She can hear her mother in the kitchen, smell apple pie. The milkman whistles as he walks up the path, and her mother calls up the stairs, "Megan, Megan, you're not going to stay in bed all day, are you? You're not going to stay in bed all day?" And she thinks about the picnic, about the boat ride on the river, about running through the field with her brothers, the sky so blue and the trees so green and she behind the others, wait for me, wait for me, but laughing, breathless and laughing, her mother standing up with a hand to shield her eyes, watching that they don't go too far, "You watch out for your sister, you hear me?" A child again, her brothers still alive, still children, her mother still living, still young, and she, with the sunlight on her and the day just waiting to befriend her, to surprise her and wrap her in wonders, she so happy with life, so far from death.

And that is the dream.

Afterword

With thought came fear. Not the normal animal fear of death and destruction, but real fear. Fear as an entity; fear as a constant companion. Picture this. A solitary creature, a man, say, sits on a hillside in the night. He's just become a thinker. Wowee, he said to himself only a day or two ago, this is pretty neat. He used to trudge around like all the other animals, day in and day out, trying to find something to eat, trying to stay warm and dry, trying to keep out of the way of his enemies. Boy, was he boring. He never noticed how beautiful the sunsets are, never understood the poetry in a bluebell or a hummingbird, never built anything, or planted anything. He just went along with whatever happened. And now here he is, torn between discovering fire and devising a wheel. Now here he is, his head filled with ideas, his heart filled with emotion. Soon he will be able to tailor a suit, paint a picture, write a love song, invent the rack. What power, he thinks, what control. The man looks up. Above him is an enormous sky, chipped with stars and a slice of moon. Below him is the desert, or the jungle, or the prairie, stretching to forever. The man sits on his hill, listening to the howls and hoots and sighs of the night. Thinking. And then he realizes that he is afraid. Scared. Terrified. Not of the dangers of the animals lurking around him, and not of the things that might fall from above. No, it is something more sinister, something that can't be fought or diverted. He sits on his hill, feeling all alone. All alone in the middle of nothing. He was always all alone in the middle of nothing, of course, but he didn't know that before. And now he does. Now that he can think, he wants meaning; reassurance. He doesn't want to consider the possibility that his life might be all for nothing. He doesn't want to die. He doesn't want to be hurt by anything. He certainly doesn't want to be alone. He sits on his hill, and for the first time it occurs to him that there are worse things than hunger, thirst, or pain. Worse things, even, than death. That is fear. That is the fear whose voice can be heard whispering above the roar of our machines and our cities and our own strong voices as we congratulate ourselves on how far we've come, how much we've achieved. That is the fear who trots along beside us as we go about our busy, busy lives. We tame wildernesses, bring water to the desert, walk among the stars. But we still hear that voice. "I'm here," it says, startling you as you brush your teeth or try on a new pair of shoes. "Don't think I'm not." "Yoo-hoo," it calls as you board the plane or wait for the bus, "don't forget me." As if we could.

For me, that is the fear that horror is all about.

Dyan Sheldon

LISTENING

Melissa Mia Hall

The whispering began in a restaurant. Irene had been peeling shrimp. She dipped the naked shrimp in cajun-spiced red sauce and bit into it as she listened. She figured it originated from a nearby table where a couple had been holding hands over a bread basket.

Something about the stock market. That wasn't unusual. Bloody Monday had made waves all around town. She fingered her new earring with her clean hand, well, semiclean. She wiped her hand again. She always ordered the peel-and-eat shrimp because they were cheaper. And it was also fun to peel them. Most of her friends thought it was a peculiar fetish. Pinching off the shell with precise delicacy gave Irene a feeling of power. She loved shrimp. Loved it.

Love. Whispering something about love? That made more sense. She chanced a quick look at the couple. They were gone. Disconcerted, Irene glanced down at her messy plate.

The whispering said, "Irene—"

She glanced around for the owner of the sibilant

voice. The waiter smiled at her and started to come over, pad in hand. She shook her head. She wasn't ready to leave.

"Irene, the stock market is a disaster and the man you love is considering suicide."

That was a horrible thing to think. John wouldn't do that. But he had invested heavily. Still, the worst was over. The market was just correcting itself. Besides, Johnny wasn't a suicidal person. She motioned for the waiter to come over. He dashed to her side, tore off the bill, smiled, and left discreetly.

"Irene, go to his apartment."

In the middle of the day? A warm blush flooded her features, the heat making her perspire. She ran out of the restaurant, didn't even wait for her change. The waiter would certainly do a double take at his tip. She didn't care. The street swallowed her whole. The only thing that mattered was getting to Johnny, saving Johnny. She stood in the middle of the street; she'd give her life for a taxi. Almost. She swayed dangerously, and a man unloading newspapers laughed at her. She got a taxi, though.

Getting into John's apartment was like getting into Fort Knox. She kept thinking of piles of gold as she staggered through the halls and swam upstairs in the elevator. Trapped like a fish in olive oil, dying. The whispering kept on, a shade too low to really hear. It had to originate from inside her, from an overworked mind. Maybe she needed to go to a therapist. When she came to his door, it wasn't open. He'd answered her buzz, though. He was alive. Shakily, she used her key and pushed the door open. "Johnny-o-John? Baby, are you okay?"

He was sitting on the bed staring at a red necktie in his hands.

"No—" Irene screamed.

"I've always been a gambler, Irene, you know?" He smiled at her from a face ashen and pinched.

* * *

John was recuperating, doing rather well. He'd moved into her apartment and they had begun talking about getting married in the fall. He saw a therapist every week and he'd taken a leave of absence from the law firm. Everyone had been very understanding. Everything was going to turn out well. All was well. Very well. Irene kept her feet on the ground and her head down. Gravity would save them. But the whispering continued. Warnings of danger, disaster, pain. Whisperings. She told John a little bit about them.

Johnny was sprawled on the bed reading the *Wall Street Journal*.

"It sounds like a voice, a tiny voice. It tells me things that are going to happen or where they might happen, just things. So I can maybe help. Like, it told me about you and I got there in time to—well, you know—"

"Save me?" He turned a page carefully and looked up at her sleepily. His eyes were distant gray clouds. "Maybe if I had been less greedy? I don't know . . ." His long fingers traced figures on the newsprint.

"Aren't you listening to me?"

"Sure. Voices? You could talk to Henry about it. He doesn't mind voices. I hear them, too. You can't ignore them. Answer them. Sometimes it's like a party line and if you don't party hearty, you're all alone. I don't like to be alone. Remember that time after the mistake, when you almost had the baby and thank God you didn't—I mean, we were babies ourselves—I had moved in with what-was-her-name,—Brigitte—and she threw me out when she found out about you—and heard about *it*."

"The baby," Irene said softly. There was a fuzzy rumble in her ear. The earring jangled, a distant phone ringing. Pick it up, Irene. He's going to tell you he never loved her and the baby never existed.

"You know, I never loved her. I thought I did, and when you told me about it . . ."

"The baby."

"Yeah, it was like it never existed and Brigitte didn't

exist, but we did.'' His eyes moved across her face.
''It'd be all right.''

''What would be all right?'' Irene said impatiently.

The clouds drifted over her completely, enclosing her
in a tattered mist. ''Everything. Tell Henry.'' He
laughed suddenly and jingled the change in his pocket.
''I tell him everything.''

''I don't want to tell a stranger about this. He'd think
I was crazy.''

''So?'' He offered his arms to her like a glowing child.
A sharp smile crossed his lips, anger peeking out of joy.
She couldn't understand it. But she went to the bed and
allowed his arms to hold and comfort her. ''It's you,
Irene. We've all got voices in our heads.''

She wouldn't tell him any more about it. Anyway, she
was fresh from a shower and she hadn't heard anything
since yesterday, at work, when the voice said Cindy
Jenson was going to get fired. And she had been, five
minutes later, right in front of Irene's cubicle. She
could've prevented it. She could've said something imag-
inative and compassionate. Still, the firm needed someone brighter than Cindy, more clever, artistic. Cindy had
never belonged in advertising.

But she was kind. Her eyes had met Irene's over the
low cubicle wall. Silently, Cindy's moist eyes begged
her to do something. Irene had looked away guiltily. She
had touched her earring (she wore only one, feeling this
somehow protected her from something nameless,
unknown). She had searched her desk for a paper clip.
The earring had trembled in the still air. While Cindy
had cleaned out her desk.

The earring. Irene touched it again. She'd been wearing this particular earring constantly. She took it out of
her ear and stared at it. The woman in the shop said it
came from a rattler. Irene frowned. Hannah Smith had
told her she didn't agree. Hannah was from Texas, a
rancher's daughter. She'd said it was too white and too
musical. Besides, it glowed in the dark. Hannah worked
in accounting. Hannah said she'd been taken. ''That

there earring is a pure-d fake," she'd said. "But I like it," Irene had said wistfully. "I do, too," Hannah had said, smiling.

So she'd kept on wearing it. Her pride in the earring had somewhat diminished, but the sweet whisper it made when the wind caught it comforted her.

Maybe it was the earring that talked to her, told her stuff and all. Her hand closed over the earring gently. Mostly it told her unhappy things so she could make them happy. Warnings. After all, she had saved John's life. She'd avoided a wreck on Broadway. She'd called the police on a rapist, prevented a robbery. Those were the big things. Little things had included warnings about the cleaner who had shortchanged her and the fish place with the rotten fish she'd never go to again. So many providential whisperings. It wasn't a bad thing. Not at all.

Irene yawned. The cold white January light framed her dark hair. She wanted to close the blinds, but John wouldn't let her. She hated how the light picked out the dark circles beneath her eyes. John looked up from his desk where he'd been playing with figures. "Why are you so tired?"

"I'm not sleeping." She thought it had been the earring's fault—too much talk wears anyone down. She had taken the earring out last night. She should've slept peacefully. They'd even made love. But afterward, she had stared at the ceiling while time melted away. "I think I drank too much coffee last night."

John shook his head. "It's New York City. It's worn me out, too. Let's move. I'd like to go back to New Orleans. Is that nuts?"

"You can't make as much money as you do here," Irene said, knowing that was his usual excuse for staying on here, but that deep down it was because her family lived here and she *wanted* to live here.

"You might like it. Change is good for the soul. Life is change."

"I liked it when we went to Mardi Gras. It was fun. I guess we could check it out," Irene said, her voice suddenly high and childlike. She shivered, fresh from a shower. She tugged nervously at her pink towel. She needed the earring.

"You really would consider a move—for me?" Johnny's eyes went round and bright like white marbles. He started for the phone excitedly. "I've got to call Billy and Crawdad."

"Have you already talked to them?" It wasn't on top of the chest of drawers. It wasn't in the bathroom, she was sure of that. She'd wiped the vanity top clean with her washcloth. Billy and Crawdad. The ones who thought cocaine was fun. The ones who never got addicted but were oh-so-concerned when their friends did. "We're behind you one hundred percent, bubba. Man, we're so sorry, Irene. He just lost control, honey." Irene shut her eyes. Their voices were like molasses. John had a bad habit of pouring molasses over his french fries.

"They've got this firm down there, just them two, and they want me to throw in my hat." John's voice had lost its New York edge. His roots. His boots. They stood in a corner of their bedroom all of the time, polished and strong. "I said I had to talk to you."

Where had she put it? She rooted around in her jewelry box, the air like ice on her bare back.

"They don't do drugs anymore—that was a hundred years ago, honey."

"I didn't say they did."

"We were in college, well, just out, and you do dumb things then." He'd begun dialing a familiar number. He didn't have to look it up. He had it memorized.

She found the earring. Her hand closed on it tightly. She turned and went to him. He spoke in a foreign language. With his free hand he reached out and fondled the breast that had slipped out of the towel. She pulled away, nervous and anxious. It was all happening too fast, like he'd planned it, knowing she'd say yes. Itchy bumps popped out along her hairline. Her skin always responded to stress. His free hand pulled the towel away, then pulled her down on his lap. He was laughing at something Crawdad had said. They were making plans, New York slipping into the Atlantic Ocean. The gulf shrimp was fabulous. "Johnny-o—" she whispered. He nodded and put his free hand between her legs. Irene trembled. "I'm scared," she said. He wasn't listening.

John left first, to find them a place, to get settled in the new job. Irene had to give notice at work, but hadn't, not yet. She kept waiting to hear from John. Life was relatively smooth. She'd begun packing their things slowly, carefully, folding each piece of clothing with a vague reverence. She was especially partial to folding sweaters. She also enjoyed going through the albums. She would pack the things in the kitchen last.

The earring hadn't told her anything for a long while now. She had left it at work in the desk for a month. But with Valentine's Day coming up, she had found it and put it on with a hopeful smile on her face. And she wore it now, on Valentine's night, expecting him to call.

The phone jangled. She picked up the receiver and listened. She could hardly hear him over all the noise. He was calling from one of those bars off Bourbon Street. A smoky saxophone curled around a throbbing drumbeat. Too loud—she couldn't hear him. But she could hear the earring. "He's going to drop you, Irene. He's going to say it's all over, he hasn't found anyone else but it's a dead-end street or it's a street he just doesn't want to travel anymore." And then Johnny-o proceeded to say exactly that and then some. Irene told him to shut up and call back when he was sober.

She went back to the woman who'd sold her the earring.

"Excuse me, ma'am, but I know this is not an authentic rattler earring—" Irene said to her vehement protestations. The woman's face flushed salmon pink and she puffed her cheeks out indignantly. But Irene had a way about her. She wasn't the sort to put up with lies.

The woman looked away guiltily. "Have a guy in the Village who does them for me," she said softly.

"I can't hear you—" Irene said. The earring told her to get a name. "What's this guy's name?"

"Bruce Thompson," the woman said flatly. She stared at Irene as if she'd fallen into a trance. "I'll get you his card." She fumbled in the cash register and pulled out a dog-eared card. She flipped it toward Irene. "You do know this shop does not give cash refunds on sale merchandise."

Irene couldn't recall it being on sale. "I didn't say I wanted a refund."

"It's art, fine art," the woman grumbled. "People don't understand art." She slammed the register and glanced away at another customer.

"Thanks," Irene said, throat tight and hands sweaty with expectation.

"You'll like him," the earring said loudly. Irene looked around, wondering if anyone else could hear the voice. The woman and the other customer looked at her with uncommon blankness. Irene rushed out of the dusty shop.

Bruce Thompson huddled under a bright light, poking and prodding a piece of green metal. "Come in, the door's open." He wore a black T-shirt and a silver necklace. His hair was startling white and his eyes a brilliant green. "I dye it." He pointed at his hair. "Last week it was blue and I got tired of it." He didn't seem surprised to see Irene. He wore an earring like hers, only it was black. "Grab a chair."

Irene fell into an overstuffed armchair. The springs had given out. She kept sinking down till her knees stuck up like knife points under her full black skirt.

"You've come to complain about my earring. What's wrong—is it too loud?"

"Loud?" The earring laughed gently and told her he was insane but harmless.

"Hey, I'm a genius, but nobody's perfect."

He stared at her while she stared at his apartment crammed full of computer parts, aluminum foil cones, and odd bits of furniture wrapped in cling film. Of course he was crazy. The remains of several meals sat on table-tops and chairs. A thin cat worked on a tuna-fish can in a corner.

Bruce Thompson continued to prod the metal plate with a stainless-steel fork. "This came from Venus. It's possibly the answer I've been looking for that will perfect my masterpiece."

Irene felt ridiculous. She reached for her purse.

The earring told her not to leave. Her mouth was dry, but she had to ask him how it worked. "What does my earring do, exactly?"

He picked up a small foil cone and held the narrow end to his ear. "Like that."

Irene felt herself sink farther into the depths of the brown chair. Brown and gray tweed. She picked at the material. Bruce scratched his stubbly chin. "Mr. Thompson, can you make it stop?" she said.

His mouth formed an O as he contemplated such an absurd idea. He whistled. A dachsund arrived. "Kiley, fetch." The dog disappeared and reappeared with a torn sock in his mouth. He deposited it gravely at Irene's feet and disappeared again. "He's learning," Bruce said happily. Irene wanted to die. "Stop it? Nothing stops, exactly. You can't hear what you don't already know. Stop it? If you don't want to hear, take it off." Bruce leaned forward conspiratorially. "Remember van Gogh? Remember when he cut his ear off—there you have it!" He clapped his hands and leaned back, pleased with himself.

Irene's earring was deathly silent. She felt stuffy, feverish. "My earring always seems to warn me about bad things, sad things—why not happy things?"

"Oh, I'm sorry. Are you sure you're not getting it

confused? Maybe you shouldn't listen all the time." His chair squeaked as he got out of it and bent over Irene. He was like a warped giant and his ears were like seashells, they were so big. And his hands were big, too, like that big white hand on those TV commercials. Irene felt faint and very small. He touched her earring gently. His own swung back and forth, hissing. He frowned. "The malfunction is in your ear; I have no control over that. There's absolutely nothing wrong with my invention."

He straightened up and chose another aluminum foil cone. "Like this, lady—" He scrunched the cone into a little ball and tossed it expertly into an overflowing garbage can. The shiny ball couldn't go in, though, and it fell out and rolled to her feet next to the sock. "Garbage in, garbage out—but is it garbage or something else—on another planet, that foil and that sock are pure gold. Know what I mean?"

Lying alone in bed under an electric blanket, Irene kept going over and over what he had said—that inventor or crazy man or whatever. She was an overstuffed garbage can.

John had started calling again. He'd been down South too long; he was beginning to sound bent around the edges, softer than soft. He stretched out his vowels and kept calling her "honey" when he wasn't telling her it was all over. She knew it was just a phase, that everything would work out. He was just drinking too much. She'd stopped wearing the earring again, because she was so afraid it would tell her he was becoming addicted again. And she wouldn't call Henry, the therapist, or Bruce, the inventor.

Her mother had called her a couple of times, too, and begged her to go to Long Island to visit her sister Bess. "You've painted yourself into a corner," her mother had told her. "That man wants too much of you—"

Outside her apartment, spring sent enticing breezes through Central Park. Inside, she kept freezing. The phone rang. She should've turned the machine on. She squinted at the alarm clock: 3 A.M. She switched the bedside lamp on and glanced at the earring on the nightstand, coiled like the snake it was supposed to be from. Something told her to put it on. The phone kept ringing. She waited on a message from the earring. But nothing happened. Maybe it would be good news. He'd say he was coming back to New York. He'd say, "I love you and everything's going to be fine"—was that her voice or was that the earring's? She put on the earring with one hand and with the other picked up the receiver.

"Hello?"

"It's Johnny-o."

"What do you want?"

The earring laughed softly and said something about something. She couldn't quite hear. She kept pulling on the earring till it pulled through her earlobe and blood dripped like teardrops onto the white sheets.

"You know what I want," he whispered.

And she did.

Afterword

When I was in college, I fell in love with photography and I often went to New Orleans for holidays. One year, while out taking photographs of whatever caught my interest, I saw a mannequin in a phone booth ostensibly using the phone. It was a wonderful sight. I loved the photograph. In reality it was just a display for a department store, but to me, as an artist, a communicator, it was so much more. I think I called the print "Communication." I tried writing a poem about it—and actually sold it to a small magazine, with the photo as an illustration—but the idea continued to haunt me. Years later, having gone through difficult relationships that suffered through communication problems, I found myself looking at the photograph and relishing it that much more. I discovered that other people agreed with me—in relationships, communication is the one crucial point we are all continually trying to understand. I discovered that what we hear is what we want to hear. Too often, we just don't listen to each other. Or if we do listen, we are always editing the conversations to please ourselves.

It's such a fascinating thought. And then there was a friend of mine who actually bought a rattlesnake earring. Put it all together and the story just blossomed.

As for why I write horror—I don't know that I would say I write horror. I try to write psychological stories— magic realism? Southern gothic? I just want to illuminate, and sometimes that disturbs. But I want people to walk away more aware of what we do to each other. So maybe we'll be kinder to each other, more caring. I don't know that I enjoy writing these stories at all. No, I don't. I do it because I do it. I don't want people to ignore the evil, because if we ignore the evil, evil wins. To eradicate evil, in ourselves, or in others, we must face it. In my more "horrific" fiction—and I stress, that's not all I write—I want to turn the light on so people can see what it is we must be rid of.

Melissa Mia Hall

PREGNANT

Joyce Carol Oates

She was months pregnant, and the baby in her womb kicked, squirmed, poked where it had no business. It murmured sly suggestions. It asked awkward questions.

Why did you wait so long?

Aren't you too old?

Did you think he would love you forever?

The baby gave pain where there was no reason. Please, the pregnant woman begged, I love you.

The baby responded with a derisive kick that staggered the woman from within.

It went on like that. Millennia had preceded the pregnancy, and perhaps indeed she was too old.

In the presence of others, this baby misbehaved. Kicking, writhing, spasms of silent giggles. Pressing on the pregnant woman's bladder so that she had to hastily excuse herself and find a toilet. Causing her nipples to harden through the fabric of her clothes as if she were already nursing.

Is this your first? she was asked, regarded with kindness and pity.

It was her strategy to hold herself straight and stiff and tall, stretching her neck to assure as much distance as possible between her head and her burgeoning belly.

The baby teased, Did you choose me?

When they should have been deeply asleep, in the dead center of the night, this baby teased, Of all the billions and billions that might have been, did you choose me?

When she sat down faint with hunger, picking up her fork to eat, the baby in her womb gave a cruel kick. Eating! Eating again! it cried. You disgust me.

She said angrily, I have to eat: I have to nourish us both.

She gripped her fork, leaning pale and sweating above the plate of food. Seeing there amid the innocent boiled rice a single white maggot and amid the fresh-steamed vegetables a single strand of her own hair.

She pushed the plate from her and ran to the bathroom to vomit.

It went on like that. A pregnancy is a lifetime. Mornings she walked, and early evenings. Her belly preceded her, parting the humid air.

Faces like balloons bobbed solicitous and curious in her path. How are you, and how many months is it, and when are you due, and nourishment is the main thing, and sleep, enough sleep. And peace.

Peace of mind! the baby sneered.

There seemed nothing she could do or say to make things right between them.

As there had been nothing she could do or say to make the father of this baby love her for longer than he wished to love her.

They were climbing a long, dizzy stretch of steps in the open air. Climbing and panting and sweating. The hot sun fell swordlike from above. This edge of the park was risky—a desolation of exposed roots of trees, eroded gullies, bottles and beer cans tossed into the grass. Bodies of sleeping derelicts. Discarded shoes, items of female clothing. The din of transistor radios.

She kept climbing. Often in the out-of-doors the baby in her womb was silent, as if unable to get its bearings.

At the top of the hill she stood on a concrete platform, shielding her eyes, gazing out over the city.

Was this the city? In which she lived? A thousand thousand buildings afloat in the summer heat haze. She could not have sworn, eyes crinkling at their corners, that she had ever seen it before.

Under her shapeless clothes her belly had grown round and hard; the bluish-white skin stretched tight as a drum. That kind of tightness can one day burst.

The baby insisted, Of all the billions and billions, you knew it would be me? Knew, and chose?

She bit her lip. Yes.

Oh, liar!

The baby writhed in silent laughter.

She held her ground. Feet apart, heels hard on the concrete. Sweat trickled down her smooth sides, gathered in a coolish pool at the small of her back. Was she to be drawn to the edge of the embankment, goaded into lifting one of her vein-raddled legs over the guardrail? Early in the pregnancy the baby had teased Lysol, razor blades, subway tracks, but she had not acknowledged hearing.

She said, Look: I have to nourish us both.

The baby's head was a rock in the pit of her womb. Upside down, it seemed, out of mere meanness. But, as if relenting, the baby asked, Is there a sun, at least?

She said, There is always a sun.

It went on like that.

Afterword

Art that deals with horror is akin to surrealism in its artful elevation of interior states of the soul to "exterior" status. Even if we were not now in our time psychologically and anthropologically capable of deciphering seemingly opaque documents, whether fairy tales, legends, outright fantasy, or presumably objective histories and scientific reports, we should know almost at once, reading horror fiction, that it is both real and unreal: as states of mind are real—emotions, moods, shifting obsessions, beliefs, and even disbeliefs. Perhaps the sole criterion for compelling horror fiction is that we read it so swiftly, with so rising a sense of dread and so complete a suspension of normal skepticism, that we inhabit the material as its protagonist, and can see no way out.

"Pregnant" is one of a sequence of little stories—I think of them as "miniature narratives"—that explore certain states of the soul from the inside. In "Pregnant," the horror was generated, at least for me, its author, by the autonomous voice of the unborn baby. I had not exactly known until the story was finished, and set aside, that it was about the phenomenon of suicidal impulses. If that is, in fact, what it is about.

Joyce Carol Oates

HANTU-HANTU

Anne Goring

I put on my shoe and scream. Nurse Kelly, the nice redheaded one, Karen, takes my shoe off and holds it up and says, "Look, nothing at all, Jane. Nothing. You imagined it." And the new sneery nurse, the man, says, "You shouldn't pander to her. She only wants attention. She'll have to learn to stand on her own two feet when she's out in the community."

There's a joke in there somewhere. Shoes. Feet. I don't laugh. I cling to Karen's hand. I'd felt it squirming between my toes. Ready to scuttle up my leg, hide in my clothes, rattle over my body with its hard, fast little feet. . . .

Karen's a lovely girl. She takes me in to breakfast because she can see how trembly I am. She talks about her boyfriend and the rock concert they're going to on Saturday. I'm composed by the time she leaves me. I can face up to searching my cereal. Making sure. Their eggs are the worst, you see. Little brown shiny packets. Easy to mistake for malted wheat husk. Karen says they're very particular in the kitchens, and if everything's piping hot I don't worry too much. If they're cooked, they're dead, aren't they? On the other hand, they can lay eggs in anything, anywhere. That's why they're so successful.

Karen reminds me a lot of Susan. Bubbly, redheaded. I like Karen, but when she's not on duty I try not to think of her too much because I only start remembering Su. I've been such a lot better lately that I've kept Su right away. But with the damned thing in my shoe this morning, the pictures won't go.

I didn't want them to change my tablets. I told Karen. She said the doctors know best and there's this new drug.

There's always a new drug. Some of them work, some don't.

Su had red hair and freckles, just like Karen. It was quite the wrong colouring for someone living in the tropics. She never tanned properly, but she didn't need a tan. All those young servicemen. Married or not, they homed in on Su like wasps drawn to a ripe August fruit. She could pick and choose and she did, but nothing heavy, nothing serious. I marveled at her. She played the field without worry or conscience. I couldn't do that. I was shy of men, too inhibited. I was an only child, born to worried middle-aged parents who built invisible fences round their dull lives, trapping me in with them. The sound of apron strings snapping was still loud in my ears. I never woke to a new day in that new country without a sense of amazement and guilt that I'd made the break, defying my mother's tears, my father's accusations of disloyalty, which were no less pointed for being silent; stares and sighs and head-shakings, laden with reproach and regret at my selfishness in putting half the world between us.

Su and I traveled out on the same plane. Propellers, then, of course. Three days with overnight stops in New Delhi and Calcutta. The shock of India. The squalor, the poverty, the smells. We were a bit fearful of what we'd find in Singapore after that. But Singapore was lush and green and sleepily colonial. We were still top of the heap then, in the fifties. Europeans, Brits, Expats with an inbuilt sense of superiority and foreign service allowances that enabled us to live in a style to which we rapidly became accustomed.

Su and I shared a flat in Tanglin. The school where we taught catered for children of servicemen, and we were civilians signed up for a three-year tour of duty.

The flat had cool terrazzo floors and a shady balcony where we sat in the evenings drinking ice-cold Tiger beer. We had a Chinese amah with a gold-toothed smile who lived in a cubbyhole at the back and kept house for us. We learned to drive and bought secondhand cars and new cameras so we could take photographs of ourselves in shorts or sundresses to dazzle the folks back home. We bought hand-embroidered linen for next to nothing at C. K. Tang's in River Valley Road and went to Raffles for Sunday curry tiffin.

We acclimatised to the soporific, steamy heat, easily able in our busy lives to blot out the unpleasant bits: The stink of the polluted river mouth, so photogenic with its clutter of sampans and *tokangs* and its sweating, ragged coolies. The poverty and disease and violence that simmered in the picturesque kampongs and behind the scabrous, bustling, overcrowded alleyways of Chinatown.

And the wildlife.

Everybody had a snake story to tell. The krait found slithering toward the baby's cot, the python in the monsoon drain. Or a *chikchak* story. The one that dropped from the ceiling into the lady's cleavage, the one that landed in the soup at a posh dinner party. I never saw a snake, and I liked the little lizards. After all, they were useful, eating up the moths and mosquitoes. It was the insect life that worried me.

Mosquitoes. "Give it a year and they won't bother you so much," the old hands said. "They like freshly arrived blood." The praying mantises with their swiveling, bulbous heads, the six-inch centipedes with vicious bites and the small, shiny brown millipedes that curled up tight at a touch, the ants that poured into the flat in brown or black streams in search of food. The giant cockroaches that flew in at night and lived in the drains, the kitchen cupboards, the wardrobes. Everywhere.

I disliked the cockroaches most of all.

Just dislike at first. Because they were destructive and filthy and a nuisance. The hate, the terror came later.

Su laughed at me. "Queen of the Flit spray," she called me. I never went anywhere without the big tin spray. No handy aerosols in those days. I never slept in any room unless it had been drenched in insecticide. I burned green coils that gave off fumes supposed to keep the night air free of mosquitos. I slept under a mosquito net long after Su had given up. I poured boiling water and undiluted Jeyes fluid down every grid and lined the kitchen shelves with specially impregnated paper.

I still got bitten. The ants still found their way into the sugar. The cockroaches kept on coming.

But in the end, my caution—my precautions—saved me. Though there have been times, screaming, blood-red times, when I wished I hadn't bothered.

Sometimes I think Su was the lucky one. And that's the sickest of black jokes.

"The sun's nice today," Karen says. "Why don't you take your knitting outside?"

She's trying to catch me out. I laugh to let her know I know. She grins back.

"I might," I say. "When I've finished this decreasing."

The dayroom does get stuffy. Too much glass. Added on to the gaunt Victorian building in the sixties and never satisfactory. Built cheaply and it shows. Draughty in winter, too hot in summer. No matter, it'll all be pulled down soon. The place is half empty already. A lot of people have left. Been sold to a property developer, I understand, for houses and shops.

I don't want to leave here, where I've learned to feel safe. But they don't listen to me. They don't understand about the danger. They just smile and tell me I'll soon settle in at the nice new house with nice new friends and nice kind people to look after us. Nice. Everything's going to be nice.

I finish my few rows and wrap up the knitting in a towel, then in the usual three plastic bags, and when Karen has her back turned I take the aerosol out of my handbag and quickly spray the outside of the parcel. She doesn't like to see me doing that. Goes on about the ozone layer. I put the parcel on the table in the sun. It'll be safe in the sun. They don't like sun. I wouldn't ever take my knitting into the garden. You never know what might get tangled up in it.

"I'm going out now," I say, replacing the aerosol in my bag. "Just for a breath of air."

Karen looks from the parcel to me and shakes her head in an exasperated sort of way. I pretend not to notice and march out briskly to show that I don't care.

It was Su's idea to go away for a few days that first Easter.

"Harry's getting to be a pain in the neck," she said. Harry was the latest besotted admirer, pursuing Su with the same determination that had won him his wings. "Every time a Hurricane flies over I think it's him keeping an eye on me. Let's take the Pontianak and flee up-country, hey?"

Up-country was Malaya, not Malaysia then. Attached to Singapore by the fragile thread of the man-made causeway. We'd been no farther than Johore Bahru, and come the long summer holidays we'd go up to Kuala Lumpur and to Fraser's Hill in the cool mountains. The Emergency was almost over, the Communist guerrillas being driven farther and farther north. Curfews being lifted everywhere. Whole areas being declared "white."

The west coast, on an impulse, at Easter? Why not? Su's car was an American Pontiac. A big saggy monster with rusting edges. She'd nicknamed it after we heard the Malay legend of the Pontianak, a vampire who terrorised women after childbirth, scooting about the jungle trailing her innards and wearing her breasts on her back.

It was a joke to us, of course.

Vampires. Ghosts, *hantu-hantu*. We giggled over reports in the local papers. Phantoms terrorising travelers on a particular stretch of road, hauntings in a rubber plantation, an old house. . . . Ghosts were taken very seriously by the Malays and Chinese. But we were sensible Brits, weren't we?

We laughed at such superstitious nonsense and Su cheerfully called her car Pontianak. After all, we were not of this steamy, red-earthed land. Its devils were not ours. We were from harder, colder latitudes, and if there was any apprehension about our journey, it was of comprehensible things like terrorists or even tigers, which were known, occasionally, to spring out from the jungle onto an unsuspecting passerby.

The road ran through long dark avenues of rubber trees, through tiny stilt-housed kampongs where children and chickens scratched in the pink dust under banana trees and coconut palms, through swatches of jungly forest, the trees grown tall and skinny in their greed for light and air, swathed in ropes and curtains of twining, strangling creeper. The ones that grew too tall, too old, too heavily burdened, crashed defeated down to the seething, crawling, wriggling life in the soft wet decay of the forest floor.

Living jungle is always full of dead things. Something dies. Something else eats it in order to exist. But we didn't think about that. We saw only the beauty of it because that was what we wanted to see. The butterflies with wings of black velvet and yellow and shot blue satin fluttering at the forest edge. A red and turquoise kingfisher regarding us from a telegraph pole. Blinding white thunderheads rising into the arch of the sky above the dense, dark green mounds of forest.

Snap. Snap. Snap. The camera clicks. The images freeze into black and white stiffness. Recorded to be sent dutifully home in the next letter, the letter never to be written.

I walk quickly between the neat lawns and flower beds. I walk in the exact middle of the path, my sturdy shoes going click-clack on the concrete, swiveling my head from side to side, ever watchful. Near the buildings it's okay. Lots of space. Nowhere for them to hide. Where the paths converge near the main gate, over-grown shrubs, laurels mostly, intrude on the concrete, making a dark tunnel. They should be cut down. I've told them. But nobody bothers. I pull my skirt tightly round my knees and rush through. When I'm safely onto the wide main drive, I look back at the masses of dark glossy leaves shining like enamel in the sun, at the leggy, bending stalks rising from an innocent litter of discarded plastic bags and drink cans.

Nothing there. Not in daylight. Not in sunlight. I wouldn't come out here at dusk, of course. Never. I know the risks.

I've been safe here for nearly thirty years. Protected by my caution, my alertness, my fear. I am surrounded, guarded, by people who have sympathy with my fear and belief in my madness.

I was mad once, of course. Properly mad. My brain convulsed to jangling chaos. The violence of my terror turning me into another Self entirely. But I am long years now from the padded cell, the locked ward, though I feel the heavy shadow of that other Self as I stand on the drive and stare through the open gates to the traffic that passes on the road.

I have become, my guardians explain kindly, an insti-tutionalised victim of out-of-date medical practices. I should have been returned to the real world years ago. I will be so much better when I have learned to enjoy the freedom of my new life.

They are so knowledgeable and clever. And such fools.

We stayed at the Rest House, a long, low building with a red-tiled roof and deep verandahs drenched in purple and pink bougainvillea. Across the road was a beach of yellow sand fringed with leaning palm trees. We swam each morning before breakfast in the warm, cloudy waters of the Indian Ocean and again in the late afternoon when we came in hot and sticky from sight-seeing.

"Don't you ever sit down and relax?" DP enquired one evening from the depths of his rattan chair as we ran indoors, trailing sand from our flip-flops.

"Why should we?" Su called cheerfully.

"Lemme buy you a drink," he said, "and you can tell me what I'm missing."

"Thanks, but no thanks," Su said, whisking past him.

Su had christened him DP, for Drunken Planter, and dismissed him as a bore. He was a small, pale, damp young man with restless eyes, his hand permanently wrapped round a half-filled glass. Whenever we were indoors, he always seemed to be there beside us. Drifting from a shady corner to offer us a drink, passing our bedroom door as we opened it, leaning across from the next table at breakfast to interrupt our conversation with some anecdote of his own.

Only that morning, Su's patience had run out. "Do you mind? This is a private conversation," she'd snapped at breakfast, when he sniggered at something she'd said to me.

Heads turned at other tables. DP smiled his bland, absent smile and turned his attention back to his toast. He was uncowable. Perhaps it was the permanent fix of alcohol in his veins that insulated him from insult. From reality. From everything, poor lost soul.

An hour later he was swaying over me, breathing whisky fumes down my neck as I sat on the verandah writing postcards while Su was indoors washing her hair.

"Pretty girl, your friend," he said. "Su, isn't it? Got spirit. I like that. . . ."

I leaned away from him and pretended to write, but I wasn't Su. Good manners had been instilled in me from childhood. Smile, be polite, respond to small talk. I couldn't be rude to him, make a scene.

We held a stilted conversation. Mostly he asked the questions, but he volunteered one or two snippets of his own. His name was Charles Smith. The rubber estate he managed had turned him into a bit of a hermit, really, because it was the most beautiful spot on earth and he hated to leave it. He struggled to bring a photograph out of his pocket. "Here," he said. "That's me in the garden, with my friends."

But my reaction was rather more positive than he'd reckoned with. As I glanced at the snap, I saw, out of the corner of my eye, a slither of movement between the wooden planks of the verandah near my feet. I squealed, dropping the photograph and leaping up and away.

"A cockroach! There! there!" He looked bewildered, bending slowly and squinting into the crack. "It's coming out! Stamp on it."

He blinked, bemused. The cockroach was big and fat and shiny brown. He reached down. "This?" he said. "This? You're not scared of a poor old cocky, are you?"

He slid it over and over in his hands, the cockroach running, dancing, sliding in and out between his fingers.

"How could you?" I said, shuddering, unable to watch.

"Fancy being scared," he said. "I bet your friend Su isn't scared." He moved suddenly, pushing his hands with the brown shiny creature rushing madly over them toward me. "Here. Look. It's harmless." His voice sounded different. He was enjoying himself.

"Don't!" I cried, cringing back. "Don't!"

"Okay, okay," he said. "Look. It's gone now."

"Where?" I looked at his empty hands.

"Threw it into the garden."

"You should have killed it!" My voice trembled.

"Everything has its place in nature," he said. "Even the humble cockroach." His voice was flat again. Bland. His hand reached out and touched my bare arm. I flinched.

"I have to go." I snatched up my postcards and fled.

The pads of his fingers and thumb seemed to have left separate damp, cold indentations in my skin. I found myself rubbing at them absently at odd times during the day. I didn't say anything to Su about what had happened. I was secretly ashamed of myself for being such a scaredy-cat over the cockroach. Besides, Su might have said something to him. Been sharp. Made a scene.

I scuff the lining of my coat against my arm. The five separate numb areas respond with a faint cold tingle. I've grown used to them, fond of them almost. They remind me to be on my guard. Doctors have examined my arm. I've had tests, scans. They say there's nothing the matter. They think it's all in my head. They would, of course. They're the sane ones. I'm the madwoman.

The wind sweeps up the drive, stirring the dust and the litter. Clouds are building over the council estate opposite the hospital grounds. It'll rain later. The day was too bright too soon.

Cars swish past the gate. It's a busy road. They'll take me out along that road when it's time, in the blue hospital minibus. Past the park, past the shops, through the streets of neat suburban houses to my new home. Out in the community, where I'll be so much better.

That's what they say. That's what they believe.

I'd like to believe it, too.

Later, we went poking around the ruins of the old Portuguese fort above the town. It wasn't a tourist asset then. There weren't any tourists. The walls sheltered heaps of tumbled, overgrown stone blocks. A crumbling statue of St. Francis Xavier stared forlornly out to sea, features blurred by years of exposure to tropical rain and relentless sun. The noon shadows were black in the angles of the gray mossy walls.

"Look who's there," Su said, tugging me behind a bolster of creeper swathing a buttress. "Our drunken acquaintance, no less." Then she paused and whistled softly. "But take a gander at his chums."

I peered round her shoulder, screwing up my eyes against the dazzle.

They stood in one of the deep black patches of shadow. For a moment I had the odd illusion of dark, bulky shapes, appearing to press themselves tightly against the wall as though shrinking back from the harsh white sun. But it was a trick of the light. As my eyes adjusted, I saw there were three people standing deep in conversation, heads bent, absorbed. Charles Smith in his crumpled white cotton trousers and open-necked shirt. The other two . . .

"Aren't they . . . isn't he *something*," Su breathed. *Something*.

What, exactly? Malay? Chinese? Indian? Some exotic Eurasian blend?

Something. Golden people.

The brown and ivory batiks they wore seemed to shimmer and flow in the shadow. The woman wore topaz-petaled orchids in her oiled hair. The man's sleek dark head seemed part of the shadow itself; his thin, beautiful profile seemed etched upon it.

As though he sensed watchers, he turned his head.

I dodged back. Su did not move. I yanked at her arm. "Come on, let's go."

"In a minute," she said. "I must see . . ." Her voice trailed away. She continued to stare round the creeper. Silent. Very still. I could hear the quick, soft sigh of her breathing in the silence, see the flush that the sun had raised on her thick, pale, lightly freckled skin.

"Come *on*," I said. We were in the full sun. Sweat was prickling down my back. "If DP sees us, he'll only tag on. We don't want him following us around all afternoon."

"What?" she said vaguely.

"DP," I repeated. "Oh, don't just stand there."

I pulled her back forcibly. For a moment she staggered, off balance. She looked dazed, distant.

"Sorry," I said. "We must hurry."

I don't think she heard me, but she followed me meekly enough down the track through the long grasses to where the Pontianak waited to take us on to fresh pleasures.

The wind nips my ears and my ungloved fingers. I hunch my shoulders against it and continue my walk, suddenly wanting to be back in the dayroom with its familiar stuffy smell. Needing the security of its cracked walls and smeary windows.

I don't want to be here looking beyond the gates into the blind abyss of the future.

I don't want to think of Su.

I hate the pictures in my head. Like the television in the dayroom. Always on even if nobody's watching. But the pictures in my head are compulsory viewing. Can't shut my eyes and have forty winks or get on with my knitting or enjoy my walk. The new tablets. Not working. I'll tell them when I get back. Tell Karen.

No help to me now, though.

I walk so fast I'm almost running, but I can't escape the Technicolor newsreel in my mind.

We went back early to the Rest House. Su seemed unaccustomedly listless.

"Bit of a headache," she confessed. "Probably the sun. I'll take a couple of aspirins and lie down for an hour."

I went for a swim, but I didn't stay on the beach long. It wasn't the same without her. I felt conspicuous on the acres of empty sand, imagining the passersby on the road above exchanging rude comments about my large, awkward shape. Thinking that the small Malay boys from the kampong near the beach, tumbling like sleek puppies in the waves, saw me as an intruder.

I expected to find Su napping, but the curtains weren't even drawn in our room. Her bed was pristinely empty. When I'd showered and changed, I discovered her in the bar, curled up in one of the shabby rattan chairs. The glass-topped table between her and Charles Smith held half-filled beer mugs. He saw me first, rose politely to his feet, his bland smile broadening.

"What'll it be? Beer? Gin and tonic?"

"Oh, I don't think . . ." I began nervously, wondering whether Su really was sickening for something to have allowed herself to be cornered by this person she so despised. "Are you all right, love? Your headache . . ."

Su's glance slid from mine, but not before I'd seen the flash of exasperation, of impatience.

"Do sit down if you're stopping," she said pettishly. "I'm fine now."

I felt hurt and surprised. I sat down, not knowing what else to do. The other two ignored me. Su was talking to Charles Smith as though he were some new acquaintance she wanted to impress. As though in my absence they had together crossed some watershed of understanding, and I was a straggler left miles behind, struggling to catch up.

"I don't know what got into you," I said, still peeved, as we walked in the warm velvety evening darkness toward the hissing pressure lamps and crowded stalls of the amahs' market laid out under the palm trees.

"It's not *him*, you clot," Su said lightly, but with a touch of that same hurtful impatience. "It's the other one. His friend."

"Friend?" I said in bewilderment.

"The one we saw up at the fort." She laughed. "He's the one I'm interested in."

I gawped at her, but she wasn't looking at me. She was staring at a display of garish plastic sandals laid out under a tree. Not seeing them, either. Her smile was distant, dreaming.

"He . . . they . . . Charles's friends, they're sister and brother. And royalty, no less. 'An ancient lineage,' to quote Charles. Oh, some minor offshoot, I've no doubt. Wrong side of the blanket, for all I know. Very ally-pally with our DP, though. Live near him in some jungly *istana* out in the *ulu*. It sounds—well—silly to say this, but something happened when I looked at him. Eyes across a crowded room and all that jazz."

"You mean, that man . . . and you . . ."

"I never believed it could happen. Instant attraction. An instant of *knowing,* absolutely, that he felt the same." She shrugged. "Fate. Kismet. Call it what you like. Pzaam. It happened right there in the fort. That's all I can tell you." The lightness of her tone belied the trusting, defenceless, almost pleading expression in her eyes.

I was moved by her confession. It was so silly and romantic and so unlike her that it must be true. And who was I, whose experience with men, with love, was limited by the inhibitions of my upbringing, to deny that she was right?

"You may not believe me," she said, "but try to understand."

I did try, but when she added, almost offhandedly, that Charles Smith had asked us to stay at his place for a day or two on the way back to Singapore, I couldn't stop myself. "Good heavens, we can't do that! We don't know anything about him—"

"We're past the age of white slave traders," Su snapped. "Grow up. He's a perfectly respectable bloke. We're together, what could possibly—" She broke off, her glance sliding past me. "Look," she breathed on a small, trembling, satisfied sigh, "Look, they're there. . . ."

I shaded my eyes against the glare of the pressure lamps. They stood beneath the tufted palms, the light catching the curve of an arm, the glint of a jewel.

Charles Smith waved. The figures on either side of him stood in a kind of proud, watchful stillness. Royalty, Sue had said, but despite my scepticism, it seemed that "regal" was the only adjective that fitted.

The man's head was turned, his gaze locked upon Su.

I stared from one to the other. Reluctantly becoming aware that whatever it was between them—this unspoken emotion, this sexual, animal compulsion—it was almost palpable on the heavy night air. Like the cloying, clinging waft of perfume from a flower-laden frangipani. The tree invisible, its presence overpowering.

I felt suddenly alone and excluded.

I caught the woman's eye. His sister. I wondered if she felt the same sense of exclusion, of shock. He was her brother, after all. And it was odd, but it seemed that her head dipped in acknowledgment and her shoulders lifted delicately, as though she sensed my thoughts and also rued what was happening.

Accept it, a soft voice in my head murmured. *Bend with the wind. It will blow over like a sudden storm. No harm done. You and I, we will guard this foolish, hotheaded pair until they come to their senses. Until then, be easy, my friend. Trust me. . . .*

I blinked in surprise. Had I actually heard her voice above the racket of the market? I stared at her, saw the gleam of her eyes, the whiteness of her gentle smile. I found myself smiling back, feeling an unexpected rush of warm kinship with her. Of course I could trust her. How lucky I was to have the opportunity to meet such a charming and interesting woman. A *royal* personage . . .

A chattering Chinese family pushed past. When they had gone, Charles Smith was crossing the grass toward us. Alone. I heard Su's gasp of dismay. It almost matched my own.

"My friends had to go. They have a previous engagement," Charles apologized. "But should you find time to call on us on your way back to Singapore, then I shall arrange a little soiree. You would find them most cultured and delightful people.'' He raised his eyebrows questioningly.

I was the one who answered. It seemed ungracious not to.

"Thank you," I said. "We should like that very much."

I see the dayroom windows now. See the people within occupied with their busy little empty tasks, playing cards, watching television, thinking about their next meal. Karen is there. Karen will stop the pictures running in my head. The worst ones of all. If I am quick enough. If . . .

It was well into the afternoon when we left the main road and began to follow the instructions on the sketch map Charles had left us.

We hadn't meant to be so late, but it had been a morning of mishaps. There was a disagreement over our bill which delayed us disagreeably. An hour into our journey the car had a puncture, and we had to spend a sweaty time changing the wheel. Then my navigation went haywire and we ended in a dusty laterite cul-de-sac in the middle of nowhere.

If we'd believed in such things, we'd have thought the omens distinctly inauspicious. As it was, we became increasingly snappy with each other.

"You drive," Su said, exasperated and cross. "I'll read the map. Honestly, it's so simple. We should have turned off right, not left. . . .''

But even she seemed unsure as the roads became narrower, the jungle closed in, and the last small kampong was left behind.

The sky was overcast. Despite the open windows, the air in the car was close and stifling. The looming forest trees almost touched over the rutted red track the road had become.

"Are you sure this is the right way . . ." I began, fighting the Pontianak's steering.

"Yes! Look. Rubber trees . . . and there's the gates.''

Her relief matched my own as jungle was replaced by neatly ordered rows of trees, each trunk bearing the cup into which the latex dripped, like white blood, from the slanting gash in the bark.

We turned between stone gateposts and drove up a metaled road fringed with shaved lawns and clipped shrubs. The house, built in the colonial style of an earlier era, stood on a small rise. Two-storeyed, an almost luminescent white against the heavy thundery sky, its louvered shutters were opened wide to catch the breeze. It spoke of order and comfort and good living.

We were smiling with relief as we climbed out of the car, yet something niggled me as I stared round.

"The photograph he showed me. He was standing there." I pointed to a grassy terrace flanked by stone tubs of flaring canna lilies. "And his friends—they were there, too. I remember now." I frowned. "It wasn't a very good photograph, though. All blurred. It didn't look anything like this. Sort of overgrown. Not nearly so grand."

But Su wasn't listening, she was already at the open door where Charles Smith waited, glass in hand, to lead us inside.

There were iced fruit drinks laid out on a silver tray in the drawing room. The room was high-ceilinged and cool. Carved blackwood chairs were set round a blue patterned Tientsin carpet.

"You find me rather disorganized," Charles said. In this elegant, quiet room he seemed more crumpled, more restless, than he had at the Rest House. Wandering round us as we perched on the flowered cushions of the chairs sipping the syrupy drinks. Perhaps, too late, he was regretting his invitation to two women who were, after all, practically strangers. "Crisis in the kitchen, I'm afraid. Cook not too well, so I let his missus, the amah, trundle him off to the Chinese quack. . . ." His voice trailed away. He stared out the open window at the terraces and lawns and the distant, dark, rigid rows of the rubber trees.

"We've come at an inconvenient time," I began, starting to feel uncomfortable. "Perhaps we should go—"

"No! No!" he said, swiveling round so quickly that his drink lapped over the glass and dripped unnoticed onto the immaculate carpet. "No, you must stay. Not inconvenient at all." His restless glance went from me to Su. There was a look of alarm in his doggy little eyes. "It's all arranged," he went on more evenly. "Besides, it's getting late. Dark soon. Storm on its way, wouldn't be surprised." Then, with a touch of gallantry: "Couldn't let you wander off to face strange roads in a storm. No, no, no. By the time you've had a shower and a rest, harmony will be restored in the domestic department. My other friends will be here. Nice little dinner party, eh? Something different. Something . . . of the country. Unusual."

"Probably fried rice and *gulah Malacca*," Su whispered, wrinkling her nose as we followed Charles up the wide, shallow stairs. Her eyes were bright with excitement. "But I'll willingly eat the Malay version of sago pud, so long as a certain royal charmer's served up with the coffee."

My stomach heaved at the thought of food. The fruit drink had been far too sweet and sickly. I yawned. "I'm exhausted. I'll crash out for an hour, I think."

"Me, too." Su's face was pale under the freckles and the peeling skin on her nose. "Hope we've got decent beds. . . . My God! Not half!" Our rooms were opposite each other on the upstairs corridor. We blinked at them through the open doors. "I don't believe it! I've got a four-poster! And all those bowls of orchids and gardenias—it's like a bower. I haven't strayed into the honeymoon suite by some chance? . . . And the bathroom! It's vast! I'll get lost on the way to the bath."

Charles smiled, that bland, all-purpose smile. "I try to make my guests comfortable." Beads of sweat dewed his upper lip. "You'll be called . . . when it's time to eat."

He gave a half-bow and retreated down the corridor.

"He may be an oddball, but he must be loaded," Su said as we wandered round the rooms, fingering ornaments, opening drawers. "Look at this plate. Famille Bleu, do you think? Hey, play your cards right and you might land yourself a rich rubber planter."

I shuddered, rubbing my arm and remembering the touch of those damp fingers. "Do me a favour!"

Su giggled. "He is a bit of a wart, isn't he?" She was overpowered by a yawn and flung herself on the lemon silken coverlet of the bed. "Not like my prince, eh . . . ?"

I think she was asleep before I left the room. I wavered across the corridor and fell blissfully onto my own bed.

The dayroom is warm. I shut the door carefully and lean against it. I move only my eyes. My head feels fragile on my stalk of a neck. The door supports my back. If I move away from it, my rubbery knees will give way. My eyes move, searching frantically for Karen. She's not here. Where are you, you stupid girl? Can't you see . . . ? Don't you know . . . ? I need help. I need . . . need . . .

It was dark when I woke. There had been a sound. "Su?" I croaked, my throat dry. No answer. I could still taste that sickly fruit juice. Yuck.

I pulled myself upright and groped for the light switch. A reluctant, flickering circle of light spilled over the bedside table, flinging most of the room into a deadly gloom. Grumbling, I rolled off the bed and found the switch for the ceiling light. That didn't work. Power problems, I thought, thickheaded still. Out here they perhaps had to rely on generators. Then I stood still, listening. Was that someone moving in the corridor? Was it time to go to dinner? Had I missed the call? God, I hadn't even showered or changed out of my sweat-soaked shirt and pedal-pushers.

I realized, muzzily, that my door was shut. I didn't remember shutting it. Perhaps the amah was back. Perhaps she'd looked in and seen me sleeping and closed the door. I hoped to heaven it hadn't been Charles Smith doing a Peeping Tom act.

I groped my way toward the bathroom. The light, thank heavens, did work in here, if dimly. At least it was enough to see—

I sprang back, aware of my bare feet. Sandals, sandals, where? There, by the bed. Shuddering, I slipped my feet into them, buckled them up, then groped for my suitcase.

Flit spray in hand I crept toward the bathroom. Blast the little horrors. They'd get anywhere. Even in a grandiose bathroom like this, all pink marble surfaces and gleaming tiles.

There were three cockroaches. Big, brown, shiny, hesitating by the drain. I aimed the Flit gun. Fired.

"Gotcha!" I said, grimly satisfied, watching them flee into the drain in a wash of insecticide. "Curtains for you, mateys."

There didn't seem to be any others. Gingerly, I edged in the gloomy yellow light to the bath and turned on the taps. I tipped in half a bottle of pink-tinted oil from the cut-glass jar on the shelf, and a cloud of scented steam rose from the water.

I was unbuttoning my shirt when I heard a little tinkling sound from the corner by the drain. I turned sharply, my hand reaching automatically for the Flit gun. No cockroaches. I frowned. Odd. A shower of plaster had fallen from the wall under the washbasin. Even as I looked, a crack zigzagged out from the puddle of insecticide—two cracks—more. Fanning out, up through the tiles on the wall, along the terrazzo floor.

With a clatter, a handful of broken tiles fell away from the plaster.

I looked at the pink heap, then back to the wall.

Like some sort of crazy contagion, the fan of cracks kept on growing up the wall, spreading from the drain toward my feet.

The Flit gun was suddenly a guilty weight in my

sweaty hand. The insecticide. It must be. Some weird effect on the plaster—even on the tiles themselves. I retreated toward the bedroom. How on earth was I going to explain this to Charles Smith?

As I backed away, the cracks came with me. They'd reached the bath now, run along the tiled sides, then over into the bath itself. Water began to ooze through in small drips, then big fat trickles. I stared in shock as the cracks raced up toward the taps. With a cough and a gurgle, the taps suddenly dried up. They instantly lost their pristine golden gleam, became dull, crumbled rustily to brown powder, and fell with a hiss into the remaining water.

It couldn't be happening! The whole of the bathroom was disintegrating before my eyes.

Worse, out of the cracks, the gaping holes, swarmed a mess of familiar, loathed bodies. Darting from their crumbling refuge on speedy, energetic legs.

I ran, then, banging the door behind me, hearing the clatter of falling, rotting fitments.

"Su!" I screamed. "Su!"

I wrenched open my bedroom door, flung myself across the black corridor, and banged on her door.

I burst in. Blackness again, was she here? Had she already gone downstairs, abandoning me? I found the light switch. Mercifully, it worked. Dim, though, a mere yellowing of the darkness. But enough to see . . .

Nightmare.

I was caught in it, trapped in it, part of it.

The air was dense with the smell of flowers and with another, underlying odour that caught at my throat and made me gag.

They were standing at the foot of the bed. Su and the beautiful prince she so desired.

His arms were round her. Her hands were locked round his head, drawing his open mouth down to hers. I saw the dark, wet gleam of his tongue, the pink, seeking, sensual lips . . .

"No! Su. no!"

I don't know how I knew or why. It was sense more than sight in that dim light.

I sensed *them*. That smell . . .

A voice in my head. Chilling, soothing, calming.

Do not be afraid. She has been chosen. She will give such pleasure . . .

The woman advanced from the shadows. The tawny oval of her face, the gleam of her lustrous eyes, seemed more perfect in close-up than I could have imagined. I was paralysed, breathless for a second at her beauty, the warmth and closeness of her welcoming smile.

Her hands fluttered out toward me.

Come, my dear. You, too, must play your part. Her voice sank to a whispery throb. In it I seemed to hear music, laughter, a thousand luminous golden delights. . . . *Come to me and do not be afraid. . . .*

I swayed, lulled, weakened.

But that smell, that fetid odour that the scent of the flowers could not disguise . . .

"No!" I gasped.

It was an effort of will to wrench my eyes from hers, to plead once more with Su.

But Su was beyond hearing.

His kiss was upon her.

I saw the cockroaches flow like a brown, slithery, rushing tide from his mouth to hers. Into her, over her, through her tangled red hair, under her clothes. I saw her writhe and jerk and moan in that last terrible orgasm as they sank, locked together, to the floor.

I screamed, but she was past hearing.

"Now you, my dear . . ."

The woman's mouth gleamed wetly open. I could see the dark heaving in its red depths. So close . . . so tempting . . .

I heaved the Flit gun up, its weight like a cannon in my weakened arms. I pumped it into her face, into her lustrous eyes, into that gaping cavern of a mouth.

Her hands flew up and she fell back. I swung the spray round, poured it onto the seething, bloody mess on the carpet that had been my friend and the giant, gnawing, rutting thing that feasted its lust and its hunger on her.

Then I ran.

Into the corridor, a place of gaping holes and crumbling plaster. Lightning flickered between the rafters open to the sky. Down the rotting stairs, slithering and skidding on things that crunched under my feet. Past that poor wretch, Charles Smith, swaying like an upright corpse amid the ruin below.

"Come back," he wailed. "There's no escape. You . . . I . . . will be punished. . . . You were chosen. . . ."

The keys to the Pontianak were still in my pocket. Somehow I got into the car, fired the engine. Lightning illuminated the house, fallen in on itself, heavy with creeper, windows like hollow eyes in a skeleton head.

The photograph. That was what I had seen in the photograph.

Perhaps I was not meant to see it. Perhaps it was intended that I should see only the illusion. My inherent fear of those . . . things . . . had momentarily unblinkered my eyes so that I caught an image of dereliction.

I drove like the madwoman I had become. Screaming at the forest that had almost swallowed up the rotten, broken rubber trees, at the storm, at Su, at *them*.

Whoever, whatever they were.

"There, it's all right, love." Karen's sympathy flows over me. "Better now?"

I nod. The pictures are fading, dissolving as the sedative takes hold.

"Nobody believed me," I say dreamily. "They said we'd been ambushed by terrorists. They found Su— what was left of her—months later . . . eaten away. . . . Charles Smith lived there once, in that house. Disappeared. . . . Japs got him, they said. House a ruin ever since. . . ."

"Don't think about it," Karen says. "Think of happier things. Like the new place you're going to."

"No . . . not . . ."

"You'll love it," she says firmly. "Much pleasanter than here. It'll be just like being at home. And there's a very nice person come to tell you all about it. One of the team who'll be looking after you. You'll be going to see the house in the morning. Isn't that a nice surprise? . . . Here we are, then. Let me introduce you. . . ."

"Hi! Nice to meet you at last, Jane."

His hand locks over mine. He's not a lot different from others I've met over the years. Dressed in the uniform of the day. Jeans, sweatshirt, earnest smile. Younger than I'd expected. They're all younger than me now. Like policemen. Even him.

"You were older once," I say, "when I was young."

I want to cry, but I laugh instead. Perhaps it's the sedative. Perhaps it's because I'm suddenly tired of running, of fighting.

I feel the damp chill of his clinging fingertips on my hand.

"How many years?" I say. "Too many for me . . . even worse for you, I think."

He shakes his head, a look of polite bewilderment masking his face.

"You've lost me there, Jane. . . ."

"You spoke once of punishment," I say sadly, softly. "Poor Charles. Poor lost soul. Is eternal youth your punishment or your price? Imprisoned. Made to do their bidding. . . ."

"About tomorrow . . ." he begins, then hesitates. His bland smile does not reach his restless eyes. I recognize the terror in them that for the moment, dulled by the sedative, lies weightily on my own soul.

"Tomorrow?" I repeat. "Ah, yes, tomorrow . . ."

We stand there in silence, hands clasped, like old friends.

And, after a moment, it seems that my head is filled with the soothing sound of a golden voice and the murmur of distant music.

Afterword

Mostly my stories begin with a character who comes into my head with his/her problem (mostly it's a problem, though not necessarily a solemn one) nagging at me until I get it down on paper and try to resolve it. With this story, I'm not quite sure whether the character did come first or whether the ragbag of ideas that constantly stirs at back of my mind threw up the notion of cockroaches as being a particularly fruitful theme for a horror story.

Whichever it was, Jane was suddenly there, middle-aged, terrified, reliving her past, telling her own story. So, as she told it, I wrote it all down.

Anne Goring

NOTES ON CONTRIBUTORS

Joan Aiken comes from a writing family (father Conrad Aiken, brother John Aiken, sister Jane Aiken Hodge) and began writing as a child, becoming a full-time writer in the early 1960s. She is perhaps best known for her popular and award-winning children's books, which include *The Wolves of Willoughby Chase* and *Midnight Is a Place,* but has also written more than twenty novels for adults, most recently *Blackground.*

Suzy McKee Charnas, author of *Walk to the End of the World, Motherlines,* and *The Vampire Tapestry,* has a background that includes a B.A. from Barnard College in economic history, teaching in both Nigeria and New York City, and working as part of a drug abuse treatment team. Since 1969 she has lived with her husband, an attorney, in New Mexico. Her most recent books are a series of "urban fantasies" for young adults: *The Bronze King, The Silver Glove,* and *The Golden Thread.*

Sherry Coldsmith was born in Texas in 1956, studied Russian at the University of Texas, and then moved to Britain where she lived for ten years. Shortly after the momentous event of turning thirty, she began writing fiction, and in 1989 decided to return to Texas and devote herself to writing full-time. "Ticanau's Child" was her second professional sale.

Pauline E. Dungate was born in Surrey in 1948 and migrated to the Midlands to read for a B.Sc. in chemistry and geology at the University of Aston-in-Birmingham. At present she teaches science in a multiethnic secondary school in Birmingham and shares her life with a writer husband, many fish, and a ferret. Her previous stories have appeared in *Imagine* and *Writer's Monthly*, and she is currently working on a fantasy novel.

Karen Joy Fowler won the John W. Campbell Award as the best new science fiction writer of 1987. She studied at Berkeley and received her M.A. in North Asian studies from the University of California at Davis. She has published a book of short fiction titled *Artificial Things*, and a novel, *Sarah Canary*, is forthcoming.

Anne Goring now lives happily in Devon, but earlier spent six years in Singapore, and loves to travel. Besides her fiction (which includes four published novels and many short stories), she also writes travel articles and radio plays, and is a regular contributor to *Motorboats Monthly*.

Melissa Mia Hall is a native Texan living and writing in Fort Worth. Since 1981, her short stories have appeared in a number of American anthologies and magazines. A member of the National Book Critics Circle, she reviews regularly for the *Fort Worth Star-Telegram*.

R. M. Lamming was born on the Isle of Man, educated in Wales and at Oxford, and now lives in North London. She is the author of two novels, *The Notebook of Gismondo Cavaletti*, and *In the Dark*.

NOTES ON CONTRIBUTORS

Terry McGarry was born in New York City in 1962 and received a B.A. in English from Princeton in 1984. She has worked as a bartender and a street vendor in Ireland, and is currently a query proofreader for *The New Yorker*. Her poetry has appeared in *Isaac Asimov's Science Fiction Magazine* and *Aboriginal Science Fiction*.

Joyce Carol Oates is the author of many novels, short stories, essays, poems, and plays, including the 1970 National Book Award winner, *them*, and, more recently, *Mysteries of Winterthurn, Solstice, Marya: A Life*, and *Raven's Wing*. She lives in New Jersey and teaches at Princeton University.

Josephine Saxton lives in Leamington Spa and writes uncategorizable fiction. Her published books include *Queen of the States, The Travails of Jane Saint and Other Stories, Jane Saint and the Backlash, Little Tours of Hell*, and *The Power of Time*.

Dyan Sheldon is the author of the novels *Victim of Love* and *Dreams of an Average Man*. Her short stories have appeared in various anthologies, including *Firebird 2, London Tales*, and *Storia 1*. She lives in Brooklyn with her daughter, cats, and a computer named Bob.

G. K. Sprinkle is a political lobbyist and consultant with a particular interest in women's issues, currently working for the Texas Association for Counseling and Development, the Texas Council on Family Violence, and the Older Women's League. She has an M.A. in biology (specialty: vertebrate paleontology) from Harvard, teaches part-time at Austin Community College, and writes articles and opinion pieces for various Texas newspapers.

Melanie Tem has published short fiction in *Isaac Asimov's Science Fiction Magazine, Whispers, Women of Darkness,* and *Fantasy Tales* as well as other anthologies and numerous literary magazines. Her first novel, *Prodi-*

gal, was published this year. She lives in Denver, Colorado, with her husband, the writer Steve Rasnic Tem.

Lisa Tuttle was born in Texas, studied at Syracuse University in New York, and worked for five years as staff writer and then television columnist for a daily newspaper. After ten years as a freelance writer in England, she now lives in Scotland with her husband and daughter. Her books include *A Spaceship Built of Stone and Other Stories,* several novels, and *Encyclopedia of Feminism.*

Ann Walsh is the author of two books for young people, *Your Time, My Time* and *Moses, Me and Murder.* She is also a playwright and poet, and her short fiction has appeared in Canadian magazines and been read on CBC radio. She lives in western Canada with her husband, their two almost-adult daughters, three cats, and two dogs.

Cherry Wilder, New Zealand-born and -educated, has spent the last fourteen years in West Germany; long enough, she says, to be in a position to correct the translations of her novels, which include *Second Nature, Cruel Designs,* the Torin trilogy, and the Rulers of Hylor trilogy.

COPYRIGHT NOTICES

Originally published in Great Britain by The Women's Press Ltd.

An *Original* Publication of POCKET BOOKS

POCKET BOOKS, a division of Simon & Schuster Inc.
1230 Avenue of the Americas, New York, NY 10020

ISBN: 0-671-70334-X

First Pocket Books printing October 1991

10   9   8   7   6   5   4   3   2   1

POCKET and colophon are registered trademarks of
Simon & Schuster Inc.

Cover art by Mark and Stephanie Gerber

Printed in the U.S.A.

SKIN OF THE SOUL

EDITED BY LISA TUTTLE

POCKET BOOKS

New York   London   Toronto   Sydney   Tokyo   Singapore